CHANGINg JaRETH

Elizabeth Wennick

POLESTAR
BOOK PUBLISHERS

CHANGINg JaRETH

Polestar Book Publishers acknowledges the ongoing support of The Canada Council; the British Columbia Ministry of Small Business, Tourism and Culture through the BC Arts Council; and the Government of Canada through the Book Publishing Industry Development Program (BPIDP).

Cover design by Jim Brennan.
Cover image by E. Larrayadieu / Tony Stone Images.
Author photo by Kevin Hawley.
Printed and bound in Canada.

CANADIAN CATALOGUING IN PUBLICATION DATA
    Wennick, Elizabeth, 1972-
    Changing Jareth
    ISBN 1-896095-97-6
    I. Title.
    PS8595.E5593C52 1999 jC813'.54 C99-910734-8
    PZ7.W4692Ch 1999

Library of Congress Catalogue Number: 99-64175

POLESTAR BOOK PUBLISHERS
P.O. Box 5238, Station B
Victoria, British Columbia
Canada   V8R 6N4

In the United States:
POLESTAR BOOK PUBLISHERS
PO Box 468
Custer, Washington
USA   60607

99 00 01 02 03 • 5 4 3 2 1

This book is dedicated to my marvellous friends Kevin Hawley and Annalise Stenekes for giving me honest opinions, and especially to Mr. Wickens, my teacher in Grade Four and again in Grade Eight, who was the first person to tell me I could write.

CHANGINg JaRETH

Part One:

CORRUPTION

1

So there was me — Jareth Gardner — leaping more or less gracefully out the second-floor window of a certain house in the nicer part of town and landing with a thud in the snow drift beneath. I recovered my footing and ran to the curb as fast as I could, the red-and-white Adidas bag my mother had given me for Christmas clutched under one arm like a football. I was running on adrenaline and I was hopelessly out of shape, but even so, I was barely out of breath when I reached the spot a couple of houses away where Matthew was waiting in the Chevette.

The snow was really coming down that night, falling in huge, cotton-ball chunks. I turned as I opened the car door to look back at my footprints in the fresh powder — jagged holes filled with red and purple light from the Christmas lights on the roof of the house I'd just exited so abruptly. It was snowing hard enough that the trail I'd left was already blurred around the edges by the new snow, and I settled happily into the passenger seat, knowing my tracks would soon be filled in completely, disappearing without a trace.

"You left the window open!" Matthew wailed as I tossed the gym bag into the back seat. I reached for my seat belt, only half hearing him. His voice was shrill. He was definitely rattled, I decided. Matthew Harper looked like a chicken as much as anything, and when he got upset his Adam's apple started bobbing up and down that skinny neck of his like a yo-yo. I was no beauty myself, with my crooked nose and eyebrows too dark for my scruffy blond hair, but I was definitely the better-looking member of our duo. Matthew had been my best friend since nursery school, and by this time I knew how to read him, probably better than I could read myself.

I looked back up at the house. Sure enough, the window by which I'd left the house was still open, its lacy pink curtains fluttering half outside in the wind.

"I'm sorry, did you want me to just stroll out the front door?" I said. "Somebody had to lock it behind you. I could break in again and close the window if you want, but then we'd have to leave the door unlocked, and somehow I don't really think —"

"Look, we haven't got time to argue like this!" he interrupted, his voice breaking like he was about to burst into tears. "We gotta get out of here!" Matthew shifted the old Chev into drive and it lurched reluctantly down the road. He was shaking visibly, and he shifted his hands up and down the steering wheel, not certain where to put them. I slammed the door shut again as the car moved.

"I can't believe we killed that old guy," Matthew said a minute later, his voice still quivering.

His words took a little time to sink in.

"We didn't kill him," I said as calmly as I could. "He

just had a heart attack. You don't even know if he was dead for sure." I pulled off the grey cotton gloves I always wore when I went out with Matthew on evenings like this.

"I do know he was dead; he didn't have any pulse. I took First Aid last year, Jareth; I think I know how to tell when somebody's dead. And he wouldn't have had a heart attack in the first place if we hadn't have been in his stupid bedroom." Matthew wiped his nose on the back of his hand. "I told you not to go into the bedroom. What did I say? I said we should stick to the ground floor. Didn't I say that?"

I shrugged, trying to look casual as my stomach did somersaults. I was glad I'd skipped dinner, because if I hadn't, I'd have yakked it up all over the car.

"He was old," I reasoned, holding my voice as steady as I could manage. "Eighty or eighty-five, anyway. He could have gone any time. We just happened to be there when he went. And he'd have heard us anyway, whether we were in the bedroom or not."

"This is it!" said Matthew. "This is the last time we do this. Next time you're on your own."

"You think there's gonna be a next time after what just happened in there? No way. We've been lucky too many times ... This is where the winning streak ends, and we're just gonna leave it at that."

It was true, we'd been damn lucky. I'd been busting into houses with Matthew since we were thirteen or fourteen, and so far nobody'd ever caught on. I always told him subtlety was the key — if we were careful just to take stuff we found sitting around — spare change, knick-knacks, whatever, half the time people would never even know they'd been robbed. They'd just think, "you know, I could have sworn I had a ten-dollar bill sitting on the dresser," or "whatever happened to that little statue Grandpa gave us for Christmas?" The three or four times we'd actually broken a window or something to get in, I would always read in the local paper that burglars had made off with TVs, VCRs: real bulky, expensive stuff we had no way to carry and no place to sell. I guess our hosts had decided to replace their obsolete electronic equipment on their insurance companies.

Which was fine with me, really. I didn't figure on ever getting caught, so what did I care if some rich guy was ripping off some big company?

■ ■ ■

Looking back on it now, five years later, I should have got an Academy Award for my performance that January night. At the time my heart was pounding in my throat, and the image of that old guy on the bedroom floor — withered old hands clasping at the air for support — was running through my head, leaving a bad taste in my mouth. But somehow I kept it all together. I felt sort of pleased with myself for keeping my head, though I'm usually pretty good in a crisis. It's like my body can function on its own while my brain takes a field trip. Just like school, really.

Matthew stopped the car and put it in park.

"I can't drive in this weather," he complained. His hands were shaking like crazy as he turned of the ignition. "It's only a few blocks to my place; why don't we just park it here and walk?"

I thought about that for a second.

"I'll take the car," I offered. "I don't mind driving in

the snow; I can drop you off at home and give you the car back at school tomorrow morning."

Matthew hesitated, thinking hard. He has this way of chewing the inside of his upper lip when he's thinking something over. Right then he looked like he was going to suck his nose right into his mouth. If the situation hadn't been so darkly bizarre I probably would have laughed at him.

"I suppose," he said finally. "Just you make sure you're *at* school tomorrow."

"I don't have much choice," I told him. "If I skip one more Biology class, I'm gone. Expelled."

"Is that part of the big Guidance deal?"

"Yeah. I also have to …" I clamped my mouth shut. There were certain things, I decided, that it would be better for Matthew not to know about at this point in time. He knew more than most people; he knew about the switchblade incident, and he knew about the contract I'd signed with the head of the Guidance department at school … He didn't need to know everything that was written in that contract.

"You have to what?" Matthew pressed.

"I have to show up at every Bio class," I told him. "Like I just said. That was the agreement. And I had to write this big apology letter to Miz Waller and shit. You know, 'it was reckless and I'll never do it again' … all that crap."

I cracked my knuckles absently. I'd have to watch what I said about that other thing — the other part of the deal. Somehow I doubted Matthew would understand.

He got out of the car and circled to the passenger side as I unbuckled my seat belt and clambered over the gear shift to the driver's seat. I'm a little neurotic about seat belts. I get really paranoid if I'm not wearing one. It's like I'm missing part of my body or something. I started to drive as Matthew fiddled with the stereo. Some heavy metal crap was playing ... a bunch of white noise, as far as I was concerned. Personally, I prefer music with intelligible lyrics.

"Turn that shit off," I snapped. "You're making my head ache."

"It's my car," Matthew protested.

"Yeah, and I'm driving it. I can't concentrate with that noise in my ears."

"What, would you rather have some classical bullshit?"

"Sure beats whatever this is."

With a grunt, Matthew turned the stereo down low, but not off. I decided not to push my luck. Suddenly I was looking forward to having that car all to myself for a while, and I didn't want to say anything that would make him change his mind.

The drive to Matthew's apartment building was mercifully short. I pulled the car up in front of the driveway and stopped.

"Well, aren't you gonna pull right into the parking lot?" Matthew demanded.

"I'd never get out again," I said. "They haven't ploughed that lot of yours in, like, two months."

With a resigned sigh, Matthew got out of the car. He knew I was in control, and there was nothing he could do about it. As he walked away through the driving snow I flipped the stereo right off and pulled away into the night, tapping the horn lightly as I went. I didn't look back to see if Matthew was waving at me. Somehow I figured he probably wasn't.

■ ■ ■

I drove fairly slowly through the snow. I'm not usually such a careful driver, even in a blizzard, but I was in a strange mood this particular evening — like I was just on the verge of exploding and had to be careful that I didn't blow at the wrong time. I couldn't think straight ... between that old guy taking a nosedive on the bedroom carpet and that damned arrangement with the guidance counsellor, I was a nervous wreck.

To be honest, though, I'd been a nervous wreck for a couple of weeks by this point. After I'd pulled the knife on James Francis in English class, everything had gone a little nuts and I'd been doing my best to put it out of my mind. It was still rattling around in my head, though, poking its nose in whenever I thought I'd gotten rid of it. They'd arranged a "complete psychological evaluation" for me, and if I didn't show up I'd be expelled. Those were the choices, and I didn't really like either of them, but in the end I figured being poked around by a shrink would be preferable to having to get a job and move out. Those were the old lady's rules: go to school or get lost. Sometimes I felt like getting lost, but I could never figure out anyplace to go. Besides that, I had Matthew to order around, and that was almost enough to make up for most of the unpleasantries.

I parked the Chevette near the mall and got out. It was eight-thirty and the night was mine, but first I needed to use the john. I swear I've got no bladder; it seems like I've always got to take a leak. And after the stress of the last hour or so, what with that old man dropping dead on us, the need to drain my bladder was particularly pressing.

I jogged through the slush to the building, trying not to soak my feet. I had on these leather high-tops I'd ripped off from Shoe World in this very mall a couple weeks earlier and I didn't want to wreck them. Most shoe stores are smart; they'll only put out one shoe from each pair. But not this place. I'd scammed a few pairs of shoes from their displays over the years, and to the best of my knowledge they were none the wiser.

The entrance to the mall had those energy-saving sets of double doors, and I stepped between them, feeling a warm blast of air against my face. There was an old woman in a long fur coat standing near the pay phone in the vestibule. I didn't take much notice of her until she grabbed hold of my arm as I passed by her.

"Excuse me, young man. Do you think you could possibly tell me the time?"

I pushed up the sleeve of my coat and checked my watch.

"Eight-thirty." I reached for the door handle. I didn't feel half so much like chatting as I did like peeing, and I hoped to escape having a discussion with her without coming across as rude.

"That's strange," she told me.

"Why is that strange?" I gave her a wink. Turned on the charm. "It's eight-thirty around this time most nights." I leaned back against the inside door, trying not to wiggle. My only hope was that this elderly woman would take the hint from my body language that I was in a huge hurry and didn't have time to chitchat.

She laughed politely at the joke, but kept right on talking.

"Well, my husband was supposed to pick me up at a

quarter to eight. I've been waiting here a long time. It's strange because he's never late. We just live down by the lake ... it's not a very long drive at all."

I shrugged, trying to look sympathetic and anxious at the same time. I have a thing about being rude to old people. You never know if they're going to turn out to be some long-lost relative with lots of money. I guess it stems from the fact that most of my relatives have been lost for a long time. Besides, my grandmother had been a pretty scary old lady. I lived in terror of her until she died.

"Well, I'm sure he'll be here," I told this woman. "It's pretty rough driving out there ... what with the snow and all."

I didn't wait for her to say anything else before I let myself into the mall and jogged away from her. There weren't many people in the mall, even for a Monday night, and some of the stores were beginning to close their doors early. I made my way to the restroom near the food courts before circling back to go out the way I had come in. The old woman was still waiting when I passed by again.

"He still didn't come, huh?" I stopped to have a good look at her. Something about her was vaguely familiar, like I'd seen her before but I just couldn't place her.

"No ... he's still not here. I tried to phone him, but there was no answer. He must have fallen asleep," she told me. "I'll just call a taxicab. That's how I got here, but Lloyd worries about me after dark. He always comes to pick me up."

Lloyd. The name didn't ring a bell ... but, damn, that old lady was looking more familiar by the second. Where could I have seen her before? People from that end of town didn't exactly run in the same social circles as I did, but still ... I'd seen her face, and it had been pretty recently. Like, tonight, I thought.

Suddenly I realized why I knew this woman — a picture on the dresser in the old man's bedroom. My heart, which had nearly returned to its normal rhythms since I'd been inside the mall, leaped into my throat. My stomach convulsed strangely, like it was planning on giving me another good look at my lunch, and I struggled to produce an awkward smile.

"Yeah, well ... I'm sure he's just held up in the snow," I croaked, then cleared my throat. To this day, I think that's the most uncomfortable I've ever been in my life. I just stood there for a second looking at this frail little old lady in her bulky fur coat, wearing way too much lipstick and about a vat of perfume as she looked anxiously out at the snow and worried about her husband — who wasn't held up in the snow at all, but sprawled dead on his bedroom floor. I chewed on my lip for a second, thinking I should do something, say something else. Mercifully, the woman spoke before I could think of anything.

"You know, I'm sure he's probably just forgotten," she said then. "Maybe I'll just call that taxicab."

I can't tell you what I was thinking at this point. My head was a rush of noise, my pulse deafening in my ears. "No, you don't have to waste your money on a cab," I heard myself saying. "Come on; I'll drive you home."

I could tell from the look on her face she was nervous. She'd heard about how awful teenagers were from all the news reports on TV.

"Oh, I can't let you do *that*," she said, gripping her big black purse a little tighter.

"Why not? Because I'm mean and scary-looking?"

She laughed at that. Despite my long, scraggly hair, I was probably the least mean and scary-looking guy you could have hoped to meet. This old lady was pretty tiny and frail-looking, but she looked like she might just have a tough streak in her. One good whack from that enormous purse of hers would have pretty much been the end of me.

I gave her this big grin, and I knew I was going to win.

"Come on," I repeated. "I don't mind driving you wherever you need to go. I'd hate to leave you waiting here on a night like this."

"I don't live far," she said uncertainly. "It's just down by the lake."

"Yeah, I know," I said. "I mean — you already said that," I added hastily.

I held out my arm for this woman and she took it. Together we walked, absurdly, arm-in-arm through the snow to the Chevette, the tiny old woman leaning heavily on me, making my five-foot-eight-inch frame look massive in comparison. I opened the car door for her before I sloshed around to the driver's side. There's a unique substance that builds up in mall parking lots when it's snowing — a cold brown semi-liquid that feels like it's going to eat through your shoes or boots or whatever. Right now it was gnawing away at my feet and I turned the heat on high as soon as I got into the car, blowing at my frozen feet as much warm air as the old Chevette would give me.

"Where do you live?" I asked the old woman. I fastened my seat belt.

"What's your name, young man?" she returned, ignoring the question for the time being.

"It's Jareth Gardner." I bit my tongue fiercely, realizing

too late that I should have kept my mouth shut. The less she knew about me tonight, the better off I figured I'd be in the long run.

"What an unusual name," she said. "It goes with your unusual features. Blond hair and brown eyes. Very striking." She paused, probably trying to think of a polite way of telling me I was a funny-looking kid. Not to worry; that was nothing new to me. My grandmother always said I was a beady-eyed little creep, and my mother had been assuring me since I was a small child that I'd probably grow into my nose any day now. When my brother Brad had been very, very young, he'd once asked me why I had lips like a duck. So I had no illusions of waking up one day as a teen idol, but I'd learned to live with it.

At any rate, the old woman beside me in the Chevette must have finally decided not to reinforce the obvious.

"Do you know where Conrad Street is?" she said instead.

I pretended to think for a moment.

"That's right off Lakeshore Road, isn't it?"

"Yes, that's right. You know, if it's too far, I can still call a taxi — "

"Don't worry about it." I put the car in drive. Matthew had one of those rubber key chains in the shape of a hand. He kept it closed into a fist with the middle finger extended. Discreetly I reached down and closed the hand before the woman noticed it.

"There are some pretty nice houses over there on Conrad Street," I said by way of conversation.

"I've lived on Conrad Street since 1934. How'd you like that?" she asked me.

"That's a long time."

She nodded. I'd given her the correct response, and I knew it. I could almost *feel* her relax.

The car was filled with her scent — sort of an old-woman smell, very distinctive. It reminded me a little of my grandmother. It was comforting, in a frightening sort of way. I guess the smell made me feel a little nostalgic.

"I got married when I was seventeen, and my husband Lloyd built that house on Conrad Street two years later. Of course, it was all forest then. No other houses around," she told me.

I did some mental arithmetic.

"You're eighty years old."

The woman laughed.

"Not until June," she said. "Don't you go making me sound any older than I already feel. My husband Lloyd, he's ninety-one. How'd you like *that*?"

"Wow." *Ninety-one. The old guy was ninety-one.*

"Ninety-one, and he still drives. Sharp as a tack, my Lloyd. Sharp as a *tack*."

I started singing a little song in my head, like some sort of disturbing mantra. *I killed a ninety-one-year-old guy.*

"He still drives, you say?" I heard myself say over the noise of the soundtrack inside my head, and I cleared my throat in a futile attempt to get rid of the waver in my voice. *What did I go and do this for?* I asked myself. *What did I have to go and tell her my name for? She'd have taken a taxicab home eventually; why did I bother to do this?*

"I turn left here, don't I?" I said then. As if I needed to ask.

"You know, Jarvis, it's *such* a relief to meet a nice young man like yourself. Most of the young people these days ... well, they're all drug addicts and rap music fans, aren't they? It's all you see on the TV these days. Especially —" and she lowered her voice conspiratorially, "Especially those punks with their gangs. Shooting people in the street, and breaking into houses..."

I almost laughed despite myself.

"There aren't a whole lot of gangs in the suburbs," I told her instead. "Not serious ones, anyway. And not all of us kids do drugs, either."

The old lady looked up at me suddenly, like I'd startled her out of a trance.

"I'm sorry; what was that?"

I felt a little insulted that she hadn't been listening to me, but it gave me a moment to collect my thoughts.

"You had some break-ins in your neighbourhood, didn't you?" I said. "I read about them in the paper."

On the one hand, I was enjoying the irony of this whole situation, perhaps more than I should have. On the other hand, I was terrified of what would happen when we got to Conrad Street. Back to the scene of the crime, as it were.

"Well, yes, just last month ... right before Christmas. The house right across the street from ours was robbed. How'd you like that? Right across the *street*."

I nodded, picturing the place in my head. For such a big house, I recalled, there hadn't been a lot of ready cash sitting around.

"What's the world coming to?" I intoned, distracted. Without thinking, I turned right onto her street before she had a chance to tell me to.

"You know your way around this area quite well, don't you?" she said.

"Well, my ... cousin ... lives right around here," I lied awkwardly. I'd have to pay more attention to what I was doing if I didn't want to really mess things up.

"Oh, really?"

"Yeah." I hoped she wouldn't ask for a name ... To the best of my knowledge, my mother is an only child. I could have a hundred million cousins on my father's side for all I know, but that's another story. I slowed down halfway along the street. "Now, which house is yours?"

"The red brick one up here on the left," she told me. "The one with the Christmas lights still up. My grandson Raymond hasn't come over to take them down yet."

I pulled into the driveway, a thick fog settling down over my head. I couldn't tell whether it was a haze of relief or of delayed panic.

"Why, that silly fool Lloyd!"

I snapped out of my trance, my heart pounding in my throat.

"What's that?"

"He's gone and opened the bedroom window. In the middle of January! How'd you like that?"

"That's kinda strange," I agreed cautiously.

"Oh, it's just *like* him," she said affectionately. "He's always saying I keep the house too warm."

"Well, you'll just have to go in and close it," I told her. My wits were returning to me slowly, and I gave her the grin again. The patented, impossible-to-resist Jareth Gardner "all's-right-with-the-world" grin. "Tell him he's liable to freeze to death with the window open on a night like this."

"Would you like to come in for a cup of ... well, a cup of tea? I know all you young people drink coffee now, but it's hard on this old stomach, and we don't keep any in the house."

"That's okay. I really have to be going."

"Are you sure?" I could tell from the look on her face that she was a little relieved I wasn't coming in. At any rate, she sure wasn't willing to put a lot of time into trying to convince me. "Well, thank you for the ride, then, Jarvis."

She slammed the Chevette's door surprisingly hard as she got out. I watched her as she walked up to the house, fumbled in her purse for a key and opened the front door. I backed the car slowly out of the driveway, resisting the temptation to linger, and drove down the street, surreptitiously checking the front lawn for footprints as I went. It was smooth with new-fallen snow.

"Hi, honey, I'm home," I muttered to myself, and giggled nervously.

I reached into the back seat and grabbed the duffel bag. We hadn't really snagged much from old Lloyd's house in the first place — just some silverware and a little cash. Then, after Lloyd went and dropped dead on us, I'd sent Matthew to get the car while I'd replaced most of what we had taken. We didn't want to leave any sign of a break-in. Matthew even mopped up most of the snow we'd tracked through the place. I didn't figure the cash would be missed too badly, though. There aren't many people on Conrad Street who would miss a little bit of loose change like that. Not with an in-ground swimming pool and a tennis court in the backyard. I'd stuffed the money into my inside jacket pocket without counting it — probably three or four hundred dollars. Matthew had been too freaked out to remember there'd even been any money. And even if he *did* remember, he'd probably just figure I had put it back when the old guy dropped dead on us. It was all mine ... every penny. There were one or two other treasures from Lloyd's house that I hadn't bothered to put back. I guess you'd call them impulse purchases: a horse-shoe, and a big old Bowie knife in a leather sheath, which I stuck in the inside pocket of my denim jacket. The horse-shoe was just for the hell of it ... I figured I'd give it to my brother Brad for luck or something. The knife was for me, though. I'd always liked knives — which had got me in some trouble earlier in the school year when I'd decided to show off my new switchblade in English class. This new knife, though, if I brought it to school — hell, forget a suspension and a couple of counselling sessions, they'd have me thrown in jail. This thing meant business, all sharp, shiny steel that would have made quick work of anybody I'd felt like running through. I liked the feeling of it against my chest, held tight to my body by the seat belt in Matthew's Chevette. It was a safe feeling, like the knife would protect me from any school guidance counsellors or psychologists or dying old guys I happened to meet.

As I pulled out onto the highway that night I switched on the radio, found a station I liked and started to sing along. The feeling of worry that had been hanging over me passed right through me and went along its way. Suddenly I felt less ... melancholy. More alive. I just wanted to drive forever, down the highway and out of this world, but that Biology class the next morning just kept creeping back into my mind. Finally, after an hour or so, I turned that car right around and drove home. Running away would have to wait for another day.

■ ■ ■

Since I was about six, my mother had been renting this broken-down raised bungalow with big front windows and an ugly cedar hedge in the front yard. It was pretty shabby, with mouldy carpets and flaking paint, but it was home. You'd walk in the front door and either go up to the main floor or down to the basement. I saw a light on downstairs as I parked Matthew's car in the driveway behind my mother's Honda. I distractedly grabbed my gym bag from the Chevy's back seat. To this day I don't remember what happened to the horseshoe ... it could still be in that car, for all I know.

I stumbled tiredly up to the door, which I opened as quietly as I could, hoping the old lady had fallen asleep downstairs in front of the television.

"Do you know what time it is, Jareth?" I heard a voice say the second I stepped inside the door.

I froze in the front hallway. My mother was still up.

Gingerly I closed the front door behind me and locked it.

"It's late, I guess," I called back down the stairs. "I don't know, ten-thirty, eleven?"

The old lady opened the basement door and poked her head out, curlers and all. A cigarette hung limply from the corner of her mouth.

"I hope you realize it's a school night."

"Yeah, yeah. I know." I rolled my eyes. There was a beer bottle in her hand, nearly empty. I was willing to bet that it wasn't the first bottle she'd opened that night ... not by a long shot.

My mother had probably been pretty once, but by

this point looked far older than her thirty-five years. Too much makeup and sun had given the skin around her wide blue eyes a worn, leathery look, and her naturally straight brown hair had been bleached and permed to within an inch of its life. Now as she glared at me from the bottom of the stairs, it was an old woman lecturing me, slurring her words just a little from the booze.

"Where the hell *were* you, anyhow?" she said. "The mall closed hours ago. You told me you were going to the mall with Matthew."

"We went there for a while, but there was nothing to do," I told her. "Most of the stores were closing early, and we didn't have any money anyway. So Matt loaned me his car and I went out for a little drive."

"Jareth, you know I don't like you driving around without a license."

I hissed impatiently through my teeth.

"I've *got* my license."

Which wasn't true at all. Technically, I'd had my license for all of about two weeks the previous fall before I went and rear-ended a cop car, earning myself a six-month suspension for careless driving.

"It's still under suspension, isn't it? Until April, I thought."

"Nope. January," I lied.

"The weather is terrible for driving. Especially for somebody with your record. You want another ticket? See if you can get your license suspended indefinitely? Not to mention that you're driving around without insurance."

"I got home in one piece, didn't I?" I pulled my jacket off and slung it over the bannister at the top of the stairs. I'd forgotten, though, about the big knife I had stowed in the inside pocket, and the weight of the thing caused my coat to slide down the stair rail and land in a heap on the floor at the bottom. Lloyd's knife in its sheath fell out of its hiding place and landed on the threadbare hall carpeting with a thud.

"And just where did *that* come from?" my mother demanded.

I flashed her my best innocent look.

"I traded with Matthew for it."

"What for?" She'd been drinking some, for sure, but for the most part her wits were still there. Drunk or sober, though, she could deliver a hell of a lecture. I blinked innocuously, wishing to myself that she'd passed out before I'd come home.

"I don't know what for ... I just wanted it."

"That wasn't what I meant, and you know it. What did you give Matthew to get that knife?"

I shrugged.

"A couple of tapes. I wasn't listening to them anymore, and I liked the knife."

"Well, I certainly hope you didn't steal it."

I sat on the stairs and pulled off my wet shoes. One of my socks came off right along with it.

"I just *told* you," I whimpered, peeling off the other sock as well, "I traded with Matthew for it. Geez, don't you *trust* me?"

That did the trick. She came upstairs and put her arms around my shoulders. I ducked out of the way of her cigarette, which was hanging dangerously close to my hair.

"Darling, you know I didn't mean it like that."

I grimaced, enduring the embrace as I tried to keep

my face as far away from that cigarette as I could manage. My mother smoked the nastiest cigarettes you can imagine, strong and pungent and wrapped in dark brown paper.

I watched the ash on her cigarette grow until it was well over an inch long. It fell off and dropped to the hall floor.

I decided to play this situation out ... I figured I could maybe earn a couple of bucks on it. My mother was pretty easy to manipulate when she was in the bag.

"Well, it *sounded* like you were implying that you didn't trust me," I said, a definite sulk creeping into my voice.

"You know that isn't true." She kissed me on the forehead, and I pouted like a four-year-old.

"Well, that's how it *sounded,*" I said, and pulled away from her. I started upstairs to my room.

"You have that appointment tomorrow after school, remember!" she called after me. I groaned.

"Oh, man, I forgot about that. Do I have to go?"

"You and that guidance counsellor made an agreement. You want to stay in school, you go to class, and you go see this Doctor Eschen tomorrow afternoon. He's supposed to be very good."

"Well, I haven't got any money for the bus," I lied, tucking the gym bag under my arm self-consciously.

"Then look in my purse, under the bed. But don't you dare take anything more than bus fare."

"And lunch money for tomorrow," I bargained.

"Take ten dollars," she said after a little thought. "But don't you even think about asking me for any more money this week."

I picked up my knife and started up the stairs.

"Don't wake Brad up!"

"A frigging brick through the window wouldn't wake that kid up," I muttered.

When I got to my room I put the knife down on my dresser, very carefully, right in the middle. Then I lay down on my bed and turned the television on louder than I needed to.

2

The doctor's office was nice, ultra-modern and painted a glossy dark blue colour with wooden trim that matched the door. There was a light grey couch along one wall, facing a low, sprawling desk, and two matching easy chairs sat in the centre of the room. There was a painting on the wall over the desk; a lone grey wolf on a rock against a bleak grey sky. It was almost too well-composed. I spent a moment trying to decide whether or not I liked it before looking away. My eyes flitted around the room and finally came to rest on the man behind the desk. He was younger than I had imagined — thirty-five, maybe — clean-shaven, with silver-streaked black hair and a ruddy complexion. There was an aquarium on the wall, and I distracted myself from what he was saying by watching it carefully. I knew something about fish. I'd had a big tank in my room until ... well, I couldn't quite remember. What had happened to that tank? I thought carefully. I supposed I'd just lost interest in it. I frowned. Strange that I couldn't remember that. I looked down at my hands, as though they might hold the answers ... traced tiny white scars across my knuckles — lots of them. There was one long one, extending from the middle of one index finger all the way down to my wrist. I squinted at it carefully. Now, where had *that* come from? It had been there a long time — a couple of years, anyway. I remembered them healing, bloody scabs all over the backs of my hands. I'd told Matthew I hurt myself fishing a ball out of the neighbours' rose bushes, but that wasn't the truth. For the life of me, though, I couldn't remember what had really happened.

"So you'll come again tomorrow, and then Friday," the doctor was saying. "I think it's a good idea if we meet three times a week for the next six weeks or so. Let's see if we can make it Monday, Wednesday and Friday, starting next week. Then we'll take a look at how we're doing, and decide whether you need to keep coming. How does that sound?"

"It sounds lousy." I sat cross-legged, yoga-fashion, in my chair, a habit that always drove my mother up the wall. "This whole thing is stupid. I'm not crazy, I don't need to get my head shrunk."

"Well, let's talk about why you're here, then. Why do you suppose your teacher ordered this evaluation?"

"Look, it wasn't that big a deal. It was just this stupid thing that happened in English class. I had this knife I lifted from another kid — a switchblade; he'd stolen it from someplace, too. Anyway, this guy was really pissing me off ..."

"The one you stole the knife from?"

"No, a completely different guy. This guy that sits behind me in class. He was tapping on his desk with a ruler and humming, and it was driving me around the bend. So I thought it would be interesting to pull the blade on him ... just to see what he would do, you know?"

"And what did he do?"

"I never really got the chance to find out. The teacher — Miz Waller — she saw the blade and she freaked out. That's it. I'm not crazy, it was just a stupid thing that happened. It's not gonna happen again, so I don't even know why I have to come here."

"You're here to talk," said the doctor with a superior little half-smile that made me seethe. "Obviously your teacher thinks pulling out a knife when someone's annoying you is a little ... extreme. Maybe we can find out why you don't think it's such a big deal."

"So, what do you want me to say? You want to hear all about my family and my shitty childhood?"

"If that's where you want to start, go ahead. Tell me about your family."

"That's not what I call them." I squeezed my hands together tightly in my lap. "I don't have a family. Hell, nobody's got a family anymore, do they? Mom in the kitchen and Dad heading out to the office with his brief-case. It's just three of us; my old lady and Brad ... that's her other kid. He's nine."

"Your brother?"

"Half," I said a little too defensively. "I mean, he's an okay kid, but ... well, we have different fathers, so it's not like he's my *real* brother."

"Do you ever see your own father?" Eschen asked. It sounded like an innocent enough question. But after seventeen years of having to explain my family to every teacher, neighbour and nosy stranger I met, I tended to get a little snippy about the issue.

"I don't *have* a father," I said.

Eschen raised an eyebrow.

"Artificial insemination?" he said with the hint of a genuine smile. "Or immaculate conception, maybe."

"Hardly." I shifted around in my chair. I thought about standing up and pacing around but I didn't want Eschen to think I was threatening him or anything. I figured he'd slap me into some kind of baby psycho hospital if he thought I was going to hurt him.

"See, my mother's this major slut," I said, my voice as flat as I could manage. "And my father was some guy she picked up in a bar on New Year's Eve. At least that's what my grandmother told me. I doubt my mother even remembers the occasion of my conception, and if she does she's never felt the need to enlighten me about the blessed event."

"That sounds like a well-rehearsed speech," said Eschen. "You've said that before."

"Well, I've had a lot of time to think about it. All that time I was supposed to spend out in the backyard playing catch with my daddy, I guess. Does that explain all my damn problems? Am I cured? Can I *go* now?"

"Your guidance counsellor said he thought you might benefit from talking to someone," said Eschen slowly, after giving me a good stare. "Like I said before, we'll meet three times weekly for six weeks, and then we'll decide where we're going from there."

"Sounds like I don't have a choice."

"You do have a choice," the doctor replied. He was all business now. "There are always choices, Jareth. You can co-operate, or you can sit there in your chair for eighteen hours and let me stare at you. But, frankly, if you want to stay in school, I think it's in your best interest to co-operate." He leaned forward, his eyes burning into mine. "So what's it going to be, Jareth? You think we could maybe have a conversation?"

Eschen had won our impromptu little staring contest, and I went back to looking at the aquarium.

"Yeah, I guess we could have a conversation," I mumbled.

The hour dragged on interminably. It was like the job interviews we'd practised in Grade Ten Business class ... or it was like a ping-pong match. I couldn't decide which.

"What do you do for fun, Jareth?"

"I don't know. Stuff. You know, hang out. Watch TV, whatever."

"Who do you hang out with? What do you like to watch?"

Good grief, I thought. The guy was worse than my mother. It was like a game, though, trying to answer his question enough to keep him happy without actually giving him any information.

Finally a buzzer on his desk went off, and he stood up and extended a hand to me.

"Well," he said automatically, "our time's up."

I shook the hand he was offering as he continued to talk.

"So we'll see you tomorrow afternoon?" he said, checking a thick leather book on his desk. "How does four-fifteen sound?"

"Sounds as good as anything, I guess." I closed the door hard behind me on my way out of the office.

■ ■ ■

On the way home I leaned my head against the bus window, enjoying the feeling of the rattling glass against my skull. It was comforting ... relaxing, somehow. I thought about hitchhiking someplace, about climbing into a car with some total stranger on his way to someplace far, far away. Starting over, maybe changing my name. A whole new life. It would have to be an improvement over this one, at any rate.

There were nine bus stops between the building where Eschen's office was and my house. I counted them half-consciously, and jolted awake just in time to pull the little overhead rope to tell the bus driver to let me off at the next stop. I got off the bus across the road from my house and plodded up the sidewalk in a daze, my thoughts pleasantly unfocussed. I was still half in a dream from my nap on the bus. There were things to worry about, that was for sure ... but there would be time to worry about them later. Right now I felt okay, and I didn't want to do anything that might spoil that.

■ ■ ■

I plodded up the stairs without bothering to remove my shoes. I hadn't shovelled the driveway yet after yesterday's snowstorm, but the snow was packed firmly enough that my feet weren't too wet. I was wearing my old canvas sneakers with the paint on them from when Matthew and I had painted the garage of my house a couple summers earlier. I threw my jacket across a chair in the living room. The old lady wouldn't be home at this time of day to complain about it.

I went down the hall to my room and turned on the

light. Brad lay under a pile of blankets on my bed, his head hanging down over the side. He was a cute kid, I supposed. You wouldn't have known we were related by looking at us; I guess we each looked like our fathers. Brad was covered in freckles from head to toe, and his hair was curly and flaming red — brighter than any other redhead I'd ever seen. It was coarse, too, like a brillo pad. My own hair was blond and straight, and my complexion could best be described as "pasty." My only resemblance to my mother's side of the family was my mouth; wide and full of teeth, with thick red lips that made the rest of my face look even whiter. Back in grade school the other kids used to ask me if I was wearing lipstick, to which my standard reply had been something really clever, like "screw you."

I looked at Brad's hair sticking out from under my sheets and playfully reached out and gave it a tug.

"Geez! What'd you do that for?" Brad mumbled, waking up and rubbing his head.

"Why are you in my room?" I shot back.

"I was watching TV and I fell asleep," he said quickly.

"The TV's not on," I pointed out.

Brad didn't say anything, but he sat up.

"Why don't you sleep in your own room?"

"There's monsters in there."

"It's the middle of the day."

"They get invisible in the afternoon. So they can sneak up on you."

"I can't believe you're nine years old and you still think you got monsters chasing you," I said.

I didn't bother to ask why Brad was still in his pyjamas at four o'clock in the afternoon. The kid was always sick. He'd been sick his whole life, since before he was born: none of his organs seemed to work right, and in nine years of life he'd had surgery an average of once a year to fix one thing or another. Plus, he caught every little virus that was going around. It was a hell of a way to live, really ... I hadn't been keeping track, but at that point I guessed he probably hadn't been to school in a week.

"Didja go see that doctor?" he asked me.

I blinked innocently. "What doctor?"

"The psychologist. The one the guidance counsellor sent you to." Brad bounced on the edge of the bed slightly.

"Don't jump on my bed. You'll wreck the springs."

"I wasn't jumping. Did you go?" Once Brad took hold of an idea, he was usually pretty reluctant to let it go.

"Yeah, I went. And he's not a psychologist, he's a psychiatrist."

"Whatever. What was the doctor's name?"

I frowned.

"What do you want to know that for?"

"Just wondering."

"Well, it was Doctor Eschen. Not that it's any of your business."

"Ooh." Brad nodded knowingly. "He's a real tightass."

"Where did you hear that?"

"I went to see Doctor Burns last year, in the same office." He made a face. "Remember?"

"Yeah. I think so. You went to see a lot of doctors last year."

"But, it was right around Easter. That's how come I remember ... it was the day before Easter weekend. When that guy Mom was going out with decided all my problems were in my head. I was in the waiting room with

Mom, and these other two people were there waiting to see *their* doctors. One of them said Eschen was a real tightass, and Mom got all mad at him for using nasty language in front of her baby." He grinned. "Like I ain't never heard that kind of language from *her*."

He was a good kid, I thought, studying his face. His father was a real son of a bitch ... Keith something ... but the kid seemed to be turning out okay. He was sharp.

I walked around my room. I had way too much furniture, mismatched garbage my mother had accumulated at garage sales over the years. The whole house had a tendency to get cluttered, but the worst of the mess always seemed to wind up in my room. I ran my fingers lightly over a table under the window. What had I been thinking about in the doctor's lobby? I frowned, trying to follow my train of thought backward.

"Brad, what happened to that aquarium I used to have?" I asked him finally.

Brad pretended to think about it for a minute, but I could see his eyes shifting around, looking for a way to change the subject.

"I don't remember," he said. He looked around the room until his eye caught my chess set, a hinged wooden box folded up in the corner. "Hey, can you play chess with me?" he asked.

"Maybe later." Two could play at this game. "I'm still thinkin' about that fish tank."

"I been practising," he persisted.

"Are you sure about the fish tank? I mean, it wasn't that long ago ... a year or so, maybe. It was a real big fish tank; I had it right here, under the window."

"I said I don't remember!" He was getting really

agitated, but still I pressed him.

"You don't remember the fish tank, or you don't remember what happened to it?"

"You got mad at Mom and you dumped it all over the floor and then broke it to pieces with your fist, okay?"

As soon as he said that I felt bad. Brad really hated it when I got mad ... sometimes I think he got sicker when I was fighting with the old lady.

"That's weird," I muttered. Again I looked at the scars up and down my arms, across the back of my hand — little white spider webs I couldn't remember. Things you'd scarcely notice if you didn't know they were there. "It's weird that I could forget a thing like that."

"You dumped it out and the fish came washing out all over the floor," Brad said, his voice wavering. "And you kept punching the glass until there was blood all over the floor. I tried to pick up the fish and put them in water but they all died."

Of course. How could I have forgotten that? I couldn't even remember what we were fighting about; something about one of her boyfriends, more than likely.

Brad's lower lip was quivering, and I could tell he was ready to lose it. "Hey, look, kid, I'm sorry I brought it up."

"You're pretty stupid sometimes, Jareth." Brad wiped his nose with the back of his hand.

"Well, you're pretty much a complete moron yourself," I shot back louder than I'd meant to.

Brad stood and moved over to the door, suddenly nervous. A lock of red hair fell across his nose, and he clutched at the waist of his pyjamas pants. It occurred to me that Brad was getting very thin, and I didn't much like the sound of the cough he was developing.

"I think I'm gonna go to bed now," he told me, his mouth set in a hard line. "Tell Mom not to wake me up until morning."

"Okay." I looked down at the floor, a little ashamed that I'd yelled at him. I thought about calling after him that I didn't mean it, but somehow the words wouldn't come out of my mouth.

I sat on the table, which groaned under my weight. I stared at the mirror across the room and let my eyes lose their focus. My image swayed and twisted as I squinted into the glass. It was nearly five o'clock; the old lady would be home soon. The clock in the living room chimed five, but it was a few minutes fast. I still had time to get out of the way before she came home.

It crossed my mind that I should do something about fixing her dinner, but I dismissed the thought. Let the old lady fend for herself, I decided. I'd hear about it later, about what a selfish little bastard I was, but at the time I didn't much care. Down the hall, in the smaller bedroom, Brad was hacking away, a wet, painful, choking cough. It was a terrible sound.

I blinked my eyes back into focus and ran a comb through my hair. I didn't look so healthy myself, I decided. Blue half-moons were developing under my eyes, and my hands were shaky. I figured I was probably worrying too much about this evaluation thing with Eschen. *Tightass*, I thought, and laughed. That kid was pretty sharp, all right. I didn't particularly want the third degree from the old lady about my session with the doctor, either, so I grabbed my jacket from the living room and made for the door.

"I'm going to see Matthew!" I announced a half-second

before I remembered Brad was supposed to be sleeping.

"Okay," he said anyway. "Have a good time."

Poor kid, I thought, not without some affection.

I plodded heavily back down the stairs and outside, pulling the door shut behind me. I didn't bother to lock it; the old lady could worry about that when she got home. Not that we had anything worth stealing, anyway.

3

I guess you could say I was mainly on my own at school, except for Matthew, although I admit that he was my best friend out of habit and convenience more than out of any great common interest we shared. Also, the pair of us stood out like a couple of sore thumbs among all the rich kids who were shuttled in every morning from way out in the country. We didn't even fit in with the other outcasts.

And so our friendship, such as it was, had endured for many years.

The intercom in the front foyer of Matthew's apartment building hadn't worked in months. I let myself in using an old bank card I had in my wallet, sliding the card in between the door and the doorframe and tripping the catch. Then I took the elevator up to the eighth floor and knocked on the door. After a minute or two, Vic — Matthew's stepfather — opened it a little crossly. Victor Fleming was a big bull of a man with a voice like a foghorn. He'd married Matthew's mother a couple of years earlier — around eighth grade, I guess — and he treated Matthew okay, although his tolerance level for me had never been very high. He was a gruff, matter-of-fact person, about as much fun as a root canal. Matthew said he was cranky because he worked weird shifts — twelve or fifteen hours at a time. He only worked three or four days a week, though, so he was usually home when I went over there. I remembered Matthew telling me Vic was some kind of social worker, although his size and that low, scratchy voice of his always put me in mind of a truck driver or a plumber.

"Matthew's eating dinner, Jareth," Vic told me sharply, starting to push the door shut. I inserted my foot neatly between the door and the doorframe.

"I'll wait in his room," I promised. "It won't be a problem." I flashed him a grin, knowing he didn't buy that act for a minute. My Prince Charming number never did much for him. He let me in, though, just like I knew he would. Vic always let me in, though I could never figure out why.

"Go on, then," he grumbled, gesturing vaguely toward the hallway of the three-bedroom apartment. "You know where it is."

I waved at Matthew, who was crouched sheepishly at the dinner table between Vic's daughters. Matthew didn't wave back.

"Jareth, have you eaten yet?" Matthew's mother asked me. Good old Mrs. F. She knew exactly what I was doing there.

"No ... but that's okay." I stopped grinning and gave her my doe-eyed street-urchin look, which is almost as good as my grin. "I wouldn't want to impose."

"He never wants to impose," mumbled Vic, settling

back down at the table. "Every night, he doesn't want to impose. Isn't there any *food* at your house, Jareth?"

"Don't worry about it, Vic," Mrs. Fleming chided him. "It's not a problem. Sit down, Jareth, there's always room for one more."

I pulled up a chair from the living room and perched at a corner of the table.

"How was your day?" she asked me.

I shrugged. "It wasn't too bad. The same as usual, I guess. You know, I went to school, I did my homework, watched some TV ... all that."

"That's more of an answer than I ever get out of Matthew," she told me with a smile. "He comes in, I say, 'How was your day?'... he tells me it was okay. Every day, it's okay. Either my son leads a very boring life, or there's a lot he's not telling me."

Matthew, for his part, simply clenched his fork tightly in his fist and shovelled an impossible amount of food into his mouth. He chewed furiously, staring down at his plate the entire time.

Mrs. Fleming set a plate of macaroni down in front of me. "It's nothing fancy tonight," she apologized with a friendly smile, "but it's better than nothing."

"It's fine," Vic told her, smirking awkwardly. He sat stiffly in his chair, speaking each word carefully. "Now, sit down and eat."

We ate quietly, but amicably. There were none of the sparks and jabs that usually marked meals at my place. Rachel, who was ten, stole occasional glances in my direction, while Megan, who was thirteen and in love with me, looked down at her plate and giggled. I figured in a month or two she'd realize I was no great catch, but for now she couldn't be in the same room with me without staring and turning red.

Matthew, who was almost as red-faced as Megan, finished his meal quickly and excused himself, leaving me alone at the table with his family.

I took my time eating, and when I had finished, I wiped my mouth as politely as could be.

"Thanks for the meal, Mrs. Fleming," I said, backing my chair away from the table.

"You could return the chair to where you got it," suggested Vic, not unkindly.

"Yes, sir." I flashed him the grin again, and he forced a smirk in return. I moved the chair back into the living room, then nodded separate farewells to Rachel and to Megan, who nearly swooned, and made my way down the hall to Matthew's room.

"You could *phone* once in a while, instead of just *showing up* at the door," Matthew said as I shut the door behind us. "Vic gets all pissed off, and you can hardly blame him. It's not like we don't eat dinner at exactly the same time every day."

I shrugged and sat on the bed, knowing he didn't really mind as much as he pretended to. I looked around. Matthew's room was small and white. No personality. He wasn't even allowed to put posters up; the landlord was anal about his lousy paint job. Our landlord, on the other hand, was just glad if we'd paid the rent by the fifth of the month. My own room had more tack holes than drywall.

"I had to get out of the house," I said finally. "It was just ... claustrophobic. Like the walls were caving in."

"How's Brad?" Matthew asked.

"He's sick. The same as always."

It was funny, usually you couldn't shut the pair of us up. True, half the time we were arguing about something, but this night there was just nothing to say. There was something unspoken between us, the memory of what had happened the previous night. We sat in silence for a couple of minutes before Matthew spoke again.

"We're going to Vermont next month. Me and my mother and the girls."

"How come?"

"She won a prize in some draw ... a skiing trip for four people. Vic's staying home so we can all go."

"Well, that sure is nice of him."

"Geez, Jareth, if you can't carry on a civil *conversation* without getting snotty ..."

I frowned.

"I don't feel like having a conversation. And I especially don't feel like having a conversation about the sainted Victor Fleming. Let's *do* something."

"Like what? Like, break into a house and scare some old fart to death? I don't think so, Jareth. Last night was enough for one lifetime. Enough for *ten* lifetimes. But thanks anyway."

"Did you notice I put gas in your car?" I said, to change the subject.

"I was gonna ask you about that. Where the hell did you *take* that car last night? There's, like, two hundred miles on it that I didn't put there."

I shrugged.

"Nowhere much. I just felt like going for a drive. Up through the country, you know. It actually wasn't snowing as hard up north of the escarpment as it was down here."

"Yeah, well ... get your *own* car if you're going to drive two hundred miles for no reason."

"And where am I going to get money for my own car? I'm not fortunate enough to be blessed with my mother's old car for Christmas."

"And speaking of money ..."

"Yeah?"

"Well, we took a bunch of it out of that old guy's drawer yesterday. Whatever happened to that?" he said, staring at me suspiciously.

"I put it back," I said, trying not to look right at him. "Although it probably wouldn't have mattered if I'd just kept it, you know. It's not like old Lloyd's gonna miss a little petty cash like that."

Matthew glared, his close-set grey eyes narrowing suspiciously.

"I don't remember seeing you put any money back. And who the hell is Lloyd?" he said.

"Lloyd? That was the old guy's name."

I took this opportunity to relate to Matthew the story of the old woman at the mall, realizing for the first time how bizarre the whole thing was. Matthew listened, his mouth agape. By the time I'd finished the story of how I'd driven the old lady right back to her door, he'd forgotten all about the money.

"Excuse me, Jareth, but do you know how stupid that was?" His voice was shrill as he bounced up and down on the bed. "Not to mention sick. Did you stick around to see her reaction? Watch her scream and cry over the old bastard? Maybe you even offered to call an ambulance for her."

I leaned forward to catch Matthew's arm before he completely lost control.

"Will you keep your voice down?" I hissed. "And anyway, I don't see what your problem is. If anything, this is *good*."

Matthew pulled away from me. He stood up and paced. Then he grabbed a dictionary from the bookshelf on his desk and flipped through it.

"Good? You want to tell me how this is good, Jareth? Let's take a look at 'good' in the dictionary, shall we?" He scanned for a few seconds before throwing the book at me. "Gosh, Jareth, there's like half a page in there under 'good,' and not one definition comes close to *driving some old lady back to the spot where we just left her husband dead in the middle of the bedroom floor.*"

He shoved his face real close to mine for that last part, stage-whispering so furiously I could feel little drops of spittle landing on my cheek. I pushed him away from me and stood up, pacing as far away from him as I could in the tiny bedroom.

"Come off it, Matthew. The old woman thinks I'm a *saint*. Driving her home from the mall when her poor old husband couldn't make it. Can't you just hear her talking to the police? 'What a nice young man this is! What's that? Break into someone's house? No, no. Not *this* boy. He drove me home from the *mall*.'" I grinned. "I tell you, Matt, if the sun shone out of my ass, this woman couldn't be any more nuts about me."

There was a long pause as Matthew thought about this. He sat in the chair by his desk and put his head in his hands. His shoulders heaved, and he shook his head. With his hands over his face like that, I thought for a second that he was crying. When he lifted his head, though, he was smiling.

"You stupid son of a bitch," he said. "You realize what you've just done? You've gone and got us a character witness. Boy, next time it snows, you should go over to her place and offer to shovel her driveway or something. Say, 'Hey, Mrs. Whatever-your-name-is, I read about your husband in the paper and I'm real sorry; can I do anything to help you out?' She'll probably write you into her will or something."

I thought that over for a second, deciding it was less stupid than most of the ideas that usually came out of his mouth. "You really think it'll be in the newspapers?" I wondered aloud.

"Sure thing," said Matthew. "If this guy was such an upstanding citizen and all that, they'll probably write big tribute articles on him for, like, a week. His what d'ya call it — obituary — is probably in today's paper."

Impulsively I opened his door and put one foot out into the hallway. "Let's go."

"Where?" he said.

"Well, to get a newspaper. There's one in your living room; I saw it on the couch. We can look at the obituary page."

Matthew sat back on the bed and shook his head.

"Hang off a bit. Vic's reading the paper now. We'll have to wait."

"How do you know?"

"He *always* reads the paper after dinner. Every night. The whole thing, front to back. You don't want to disturb him. You can't even take one section until he's finished the whole thing. He likes it to be in order the whole time he's reading it; it's like some kind of sacred ritual."

I shrugged. "What's he gonna do, bite my head off? I'm not scared of Vic; I'll go get the paper."

A moment later, Vic lowered the paper slowly from in front of his face to find me grinning at him.

"What's up, Jareth?" he asked warily.

"I was just wondering if maybe you've read the news section yet."

He lifted an eyebrow at me, his eerily translucent green eyes prying into mine. "What's this, Jareth? Are you taking an interest in the world around you all of a sudden?"

"Well, it's just that we've got this project to do for school, and we need to look in the paper. I was just going to ask, you know, if you've finished with that section, maybe could I have it?"

Vic frowned thoughtfully, his reddish forehead creasing up. He ran a hand over his hair — black and slicked back, bulletproof, like a greaser from the 1950s. I tried not to laugh as I thought to myself how much he looked like the Fonz.

"Funny, I didn't think you and Matthew had any classes together this semester," he said after a moment. That was Vic Fleming for you. Always smelling rats. Not that there weren't any to be smelled, of course. Hell, this was probably the granddaddy of all rats, I thought to myself.

"Actually, we don't," I admitted, thinking on my feet. "But Matthew's got economics this year, and I took it last year, so I thought maybe I could help him with this project, since he waited so long to start it. You know Matthew. Always waiting for the last minute to get moving."

I kept right on grinning, and after a moment's contemplation Vic shook his head and let out a throaty chuckle.

"Take it," he said, shoving the entire paper toward me with his foot. "Just don't cut anything out; I haven't finished reading it. Bring it back when you're done. And try not to wrinkle it up too much, will you?"

I grabbed the section I wanted and jogged happily back down the hall to Matthew's room.

"If you weren't such a punk, Jareth, you'd have a marvellous career in used car sales," Vic called after me. "And don't run in the house!"

I closed the door and raised a finger in salute to Vic — the middle one. "Son of a bitch," I muttered.

"He's not so bad," Matthew said weakly, leaning back in his desk chair. "Once you get used to him. He's got a lot of ... what do you call them, *quirks*. But he's really kind of cool. You know, once in a while."

I gave him a disgusted look. "Yeah, sure. Whatever."

I spread the paper out on the bed and flipped through it. Matthew hovered over me, reading over my shoulder. Normally that would have driven me nuts, but I was so intent on finding old Lloyd's obituary that I scarcely noticed.

We found the article at the same time.

"That's him!" I shouted, forgetting to keep my voice down. I picked up the paper and read the entire thing twice while Matthew strained to get a look at it.

"Poor Lloyd Clemence, and his grieving widow, Constance," I said. "Hey, this guy was a founding member of the Central Park Community Centre."

"Constance Clemence. That's a pretty brutal name."

"Well, she wasn't born with it, she married it."

There was a picture above it, an ancient wedding photo of the two of them. At first glance it didn't look much like the photo was connected to the article.

"Well?" said Matthew after a good four or five minutes of stomping impatiently around the room.

"Well, what?"

"What does the damn thing say?"

"It says he died of natural causes in his Conrad Street home," I said with a relieved grin. Matthew grabbed the paper away from me.

"Nothing about a break-in?"

"Nope." I grinned. "It doesn't even say he left the window open."

At this, Matthew howled with laughter ... hysterical relief, I supposed. He rolled over backwards and landed with a *thud* on the floor. He had a terrible, horsy laugh, I thought, stifling my own urge to break into hysterics.

After maybe a minute we heard Vic pounding on the door. "That's the funniest Economics project I've ever heard," he thundered. "You might want to remember we've got neighbours here."

That was enough to send me into hysterics, too, and it took another couple of knocks on the door to get us to calm down.

The way I figured it, I'd won *that* game hands-down. I'd won against Matthew — I'd gotten to keep the money. I'd won against Mrs. Constance Clemence — she wouldn't suspect a thing. But, most of all, I'd won against poor old Lloyd Clemence, formerly of 104 Conrad Street. We'd come out on top, and old Lloyd — well, he was just about on his way to being worm meat. Pushing up the old daisies. So long, Lloyd.

Funny how I didn't feel too great about that particular victory.

4

As the weeks went by, old Lloyd Clemence started to fade just a little bit from my mind. I went on with my days, hung out with Matthew, went to school, talked to Doctor Eschen. But it was funny, every once in a while I'd pass some old guy walking along the street, or I'd see two kids wrestling in the hallway, or see something on TV and the whole thing would come right back like it had happened the day before.

When Brad was a little kid, I used to play blocks with him. We'd pile them up as high as we could, higher than his head if we could manage it, and he'd stand staring at the tower for about five seconds before pulling the block out of the bottom of the pile.

That's what it felt like, passing through those days. Going to class, going to Matthew's, going to the doctor's office ... adding block upon block upon block. But any second now, somebody was going to come along and yank the bottom away.

February had given way to March, and though there was still snow on the ground, there was considerably less of it. The air was warmer, and every once in a while the clouds would part and there'd be a hint of something in the breeze — a bird singing, whatever — that meant spring was right around the corner.

And then it happened.

■ ■ ■

I didn't want to go to school that morning. I didn't want to go to school any morning, but this particular morning it was especially difficult. There was an icy rain falling outside that rattled the aluminum siding on the house and brought a numbing chill to every movement. I also had an appointment with Doctor Eschen that afternoon, which didn't exactly thrill me, either. That was the arrangement, though ... the big guidance deal, as Matthew had called it. Eschen and Biology. I'd resigned myself to the reality of the situation, but that didn't make it any easier to live with.

When I got out of the shower my mother lay sprawled out in a chair in the living room, still wearing last night's clothes. It was seven-fifteen in the morning, and she was due at work at eight.

I brushed past her indifferently, looking for my shoes. She reached out a bony hand as I walked by and grabbed hold of my arm. I jumped about a foot in the air, surprised she was awake.

"Jareth, honey?"

I pulled my arm out of her grip.

"What's the problem?" I snapped, a little embarrassed at having been startled like that by such a stupid thing.

"Be a dear and call your mom's work for her, won't

you? Tell them I'm coming in late today ... Tell them I've got to stay at home with Brad."

"Brad's going to school today," I told her a little self-righteously. "He said he was feeling better. Besides, you never bother to stay home with him when he *is* sick."

The old lady's voice grew harsh.

"If I stayed home with him every time he was sick, young man, I'd lose my job. Did you ever think of that? *You* wouldn't have a place to live, for starters. How would you like that?"

"Shut up." To top it off, it was a Monday morning, and I was crankier than usual. "If you're too drunk to go to work, *you* call them."

That shut her up, for the moment at least. I'd made my fair share of phone calls on her behalf, but this day I just wasn't feeling that charitable. My mother worked as a phone service representative for a big mail-order company. You know the TV ads, "Call *right now* to buy this marvellous piece of crap and you'll receive some other useless piece of crap you just can't do without, *absolutely free*. Our operators are standing by!" Anyway, it was probably her fifth job in about seven or eight years, and the only one she'd managed to keep for more than a year. Every time she lost a job she'd tell me it was corporate downsizing or some kind of personality conflict with her manager or something, but I always figured it was because she didn't show up half the time — and the other half of the time, she probably smelled like a brewery and couldn't do the job.

I found my shoes and shuffled on down the hall to check on Brad, who was fumbling around in the bathroom. "You okay in there, kid?"

I heard his affirmative reply over the noise of the running water. A few minutes later he came out of the washroom dressed in his good clothes. He didn't go to school much, and when he did, he liked to make an event of it.

"I hope those guys don't go after me today," he said casually. He went into his room to comb his hair and I followed him.

"What guys?" I asked, watching as he forced the comb through the unruly mass of his wild red hair.

"Oh, just these kids, you know? Tony Savage, and Nathaniel and Dmitri. Last time I was at school they got mad at me for something, and they said they'd get me tomorrow. But that was like a week and a half ago, so maybe they forgot by now."

"You're a cool kid, you know that?" I told Brad, and ruffled his hair. He got this look on his face like I'd just given him a pony. "Why were they mad at you?"

"'Cause I said they were a bunch of Neanderthals. You should see them. They're always picking on younger kids, you know?" And he got this indignant look on his face, like he was ready to take them all on single-handedly.

"Well, you just stay away from those kids, okay?" I said. "Stick close to the teacher or something when you go out for recess."

Brad frowned. "What do you think I *am*, some kind of baby? I can take care of myself ... I was just *saying*, I hope they wait for tomorrow. That's all."

I shook my head, grinning, and went back out to the living room. The old lady was sprawled out on the couch now, her hand over her eyes like she was in some silent movie.

"That hangover virus sure is a bitch, ain't it?" I said

loudly in her ear. She sat up real quick, like she'd just become sober in a hurry.

"I've had just about enough of you this morning. I don't know who you think you are all of a sudden that you're superior to your mother, but —"

I didn't hear the rest. I slammed the door on my way out and slid down the driveway to the sidewalk. I stopped to skate in a patch of ice near the corner of my street. I wasn't in any great hurry to get to school. The freezing rain gave everything a dark, dangerous-looking sheen, and the sky rolled with ominous black clouds. Already I had this feeling like it was going to be a long day.

It had been three weeks since my little adventure at the home of Lloyd Clemence, and for some reason I couldn't get him out of my head. I kept seeing him there on the bedroom floor, his mouth opening and closing like a fish out of water.

By the time I got off the bus in front of the doctor's office that afternoon, I'd been thinking about Lloyd all day. It was strange that I couldn't get him out of my head that day. After all, it was three weeks to the day since the whole thing had happened. Maybe that was it ... the anniversary, as it were. I even toyed with the idea of mentioning the incident to Doctor Eschen when I talked to him. It wasn't like I wanted to get it off my conscience so much as I wanted to see how he'd react. In the end, though, I decided it would be better if I held onto this secret for the time being. I was half enjoying this relationship I'd established with Eschen; I was getting pretty good at talking for fifty minutes and saying absolutely nothing. I wondered how much the school board was paying for these little sessions, to have me sit across from this high-rent shrink and entertain him with cheesy little stories from my child-hood while he scribbled notes furiously with that four-coloured Bic pen he always used. I figured he was pretty stupid to think these charming little anecdotes had any significance. Either that or he was more perceptive than he was letting on. That second possibility — the idea that he could see right through my act — was enough to keep me just a little bit on edge. All the same, I got through my appointment each time without giving anything away, and the feeling of relief as I left the office was nearly over-whelming.

There was a convenience store by the bus stop down-stairs, and I wandered in to kill some time until my bus showed up. On the wall over by the magazine rack there was a big stationery shelf set up, covered in pens and rolls of masking tape and all that stuff. I wandered over there with my eye on the stationery, but on the way I acciden-tally-on-purpose knocked a couple of magazines off the rack. As I bent over to pick them up I slid a comic book up inside my jacket. I don't have much interest in comic books, but I thought maybe I could give it to Brad. I made a big production of cleaning up the other books on the floor, looking up at the old man behind the counter with this look on my face like "whoops, aren't I a klutz."

Then, as I stood up and put the other magazines back where they belonged, something on the shelf beside them caught my eye. It was a thing of beauty, something that had no place in a cheesy little convenience store among the off-brand pencil-crayons and dusty boxes of paperclips and elastic bands: a sketchbook, a big hardcover one with a shiny black cover. I opened it up and ran my fingers over one of the pages. It was full of heavy yellowish paper, perfect for sketching in pencil. I hadn't taken art since Grade Nine, nor had I even thought about drawing a picture since I was about fourteen, but something about this book appealed to me. I still had most of the money I'd taken from the old man's dresser drawer. All in all, there had been nearly five hundred dollars, and I was trying to make it last as long as I could, but I knew I wanted this book. I thought of staging another wipeout, of tucking it into my jacket along with the comic book, but something inside me said no. This was something that had to be properly bought and paid for — never mind that I was paying for it with stolen money.

I brought it up to the cash register and paid for the book, twenty-two dollars' worth, taking care not to rustle the comic book that was pressed between my jacket and my shirt front. Then I stuffed it into my knapsack and went outside to catch my bus.

■ ■ ■

Maybe it's just hindsight playing tricks on me, but for some reason the front walkway felt much longer than usual that day. I had this feeling of — what? Impending doom? Some vague kind of sensation that something was terribly wrong. At any rate, the second I stepped inside the door the feeling intensified. Something was amiss. I could feel the hairs on the back of my arms standing on end.

"Mom?" came Brad's voice from upstairs. For a second I relaxed. Nothing to worry about. Brad was upstairs watching TV, that was all.

"Nah, it's Jareth," I called back. I dropped my knapsack on the brown vinyl hassock inside the front door, kicked off my shoes, pulled the comic book out of my jacket. "Hey, Brad? I brought you a present."

There was a long wait before I heard a weak response, a long, high whimper, like air being let out of a balloon too slowly.

About a week and a half earlier, I'd told Doctor Eschen the story of how I'd broken my nose when I was seven or eight. The old lady had sent me away to camp for the summer when Brad was born because she'd wanted me out of the house. I'd been hiking through the woods with nine or ten other campers when another kid and I got separated from the group. We'd gone right off the trail, looking for a squirrel or something, and the bush was dense enough that we had to walk single file. The other kid – Mark, I think his name was – had been at camp before, so he was more used to the woods than I was. I let him go ahead of me, and when he pushed a tree branch out of his way, it snapped back and hit me across the face, knocking me flat.

That was the same feeling I got when I heard that noise – blind panic, like somebody'd smacked me hard in the face with the branch of a tree. Brad was a tough little kid; he wasn't the type to admit he was in pain, even when he was. That whimpering cry was something I never thought I'd hear from him: a cry of defeat.

I bolted upstairs, eight steps in two leaps, and tore down the hall to find the source of the noise. When I found the little boy on the wooden floor of the old lady's room, stomach-down in his pyjama bottoms and one of my old tee-shirts, I had to choke back my lunch. His right arm was gathered at a grotesque, impossible angle against his chest. There was blood all over his face, spreading out in a puddle across the parquet flooring the old lady was so damn fussy about.

"Shit!" I took a step back, reeling against the doorframe while a million thoughts flew through my head. Thoughts I didn't need right now: my biology homework, my next appointment with Doctor Eschen, wondering what Matthew was having for dinner that night. The thing before me on the floor was nothing; a figment of my imagination; a TV show come to life.

"Jareth?" Brad croaked, lifting his head slowly off the floor.

That was enough to snap me back to reality. The look on Brad's face was haunting; his eyes were wild, desperate, his nose and mouth covered in blood that bubbled out his nostrils.

I had to call an ambulance.

I scrambled for the phone and dialled, my hands shaking. I listened to it ring four, five times. Finally, someone on the other end picked it up.

Whatever had taken over my body during that crisis upstairs at Lloyd's house kicked in now, speaking the words for me. I gave the address calmly, as though I'd done this a thousand times. Like I said before, I'm pretty good in a disaster. It isn't until later that I usually go nuts.

When I was finished talking I let the phone drop from my fingers, heard it rattling on the floor, the operator's voice calling for me to stay on the line, but it didn't register.

I knelt beside Brad, lifting his head, setting it in my lap, trying to wipe away some of the blood with my hands.

"It's okay, you're gonna be fine. They got an ambulance coming right now," I said, my voice wavering unexpectedly.

"Jareth?" Brad's good hand gripped at my jacket, leaving a bloody smear. "Jareth, I think something's really wrong."

"S'okay, kid. You're gonna be fine."

"I wanted to stay at school today," he said. "But I got sick at recess. Mrs. Kelly called Mom at work."

Brad coughed with much effort. I used the neck of the tee-shirt he was wearing to wipe some of the blood away from his mouth. Horrified, I realized he was spitting up blood.

"Maybe you better not talk any more right now," I suggested, starting to feel faint from all that blood on the floor. "We just gotta wait for the ambulance, okay? It'll be here real soon."

I looked at the boy, prone on the floor. When Matthew had taken a first aid course the previous semester, he'd taken great pride in telling me everything he'd learned. I strained to remember something ... anything ... he'd said to me that might be of assistance. Roll him over on his side, I thought vaguely, he'll choke on all that blood. I bent to turn him over.

"Look at the mess I made," he moaned. "The old lady's gonna kill me."

"I'll clean it up for you," I said. "She won't even know it happened."

It didn't occur to me until much later that he'd never called our mother "the old lady" before, and he'd always been mad at me that I wouldn't call her "Mom."

"You wanna know something funny?" Brad said. "I thought this was the bathroom. I opened the wrong door, and then I just got dizzy."

His right arm dangled uselessly at his side. It was

bent at a bizarre angle, like it was broken in two or three places, and I wondered how he'd managed to change out of his school clothes into his pyjamas without using it. I knelt down again and gently lifted the tee-shirt to look at the stomach he was trying to shield from me. The skin was black and purple from the bottom of his neck to the waistband of his pyjamas — and further down, I guessed without checking. He'd taken some beating, all right.

"I guess those guys really did a number on you, huh?" I said weakly.

"Guys?"

"You know. The ones at school. Nathaniel and Dmitri and Tony Savage."

"Oh yeah," he said, his voice strangely flat. "Them."

I knelt there forever, stroking Brad's sweaty hair, feeling about as helpless and pathetic as I'd ever felt in my life, my stomach in knots as I fought back tears.

Finally there was a knock at the front door, a voice shouting up the stairs.

"Did someone call for an ambulance?"

"Upstairs, the end of the hall," I shouted back as loudly as I could.

I stood up and the room careened madly around my head. The world became a blur. Around me, voices unattached to bodies asked meaningless questions; unfamiliar faces moved into my mother's bedroom and took control.

"Is this your brother, son?" asked one voice gently.

"What happened?" came another, accusing.

Whatever instinct that had taken over when I found Brad on the floor left me, and suddenly it occurred to me that my legs weren't doing me much good anymore. I fell — or, rather, *dropped* — to the floor. A comforting hand fell heavily on my shoulder, and it didn't occur to me to do anything about it.

"Where's your mother?"

"I don't know. She went to work late, but ..." I trailed off. Somehow the pieces just didn't fit. She'd gone to work, Brad had gone to school. Then he'd gotten sick at school and they'd called the old lady away from work ... so why was he bleeding? How was his arm broken? And more to the point, where the hell was my mother?

"What's your brother's name?"

"It's Brad Gardner. Short for Bradley. He's nine years old." I looked up. "I want to go in the ambulance with him."

"Well, come on, then. Hurry up."

■ ■ ■

For an hour I sat in the emergency room, flipping through magazines dating back before the Gulf War. Then somebody came and told me I could go upstairs and wait in the Surgery wing, where there weren't any magazines at all. There had been a thousand questions, followed by papers for me to sign ... things I probably wasn't supposed to be authorizing, but I'd told them I was eighteen, and they hadn't seen fit to argue with me. Aside from that, nobody had spoken to me in a long time. Eons.

So, there I sat in the waiting area and leaned my head against the sterile green wall. I closed my eyes, wishing there was somebody around to have a conversation with.

Nobody knows I'm here, I realized. Not Matthew, not the old lady ... nobody knows this is happening to me.

I wouldn't have minded some dinner — a Coke,

anything, really — but I'd realized almost as soon as I'd arrived here that my wallet was in my jacket, on the hassock in the front hall of my house. I'd realized about the same time that I hadn't locked the front door. I wondered how I was going to get home from here. I wondered whether Brad was going to live through surgery. Finally I just got tired of wondering and fell asleep.

I was wakened a couple of hours later by someone shaking me by the shoulder.

"Jareth Gardner?"

"Mmm."

I opened my eyes, trying to remember where I was. As things came into focus I figured I'd see a doctor or nurse standing there, but I was mistaken. There was a guy in a suit, middle-aged and built like one of those phony wrestlers, with a shaved head and a goatee that made him look like he should be wearing a Hell's Angels jacket or something.

"My name is Detective Brooks," he said. "I need to ask you some questions."

"Okay," I replied numbly. My voice sounded strange, echoing in my ears — like I was talking from the bottom of a deep well. The cop — Brooks — sat in the chair opposite mine and crossed his legs. He took out a notebook and held it in his lap, reminding me of Doctor Eschen. *Tell me about your brother, Jareth.*

"I need to know what happened to your brother, son," he told me.

Son. Funny, the paramedic had called me that, too. I couldn't help thinking Brad must be hurt real bad if all these guys in uniforms were being so damn nice to me all of a sudden. I thought for a long while, pressing my tongue up against the inside of my front teeth in an effort to get enough saliva in my mouth to be able to talk without sounding like I'd been asleep forever.

"Some kids at school ..." I said, finally. "He was saying this morning that some kids at school wanted to beat him up." Was that just this morning? I looked around, blinking to focus my eyes. The clock on the wall of the waiting area said it was a little after midnight.

The cop gave me a patronizing look, like he thought I was full of crap, but he wrote it down anyway.

"What kids?" he said. "Did he tell you their names?"

"Yeah, he ..." I paused. Something stirred in my memory — the look on his face when I'd asked Brad about those kids. "Do you think they're the ones who hurt him?"

The cop scribbled in his notebook as I struggled to remember the names Brad had told me.

"And, your mother."

"What about her?"

"We need to know where she is. There's no one at your house right now. Do you think she might be at work? Or maybe at a friend's house?"

"She left work early today. I don't think she really has friends. Nobody she'd go visit, anyway."

"No?"

I shook my head.

"Nah. She's not somebody you'd want to spend a lot of time around."

I shouldn't be telling him this, I thought. The old lady would tell me that airing the family's dirty laundry in public is bad form. The cop gave me a weak smile, like he wasn't sure if I was trying to make a joke.

"Why is that?" he asked.

I gave him a good long look, then figured, *what the hell.* If I was gonna bury the old lady, I might as well bury her good.

"I don't know where she is, but I'd bet she's gone off someplace to get good and piss-drunk," I told him.

Numbly I answered a few more questions — Brad's teacher's name, what time Brad had come home from school, bars where the old lady liked to hang out. I felt lost ... anaesthetized.

Finally the cop closed his notebook and thanked me for my time. He stood up and turned to leave, and I found myself calling after him.

"Hey. You weren't planning on going back to my house anytime soon, were you?" I said.

"Yeah, I thought I'd go and see if your mom's come back."

I stood stiffly, my entire body aching from sleeping in that hard plastic chair.

"You think I could maybe get a ride home with you?"

He looked at me intently, muddy green eyes boring into me. I expected him to tell me he wasn't running a taxi service, but instead he cocked his head to one side and smiled gently.

"How long have you been here?" he said.

"I don't know. Since after school, I guess."

"Hmm. That's a long time," he said. "How old are you, son?"

I blinked, surprised to hear the question. I wondered how easy it would be for him to find out if I was lying.

"I'm eighteen," I said as easily as I could manage.

"You gonna be okay on your own overnight?"

"Yeah." I looked back at him a little defensively. "Why wouldn't I be?"

"I don't know. Just making sure." He tucked the notebook into the inside pocket of his jacket. "Come on, then. I'll give you a lift."

As I climbed into the car, a terrible thought occurred to me.

"Hey. My brother's not dead, is he?" I asked.

The cop turned, startled, and gave me a good stare by the glow of the car's dome light.

"Didn't the doctor come and talk to you?" he said.

"Nobody came and talked to me," I said, my voice breaking. "You were the first person I talked to. Is my brother dead?"

"No," the cop said, pressing his lips together grimly. "No, he's not dead."

He didn't add the words I could tell he was thinking. *Not yet.*

We sat in silence all the way back to my house. I stared out the window at the passing lights, and concentrated as hard as I could on not crying. Not in front of this cop. Not in front of anybody. I could cry all I wanted when I got home, I thought.

"You sure you're gonna be okay?" the cop asked me as he stopped the car in our driveway.

I nodded, but it was a lie. I stumbled up the driveway to the house and let myself in through the still-unlocked front door. The cop was right behind me, probably more to make sure I didn't pass out on the way to the door as to see whether my mother was there.

"Guess the old lady's not home," I told the cop, flipping on the light in the front hallway. "She'd have turned the porch light on, at least, and the TV would probably be blaring."

"Try to get some sleep," he said, and handed me his business card. "And give me a call if your mom shows up. I'd just like to ask her a few questions. My pager number's on there; you can get me twenty-four hours a day. Okay?"

"Yeah, sure."

And with that, I stumbled up the front walk to the house.

The comic book I'd ripped off for Brad was still on the floor in the front hall, and I tucked it under my arm and carried it upstairs to put on Brad's pillow. For when he got home, I told myself.

It was nearly a quarter to one. I hadn't eaten dinner, but food wasn't a priority for me at that point. All I wanted to do was crawl into bed ... but first I needed a long, hot shower. Something to wash away the smell of the hospital, the horror of the day. I noticed with a feeling of morbid fascination that there was blood caked under my fingernails. Brad's blood.

I don't know how long I was in the shower — half an hour, maybe forty-five minutes. By the time I was finished the hot water was long gone. I wrapped myself in a worn towel, shivering for a long time before I finally pulled on a pair of shorts and wandered out into the hall.

My hair was dripping ice trails down my back as I ventured toward the old lady's room. The door was still open — a sure sign something was wrong. But in my head I was desperately hoping I'd imagined the whole thing, hoping Brad would still be in there. Not sprawled on the floor in a pool of blood, but just ... I don't know, snooping around. He'd spring out from under the bed and yell "surprise" or something.

Not that he ever would have done that anyway. Brad was a pretty serious kid. Pranks like that just weren't his style.

The first thing that occurred to me as I flicked on the light was that the closet door was open. Somebody'd been in here since I left with Brad. The old lady's dresser drawers had all been pulled out and shoved back in, and some of her clothes were sticking out the sides. She would have a freak-fit if she saw that, I thought, and briefly considered cleaning it up for her.

But the real mess, of course, was the floor. I tried not to look at the puddle of blood, now dried to a dark maroon. There were bloody footprints everywhere — my sock prints, the paramedics' boots. On the floor by the closet I saw a small circle of black plastic. I picked it up and looked it over carefully. The top of a film canister, I thought. Somebody'd been taking pictures in here.

Out in the living room I could hear the radio playing.

"Somebody here?" I called softly. I felt sick to my stomach, and far too weak to shout. The taste of my long-ago school lunch sat dully at the back of my mouth as I plodded heavily down the stairs.

"Jareth, darling! Come on out here and dance with your mom."

In the living room, the old lady waltzed by herself. As soon as I stepped into the room, she seized my arm and pulled me to her. In the second before I pushed her away, I got a gagging whiff of gin-and-vomit from her breath.

"Hey, Brad's in the hospital," I said dully.

My mother didn't look overly concerned.

"Well, I'll be sure to go by and visit him tomorrow," she said casually. She grabbed at my wrists again, but I stepped back against the wall and crossed my arms tightly over my chest. There was a dull throbbing in my head as I watched the woman dancing, inches away from me.

"Mom?" My voice was strangled, strangely high-pitched. "Mom, what happened to Brad?"

She turned around so she wouldn't have to look at me.

"How should I know?" she said, although with the amount she'd had to drink it was a struggle for her to get the words out.

It was then that all the pieces fell into place for me. It was like a jolt of electricity went through my body as I put it all together: Brad in his pyjamas, the cop at the hospital, the way Brad hadn't even known what I was talking about when I asked him about the kids who beat him up.

"What did you do to him?" I croaked, feeling the room swaying around me. I cleared my mind and stood up as straight as I could manage, the great detective Jareth Gardner making the final accusation. "No, no, never mind," I said. "I know what happened. He got sick at school and his teacher called you at work. But you called in this morning and said you were going to be late because Brad had to stay home sick. So you got in crap from your boss when they caught you lying. Am I right so far?"

My mother turned back to face me, a freakish look of incredulity on her face. She was truly a horrific sight, her mascara streaked down her face, lipstick smeared, her hair askew.

"I got fired," she said, with something like wonder in her voice. To this day I'm not sure if she was surprised I figured it out, or surprised she'd lost her job.

"So I guess you were pretty pissed off at Brad when you went to pick him up at school, eh? Maybe you stopped and had a few drinks on the way to get him, just to take the edge off how upset you were over losing your job. Is that what happened?"

"You are a snotty little punk," my mother said, spitting a little in my face as she spoke, leaning closer with the hint of a threat in her eyes. But it was too late to stop me now. I was on a roll.

"So what did he do to get you so upset?" I said. "He throw up on the carpet? Maybe he was playing the TV too loud. Was that it? You grabbed him, gave him a good shove. What happened next? He fell over, broke his arm? Or did that happen after you kicked the shit out of him?"

That did it. The look on the old lady's face told me I'd nailed the story — if not exactly on the head, then close enough to drive it in.

"You're a selfish little bastard," she hissed. "I've wasted my whole life on you kids, and this is how you talk to me?"

I could feel my hand flying up to slap her face. I realized what I was doing a millisecond before it happened, but I did it anyway. My mother took a step backward, a pale pink handprint appearing on her cheek where I'd hit her.

"Talk about selfish," I shot back. "Your son is dying, and you're upset because he cost you your job?"

"He's been dying his entire life," the old lady said, turning away from me melodramatically and stumbling toward the couch. "When he was born the doctors told me to just bring him home and make him comfortable. He wasn't even supposed to live this long, you know. He was supposed to be a vegetable and then die."

I chewed on my lip, determined not to cry. Of course I knew that. I'd heard it half my life, whispered around corners when grown-ups thought I wasn't listening, spoken in code when Brad was a toddler. Even Brad knew it. For all the doctors' talk about how he was supposed to be retarded, he was a pretty bright kid. Bright, but doomed.

But it wasn't supposed to happen like this. You just didn't do something like that to your own kid. Hell, you didn't do it to anybody.

I stood there for a long time, leaning against the living room wall and watching as my mother flopped over on the couch. She was snoring away in a matter of seconds.

The next hour passed like a dream, like I was watching someone else digging through my pockets for the cop's card, picking up the phone and dialling. Then I stood on the front step in my shorts and watched while a uniformed police officer coaxed my mother into a car. Detective Brooks was there, the cop from the hospital, patting my shoulder and asking me about a hundred times if I was sure I would be okay. I said yes every time. I figured I probably broke some kind of world record for lying that night. Of course I wasn't going to be okay. After what had just happened, how could anything ever be okay again?

5

The house was shrouded in an eerie silence when I woke up the next morning. It was five after seven, and I rolled out of bed stiffly, hoping the whole of yesterday afternoon had been a dream.

"Mom? Brad?" I called out my bedroom door. "Anybody here?"

Of course there was no answer. I grabbed a tee-shirt and stumbled out into the hallway. The door to my mother's bedroom was still open, and I pulled it shut hastily. I didn't want to look at that mess on the floor again.

I don't know why I went to school that day. Force of habit, I guess. What else was I going to do? In my head I was thinking I had to go or I'd be expelled. Of course, if I'd called the school and told somebody what was happening, I'm sure they would have made an exception to the big Guidance deal. But phoning the school and giving excuses wasn't really my style. So I pulled on a pair of jeans and plodded off to school.

Beyond feeling obliged to go, I somehow felt like going to school would make everything normal again. But sitting in class — Biology first period, English second — was a tortuous experience, and by the time lunch rolled around all I could think about was getting the hell out of there.

"Brad's in the hospital," I told Matthew at lunch. He leaned across the sticky cafeteria table and stole one of my fries. We always sat at the same table in the centre of the school's sunken cafeteria, two losers alone at a full-sized table, surrounded by a table full of jocks on one side and other cliques on two others. We got some funny looks, and occasionally one of the jocks would make a crack about us, but mostly we were left alone. There were easier targets for them to pick on, and they seldom bothered with us — especially after the word spread about me pulling a knife on somebody. Now they hardly dared even glance in our direction.

"He is?" Matthew said, his mouth full. "How come? Is it his stomach again?"

I shook my head grimly, although Matthew was too busy stealing another of my fries to notice.

"Nah, nothing like that," I said. "Look, do you want something to eat? Because I'll buy you something if you want. I've got money. I can buy you lunch."

Matthew shook his head.

"No. I think I'll just pick off your plate."

I leaned territorially over my lunch. We played this game every day, and it usually ended with him eating most of my food. Today I just wasn't in the mood for it.

"Cut it out," I growled. There was a long, awkward silence before Matthew spoke again.

"So what's with Brad?" he said. "His, what d'you call it? Hernia?"

"No, he had that fixed a couple years ago, remember?"

I paused, looked down at the plate of fries for a second before shoving them at Matthew. "Here, you finish them. I'm not hungry anymore."

Matthew, who was never one to look a gift horse in the mouth, munched happily for a minute or two before he remembered we were in the middle of a conversation.

"So what happened, then?" he said. "I thought the kid was doing okay these days. I mean, not bad enough to be in the hospital, anyway."

I shrugged. I didn't want to talk about Brad anymore.

"I hit my mother yesterday," I said instead.

Matthew's eyes widened.

"You hit your mother?" he echoed.

"Yeah."

"You're going to hell, you know that?"

"What are you talking about?"

"The way you treat your mother." He leaned over and took a sip of my Coke. "And stealing money from her and everything ... It's a sin or something."

"Come on. When did you get all religious?"

"I'm not. It's just ... you're s'posed to respect your parents and stuff. Vic says ..."

"Who cares what Vic says? I hate Vic."

"Yeah, I know you do."

We sat for a few minutes in silence before Matthew spoke again.

"How come?" he pressed.

"What?"

"How come you hate Vic?"

"I don't know." I thought for a moment. "He's an asshole," I said.

"He likes you," Matthew told me. "You probably don't

think he does, but he thinks you're okay. He's just not real emotional. But he likes you."

"That's great. Just swell," I snapped, slurping at my Coke. "My life is complete because Victor Fleming thinks I'm okay. Look, what the hell are we talking about Vic for?"

Matthew was getting on my nerves something awful today. I pushed my chair back and stood up.

"Look, I'm skipping this aft. I'm gonna go down to see Brad in the hospital," I said. Then, instinctively, I added: "You want to come along?"

"I can't," he said. "I have a math test, then my mom's picking me up early. We're leaving for Vermont this afternoon."

Vermont. Right. I vaguely remembered him telling me something about going away. Some skiing trip his mom had won.

"That's cool," I said halfheartedly. I pitched my Coke cup into an overflowing garbage can near the door of the crowded cafeteria. The cup rolled down the heap of garbage and landed on the floor. I didn't bother to pick it up.

"Hey, tell Brad I said 'hi,'" Matthew called after me as I headed out of the caf. I turned back and gave him a half wave and climbed the steps to the cafeteria door.

It didn't feel final or ceremonial or anything, walking out of the school building that day, but that's what it was. I didn't know it at the time, but it would be the last time I set foot inside that school. And it would be months before I talked to Matthew Harper again.

■ ■ ■

With my chin clamped tightly against my chest and my hands buried deep in my pockets, I strode into the brisk March air. The sky was clouding over; thick, grey clouds that seemed to envelop my soul. I walked home in a daze — just a quick stop there, I told myself, then I'd get a bus downtown to the hospital.

I wondered what would happen when I got there; whether Brad would be awake, whether they'd even let me in to see him. Not that I really wanted to see him like that; I figured he'd be in rough shape, all hooked up to tubes and machines. But I needed to know. I had to see him; to hold his hand, tell him everything was gonna be okay, even if I knew it wasn't.

But I never got that far. There was a strange car in the driveway when I got home. If I'd been a little less tired I'd have realized it was the same car that had brought me home the previous night. The cop — Banks or Booker or something like that, I thought his name was — sat reading a newspaper.

I stopped short of the car as soon as I recognized the cop. There was no *good* reason I could think of that a police detective would be waiting outside my house. I thought the situation over for a second or two. Maybe he'd come to tell me it was all a big mistake — Brad was going to be fine, there was nothing to worry about.

Or maybe somebody'd finally tipped him off about what happened to old Lloyd Clemence a few weeks back. At that point, I would have welcomed that news, if it meant I didn't have to hear the reason he was really there.

"Hey!"

I tapped on car window, catching the cop's attention. He forced a weak smile and stepped out of the car.

"Hi, Jareth. Can we go inside and talk for a few minutes?" he said.

I shrugged. "I guess."

I let him in the house, and showed him upstairs to the living room.

"I think I already know what you're gonna say," I said, and perched in a chair. "I'll make it easier for you; my brother's dead, isn't he?"

The cop nodded grimly, running an enormous hand over his shaved head. I noticed the shadow of his hairline was a little darker today than it had been yesterday at the hospital; he hadn't bothered to shave it since then.

To keep from crying, I bit my lip until I tasted blood. I was determined not to cry until after he was gone.

"When did it happen?" I managed.

"A couple of hours ago. I'm really sorry."

I nodded, regained my composure. I stood up and ran the heels of my hands across damp eyes.

"That's okay," I told him. "I mean, it's not your fault."

"Look, are you sure you're going to be okay? I can call somebody for you if you want. Figure out a place for you to stay."

I laughed humourlessly. Shook my head.

"No," I said tightly, "That's not a problem. I mean, a place to stay ... I'll probably just crash at my dad's place for a while, you know?"

The cop nodded solemnly.

"Does he know?" he asked me. "About Brad, I mean?"

My heart did a back-flip. What a stupid way to get caught in a lie.

"He's not Brad's father," I said quickly. "We have different dads. I don't know where to find Brad's father."

"Hmm." He thought that over for a few minutes. "Well, can you give me your dad's number? I'd like to be able to get hold of you. We're probably going to have some more questions for you."

My heart pounded. It hadn't occurred to me that he would ask about my father. Before I knew what I was doing, I'd blurted out Matthew's number. Oh, well. I'd have to talk to Matthew, make sure he could cover for me if the cop happened to call.

I wondered how long it would be before the detective put it all together. The fact I wasn't eighteen, combined with the fact I couldn't have identified my father if you paid me, let alone gone to stay with him. But for the moment, it got me out of an awkward situation. I mean, really. Where would I have gone to stay? My grandmother was dead, I didn't have any other family to speak of. Were they going to put me in a foster home? Ridiculous.

No, I decided, I would just have to figure this one out on my own.

6

Once the cop had left, I wandered around the house for a while, wondering what to do next.

There was a big cabinet in the living room with all the old lady's good china in it — stuff my grandmother had left her. On top of the cabinet were my and Brad's school pictures, all the way back to kindergarten. I looked at them thoughtfully. My own pictures were all there — twelve years worth ... the shaggy-haired little kindergarten kid with two front teeth missing; the third grader with two black eyes and a red nose from his run-in with a tree branch at summer camp a few weeks earlier; the long-haired high school senior in the torn denim jacket, scowling into the camera. Had that just been a couple of months ago? I checked the mirror in the hallway to make sure I still looked like that. Ugly, I thought. Inside and out, pure ugly.

I looked back at the other pictures. I didn't really remember having any of them taken, except for the one from fourth grade with my tongue sticking out. The photographer had been a big guy with curly white hair who had given us all nicknames. All the photographers did that, every year, except that they usually called me something lame like "Big Guy" or "Stretch" because I was always the shortest kid in the class. This one particular guy wasn't any different; he'd called the girls Princess or Wonder Woman or Cinderella, and the boys were all Batman or Prince Charming. When he'd come to me, though, he'd called me Tarzan, and I'd liked that. I'd spent the rest of the day pounding my chest and crawling around on desks because it amused the other kids, until finally the teacher sent me to the principal's office.

When I'd finished examining my own photographs, I selected one of Brad's — the second newest one; he looked too sick in the last one, all pasty and emaciated — and took it with me to Brad's room.

I sat on his bed for a little while, looking around. The wallpaper was covered in balloons and airplanes Brad had been on the verge of outgrowing. He'd hardly ever slept in his own room anyway — too many monsters. Half the time I'd find him curled up on the couch or on the floor of my room.

I hugged the picture — looking a little ratty in its crappy cardboard frame — tightly to my chest and leaned down until my head nearly touched the floor. I looked under the bed.

"No monsters in here tonight," I said aloud, startled by the sound of my own voice. I sat up again, half-expecting to see Brad in the doorway, wondering why I was talking to myself.

The house was too quiet; I needed some background noise to distract me, to keep me from thinking. From room to room I paced, turning on television sets, radios, whatever I could find. Soon the house was alive with sound. I turned on all the lights in the house and stood alone in the middle of the living-room floor until I didn't want to stand any longer, and there I sat. After a long time I went into my room to watch television. I didn't like the way my own reality was going; it was time to distract myself with someone else's.

■ ■ ■

"Where do you go after you're dead?" Brad had asked me once, a couple of years earlier. I'd been visiting him in the hospital — I couldn't remember why he was in the hospital that time, but I supposed it didn't really matter. I remembered the question, though, and I remembered my own answer.

"What do you want to know that for?" I'd replied. "Nobody's dying around here."

He'd given me this patronizing look. He knew better than that; he always had.

"Yeah, but let's just say I did," he'd said. "Where would I go?"

"Heaven, I guess. I don't know, what are you asking me for?"

"Well, what if you do something bad?"

"Like what?"

"Like swearing at Mom."

I laughed.

"Then I guess I'm going to hell," I'd told him with a grin. "Maybe even a couple of times."

Brad hadn't found that quite so funny.

"John Allison in my class says if you go to hell, you burn forever," he'd said.

"John Allison." I shook my head. John's older sister Hope was in my grade, and she'd been preaching hellfire and brimstone at me since kindergarten. "Know what? John Allison's whole family is screwy," I'd told him. "The whole bunch of them. Don't you listen to a word they tell you. Man, they think Saturday morning cartoons are messages from Satan."

He'd laughed at that and dropped the subject, but I could tell from the look on his face it still weighed heavily on his mind. I wondered if he'd known; I mean, he knew he was going to die, but I wondered if he'd had some sense that it would be so soon — or so violent.

It was true, about the Allison family. Hope had spent an entire year — Grade Two or Three, I thought it was — trying to convince me the Smurfs were evil. But now that Brad was dead, I wondered if maybe I shouldn't have brushed him off so lightly. He was just a kid; maybe he needed to hear about God. For that matter, I reflected, maybe it wouldn't have done me any harm, either.

I curled up on my side on Brad's bed, a fetal ball with his picture pressed up against my stomach. It was a little after two in the afternoon, and the house was ablaze with sound. I could hear some talk show blaring through the vents from the basement, and a soap opera from the TV in my bedroom across the hall. From the radio in the kitchen I could hear music of some kind — the country-and-western crap the old lady listened to all the time. I lay there for a long time, feeling empty, until finally I drifted off into a fitful, restless sleep.

I must have got up at some point that afternoon or evening, because I woke up in my bed the next morning.

The house was impossibly loud, and I retraced my steps from the previous afternoon, turning off all the TVs and radios in the house except for the one in my own room. Marvin the Martian, the little guy in the red suit with the Roman legionnaire's helmet, was on *Bugs Bunny*. I perched in front of the set to watch. I hadn't watched *Bugs Bunny* with Brad in years, and somehow there was a big hole where he should have been sitting, asking stupid questions about the plots of the cartoons. I wondered why I hadn't watched TV with him lately.

I sat through two or three cartoons, not enjoying them very much. I couldn't watch them by myself. Finally I stood and turned off the television. I'm bored, I realized. My brother is dead and I'm not mourning, I'm bored.

I took off my clothes from the day before and had a shower. Pulling on a tee-shirt over a pair of sweat pants, I went out to the living room. I couldn't be bothered with jeans. Too much effort.

Around noon the phone rang, a sound from another world, and I sprang to answer it.

"Hi, Matthew?" I said hopefully. Somehow if I heard his voice, that would make everything all right again. Everything would be the way it was supposed to be: Brad in his room, the old lady watching TV in the basement and Matthew on the phone.

"Jareth, honey, it's Mom," I heard instead. My stomach coiled into a tight knot.

"What do you want?" I said, struggling to keep my voice even.

"What are you doing, honey?"

"Why are you calling me? I thought you were supposed to be in jail."

My mother laughed like that was the funniest thing she'd ever heard.

"Well, yes, darling, but they let me use the *phone*. I just wanted to see how you're doing."

"Oh, gee, that's mighty big of you. Gosh, how am I doing? Well, better than Brad, anyway. Or maybe you haven't heard." I was unable to keep a tremor from my voice as I shouted into the phone. But nothing I said seemed to faze the old lady.

"Now, darling, that's not fair," she said coolly. "I've already told you, it was an accident. I didn't mean to hurt him."

"And that makes everything okay, does it?" I was nearly screaming now, feeling my face burn with rage. "You think you can just say you're sorry and make everything better? Well, I'm sorry, but it doesn't work that way!" I slammed down the receiver.

About five minutes passed before the phone rang again, and this time I didn't even bother picking it up; I just yanked the cord out of the wall and walked away. I could hear the extension downstairs ringing for the better part of half an hour.

I had always marvelled at how tidy Brad kept his closet. Everything he owned was neat and tidy, but especially the closet — all the clothes neatly on hangers, three or four old baseball caps hanging from a hook on the back of the door. There were two boxes on the closet shelf. The first, a blue Nike box, held all Brad's medication. He'd taken care of his own medicines for a couple of years, ever since the time the old lady had accidentally given him twice the amount he'd needed and he'd nearly died. The pill bottles, creams and puffers were lined up in rows in the box.

I counted the bottles. There were fourteen bottles of pills, plus three inhalers for his asthma. I shook my head incredulously and put the box aside.

The second box was larger, and though it had probably been there all along, I'd never noticed it before. It was a big, old-fashioned hatbox with purple swirls all around it. In black magic marker on the lid, Brad had written "Brads Treasures Keep OUT" in his big, round, beginner's script. With shaking hands, I took off the lid.

There was a dollar and sixteen cents in change in the bottom of the box. Besides that, there wasn't much ... A picture of me and the old lady he'd taken the previous Christmas with the disposable camera I'd bought him; an old teddy bear Brad was too embarrassed to sleep with anymore; the shark's tooth he'd traded with Marty Wilmer for his appendix in a jar. Nothing spectacular, just ... a nine-year-old's treasures.

On impulse, I picked up the comic book I'd left on his bed a couple of days earlier and slipped it into the box before replacing it on the closet shelf.

"I miss you, kid," I whispered. I didn't want to speak out loud anymore. Now that I'd turned off the radios and TVs, the house was too quiet to disturb.

The day progressed, and I started to feel like I was going around the bend. I wandered around the house, going over things in my head. I went and sat on Brad's bed, staring up at that closet shelf with the two boxes, studying them until I thought I would go nuts.

A drink of water. That was what I needed. I went to the kitchen, where I fished a plastic coffee mug out of the cupboard and filled it from the tap. The water tasted stale, and I dumped it out after one sip, tossing the mug after it into the sink. There was some orange juice in the fridge, and I poured some into a tall glass, bringing it back with me to Brad's room. I stood in the closet doorframe with my glass, looking up at the boxes. Finally I reached up and pulled down the shoe box with the pills in it. Sitting back down on the bed, I opened the box and took out one of the bottles. I set my glass of juice down on the floor beside the bed and twisted off the child-proof cap. Child-proof, my ass, I thought humourlessly. Who do they think these were for, anyway? I poured the contents of the bottle out onto the bed and ran my fingers across them, enjoying the texture. I poured out a second bottle beside the first one, letting them mix together on the blue-and-green quilt. Carefully I arranged them in patterns, first a square, then an arch. I poured out a third bottle and made a rainbow from the different coloured capsules. Reaching down for my orange juice, I took a handful of the pills at random and looked at them. I took a sip of the orange juice and clapped my hand to my mouth, letting the pills fall into my throat. I washed them down with a mighty swig of juice, then stood up uneasily and looked in the mirror.

"What do you think you're doing, Jareth?" I asked my reflection. I'd stopped worrying about speaking aloud. "You trying to kill yourself? Because if you are, there are better ways of doing it. You can't do much about the state of your life, but death's an easy enough thing to manage."

I went to the bathroom and opened the medicine chest. There was an unopened package of ladies' razors on the top shelf. They belonged to my mother; I myself had yet to grow anything worth shaving off. I took it down and opened it. The razors were the plastic disposable type

— safety razors, it said on the package. I took one out and brought it down with me to the basement. There was a work table on the far side of the basement where Keith, Brad's father, had once attempted to set up shop. An assortment of unused hand tools hung neatly on the wall under a quarter inch of dust. I took a claw hammer from its nest and brushed the dust off onto my pants. I took the cap off the razor, and, holding it by the pink plastic handle, I aimed a blow at the head, knocking it clean off. The double blade of the razor remained snug inside the head. *Nuts.* I brought the hammer crashing straight down on the head of the razor, crushing it flat. Gingerly I picked it up. The blades were bent out of shape, nicely mangled, but still firmly surrounded by their plastic sheath.

I would have to try something else.

I ran back up the stairs to the kitchen, full of some bizarre kind of energy now, and found a paring knife. I sat in a chair at the kitchen table and examined my arms. Like my hands, they were covered in tiny white lines. Scars, I thought. From what? From the fish tank? That had been a crazy thing to do, but this was even crazier. With a single motion I sliced from one side of my wrist to the other, just above my watch band. The skin didn't *cut* so much as it *tore*. For a moment, nothing happened. I watched tiny droplets of blood come to the surface of the skin before the cut split open and bled freely. I stood up and walked from room to room, dripping blood on the carpet, wondering what to do with myself next.

In the living room, there was a scented candle in a glass jar on the coffee table. I sat on the couch and picked up a book of matches that lay beside the candle. That was my mother for you; never a shortage of matches and lighters close at hand. It's a wonder Brad or I hadn't burned the house down by the time we were out of diapers.

I lit the candle and watched the flame flicker back and forth, focussing my eyes on the blue part in the middle. That's the hottest part of the flame, I thought. I put my hand as close to the flame as I could stand and held it there for a long time. The nauseating smell of vanilla candle and burning flesh wafted up to my nose, and when I pulled my hand away there was a blistering red spot on my palm. I tried to peel the skin away with my fingernails, but it hurt me too much and I left it, half on and half off my hand.

Back to Brad's room. Now I just wanted this to be over. More pills. I polished off all the capsules I'd dumped out onto the bed. The world was starting to get a little blurry on me, like when the vertical hold on the television had gone on the blink. Then I heard this voice, loud and clear from inside my head, like the words were being screamed in my ear. I was so surprised to hear them, in fact, that I turned my head to see if someone was standing there.

"If you're gonna die," said the Voice, "you should go talk to Matthew first. Tell him you're sorry for always pushing him around like that, or something. Say goodbye, at least; you've only known the guy two-thirds of your life."

It seemed like the most sensible thing I'd heard all day. I headed for the front door, locked it and stepped outside, pulling it shut behind me before I realized I hadn't put any shoes or socks on, and I didn't have a key to get back in the house. Oh, well, I thought. It was only a couple of blocks.

There were a few stubborn inches of snow on the ground, and as I trudged along, the wet cold started to burn my feet. I kept right on walking. It wasn't so bad, I told myself. Soon it wouldn't matter anyway. The feel of the snow on my bare skin wasn't as bad as the feel of the brisk March wind whipping them dry. The skin felt like it might be cracking, but I was beyond pain by that time. My head was in a fog but I trudged onward, one foot in front of the other.

I walked across the parking lot of Matthew's apartment building, where Old Pete the superintendent was salting the pavement — probably for only the second or third time all winter. He looked critically down at my bare feet.

"It's a little cold to be out without shoes or a jacket, isn't it, son?"

I ignored him and reached for the door handle to let myself into the building. I didn't have my bank card to open the door, but the doormat had been kicked between the door and the frame so that it hadn't closed properly. When I extended my hand, I saw that it was twitching slightly; either that or my hand was perfectly still and the rest of the world was twitching. I grabbed for the handle and missed, my fingers closing on air. I got it on the second try, pulling the door open and stumbling into the lobby. I followed an old man into the elevator and the door slid shut.

The man said something to me, but I didn't catch what it was. I cocked my head slightly, hoping he'd repeat himself. He did, nearly shouting.

"I said, what floor?"

"I'm sorry," I mumbled. "I'm not feeling well." I

thought for a moment. What floor? I'd only been here a hundred thousand times; I should have known this.

■ ■ ■

I stood outside Matthew's door for a long time, wondering why no one was answering. I knocked three, four times, then waited, the long, diamond-patterned carpet of the hallway spinning gently around me.

A thousand miles away I could hear the familiar whirring and clicking of the elevator. For a second I thought it must be Matthew getting in late from school. I thought it had been a little after four o'clock when I'd left my house, but it was hard to say for sure.

That's when I remembered Matthew was gone, skiing in Vermont with his mother and the girls. Bastard. How dare he go away on holiday when my life was falling apart?

The elevator doors opened and I heard footsteps coming toward me. A raspy baritone called my name.

"Jareth?"

It was Vic. I realized it was Vic the second before I felt his hands on my shoulders, turning me around to face him. I tried not to look at him, thinking how pathetic I must be by now.

"What happened to your arm, Jareth?"

My arm. I'd completely forgotten about the cut across the inside of my wrist. I held it up to my face to examine it. It looked pretty gross — it was too early for it to be infected, but it certainly wasn't very clean. The bleeding had slowed down a lot, though. I reached my right hand over to touch it, and it occurred to me that I should be feeling some kind of pain from a wound that size. There was none, though. My body wasn't numb, exactly, but like it was somewhere else, like I was standing outside it, looking at someone else's arm. The burn on my palm wasn't bothering me, either. But the inside of my head was aching — spinning, a mass of raw nerves and unchecked rage.

I suppose at some level I was mad at the old lady for what she'd done — or mad at Brad for being dead — but at the moment, the thing that made me angriest was the fact that Matthew had dared not be there when I needed him.

Outwardly, though, I just stood like a lump in the hallway, staring up at Vic with blank, uncomprehending eyes.

"Jareth?" he repeated quietly. "How you doing, son?"

I shook my head, still staring down at my wrist. I didn't much feel like having a conversation with Vic at this point in time.

"I read about your brother in the paper," I heard him say. "I'm really sorry."

You can go screw yourself, I thought bitterly. I don't need your cheap pity.

But when I opened my mouth to say that to Vic, no words came out, just a weak, strangled sound, and I started to cry, really cry for the first time since all this had started. I seized on to him suddenly, burying my face in his shirt front, and he put his arms around me and held me there like he'd been expecting it. I just stood there for the longest time, feeling like a fool but not wanting to let him go, until finally I'd cried myself out and I pushed away from him.

"You finished?" he asked gently. There was a strange smile on his face, his lips pressed together so tightly the colour drained from them, deep creases appearing around his pale green eyes.

He didn't look uncomfortable after my little outburst,

but I sure was. I shuffled my feet, stared at the carpet and thought about what I should say next.

Nothing came to mind, though, and after a few seconds Vic's smile disappeared suddenly and he turned to unlock the door. I sniffled loudly and wiped my nose on the back of my hand as he spoke.

"Come on inside. We'll get you cleaned up some," he said.

I thought hard, shaking my head a little to clear it. If he found out I was trying to kill myself he would stop me, I realized.

"No, I don't think I can," I said, starting to back away from him. "Thanks anyway, but I really have to go. I've got stuff I gotta do."

Vic looked down at my feet.

"Well, at least let me get you some shoes," he suggested. "You're liable to get frostbite if you go back out like that." And he let the apartment door swing wide open. This was a first — Vic Fleming inviting me in. I stepped inside without saying a word, although I had to smile at the irony.

"I want to disinfect that cut on your arm first." He seized my arm and examined it closely. As he did that, he noticed the burn on my palm. "What have you been doing to yourself?"

I shrugged indifferently as he led me into the bathroom. He turned on the tap, all the while holding on to my arm like I was some kind of infant. The sound of the water made me realize how badly I had to pee.

"Could I just use the bathroom for a second, Vic?" I heard myself saying.

He nodded and stepped outside. I locked the door

behind him — I always lock the bathroom door, even when I'm alone — and I did what I needed to do.

When I'd finished, I hesitated before opening the door to let Vic back in. I could have just stayed in there forever ... or at least until I was dead. The idea was appealing, but after a moment's consideration I figured it wouldn't be so great for Vic. Besides, who knew how long it would take for me to die? I could have been in there for hours. Vic was a big guy, and short on patience ... he would have just broken down the door. I turned the lock on the door-knob and let him back inside.

I stood impassively as Vic rinsed out my cut, then poured some alcohol on a cotton swab and rubbed it over my wrist. I flinched instinctively, although it didn't really hurt. I knew it should have at least stung, but instead it just felt cold.

I turned my head as far to the right as I could man-age, trying to find something besides Vic to look at. I stared at the tile floor, blue and yellow checks, at the matching wallpaper, at the stupid fuzzy yellow cover Mrs. Fleming had on the toilet tank.

When I did turn back to look at Vic's face, though, he seemed to be preoccupied with something. The smell of the alcohol was making me feel even more queasy, and I gripped the edge of the sink with my free hand to keep my balance.

"You know, Jareth, you might want to get this stitched up," he said cautiously. "It's actually pretty deep. How'd you cut yourself, anyway?"

"I, um, slipped cutting a bagel," I muttered.

Vic fussed about getting a gauze pad out of the medi-cine cabinet and taped it in place over the cut. He caught my attention, then cocked an eyebrow at me.

"Hey. Why don't you go sit down in the living room a second? I'll find you some shoes," he said.

While he rummaged around in the hall closet, I flopped down on the couch, reached for the TV remote control. There was some sitcom on channel four, but I couldn't follow it. Vic was talking, something about my mother, but I didn't catch that, either.

The room was getting fuzzy, like everything was going in slow motion, and I drifted back and forth between darkness and reality for a few minutes. Vic's voice faded into the background as I stopped hearing him, until suddenly his tone changed and pulled me back to consciousness.

"Jareth?" I heard loudly, so close I could feel his breath against my face, warm and smelling of coffee. I felt his hand on my chin. With his thumb he pulled down my lower eyelid, and for a second I jerked away, thinking he was going to jab something into my eye. He stared intently at me for a minute before he stepped back and stood towering over me.

"What are you on, Jareth?"

I blinked vigorously, not understanding what he was asking me.

"What? I — nothing," I managed.

"What are you on?" he repeated. "Jareth, I don't want to play games with you, here; don't tell me you didn't take anything."

"Four or five handfuls," I stammered. "Just ... whatever was in the medicine box."

Vic cursed under his breath. I looked up cautiously to see him shaking his head, and I thought for a minute that he was going to chew me out good. Instead, he sat beside me on the couch and ran a hand through his hair.

"What time?" he was asking me then.

"Hmm?"

"What time did you take the pills?" he said slowly.

"I'm sorry," I mumbled listlessly. "I don't really re-member. All afternoon, I think."

He took a deep breath.

"Okay, Jareth. Here's what's gonna happen now," he said evenly. "We're going to the hospital now, and we're gonna get you fixed up."

"No. I don't think so," I told him. The hospital was a bad idea, although for the life of me I couldn't remember why.

"Now, are you gonna help me out and walk to the car," he continued, ignoring me, "or am I gonna have to carry you? It doesn't really matter to me, because either way you're coming with me to the car, but I thought you might like to have a choice."

There was no anger in his voice, no force behind his words. They were just... fact. I was going to the hospital, and there wasn't a whole lot of anything I was going to be able to do about it.

"I guess I can walk," I said meekly. I pulled away from him a little, and he reached out a hand to steady me.

"That's fine," he replied, a grim smile on his face. "You just remember I'm stronger and I'm faster than you are, and we should both get there in one piece."

Ordinarily I would have taken a comment like that as a challenge to run, but suddenly I didn't care. It didn't matter anymore. All I wanted now was sleep. I wanted to sleep forever, but I let Vic haul me out the door.

"It's getting cold out there," he said conversationally. "Looks like we might get one last taste of winter before it gets any warmer."

He put his hands on my shoulders and guided me into the elevator. I plodded along, just letting my still-bare feet move themselves without giving any thought to where they were pointed. Vic, still holding onto my shoulders, did all the steering.

When we got down to the parking lot, Vic ushered me into his car — a big navy-blue Buick with peeling paint and torn vinyl seats. I hadn't been in that car in close to a year and a half, but I still remembered the smell, like musty lemons. Until Matthew's mother had given him that ratty old Chevette of hers, Vic had driven us everywhere ... ever since he'd started dating Matthew's mom when we were eleven or twelve.

I reached to fasten my seat belt, but couldn't figure out the catch. Vic leaned over and secured it. Gave me that sad smile again.

The superintendent was still there, chipping away at the ice on the sidewalk with a battered old shovel. It seemed a little ridiculous, since the ice had been there all winter and would be melting in the next week or two, but he was at it pretty intently.

"Somebody must have complained to the landlord," said Vic, echoing my thoughts. "Old Pete doesn't usually put that much effort into anything unless his job's at stake."

As Vic started the car I blinked myself back to reality for a moment, suddenly realizing where he was taking me, what it all meant. I wondered what they'd do to me at the hospital. Pump my stomach, I guess. I'd always wondered how they did that. Would it hurt? I leaned back against the headrest and let my eyes drift shut. I guessed I'd find out soon enough.

"Hey." Vic gave me a nudge. "Don't you go to sleep on me."

Vic parked the car in the Emergency parking lot and crossed over to my side of the vehicle to unbuckle me.

"I can do this myself, you know," I protested sleepily as Vic tugged back the seat belt and all but dragged me out of the car. I pulled away from him and took a couple of staggering steps before I collapsed on the asphalt like a rag doll.

"Okay. You can do this yourself," he said. "But how about I give you a hand, just this once?"

He easily helped me to my feet and together we went inside.

7

The bored-looking nurse behind the counter was arguing with a round, middle-aged European lady who wanted to know when her husband could get in to see a doctor. The man — at least, I assumed it was her husband — sat in the waiting area with a bloody towel wrapped around his hand. The only other man in the waiting room was a yuppie type with a sniffling kid of about four.

"I'm sorry, ma'am," the nurse was saying, "but I don't know when there will be a doctor available. We will get to your husband as quickly as we can."

The woman raised her voice and spoke faster, switching unintelligibly back and forth between rough English and her own language. I think she was speaking Italian, but I couldn't say for sure.

"I said I *can't tell you that at this time*," shouted the nurse. Apparently she thought the woman's grasp of the English language would improve if she only spoke louder.

Vic shoved his way in front, still holding me by one arm so I didn't fall over.

"Excuse me," he said quietly. The nurse continued to argue with the woman. "Excuse me," he said, still quiet, but with a "don't screw around" sound to his voice. "This young man has just taken four or five handfuls of whatever he could find in the medicine chest."

"Box," I corrected him. "It was a shoe box."

Vic ignored me and continued to speak to the nurse. All of a sudden she looked a little worried, her over-plucked eyebrows shooting up above the thick pink frames of her glasses.

"So, if it's not too much trouble," he continued, his voice steady and even, "I was wondering whether we could maybe get him admitted."

I leaned back against the wall and drifted among my thoughts. I desperately wanted to go to sleep. More than anything now, I wanted to sleep. Voices buzzed around me, but I barely heard them.

"They're gonna make you drink some vile-smelling green junk that tastes like ground-up chalk," Vic was saying in my ear, "and you're going to puke your guts out for a while. Stuff cleans out your system real good."

"Yeah?"

That seemed like an appropriate thing to say. I wasn't quite understanding things at this point, but it seemed best just to agree and not ask questions. Two nurses pulled me out of Vic's grasp, away from the wall and through a door. I looked back over my shoulder to see Vic conferring with the nurse behind the desk before my guides rounded a corner and led me out of view of the Admissions desk.

The stuff they gave me to drink looked more black than green, but otherwise Vic was right; to use Matthew's words, it smelled pretty brutal. There was a paunchy, un-happy-looking nurse with a dark moustache who seemed to be responsible for me. She somehow got me undressed and into a hospital gown, and brusquely re-bandaged the cut on my wrist and the burn on my hand. It's funny, I thought as she cleaned and dressed the wounds, I'd forgotten about those. They just didn't hurt anymore. The nurse stood over me impatiently as I examined the cup with the black stuff in it.

"How long is this shit gonna take to work?" I asked her.

"Watch your language," she said with a dark look. "Anywhere from five minutes to half an hour. Some of that depends on how much you *want* it to work," she added meaningfully.

I wrinkled my nose and swallowed it in two quick gulps. It did taste an awful lot like chalk. I wondered how Vic knew that. I opened my mouth wide to show the nurse that it was empty, and she turned her back on me abruptly, pulling the curtain on her way out of my emergency room cubicle.

I don't know if it was the realization that I wasn't going to die or just the fact that I was getting used to the drugs in my system, but my head was a little less fuzzy now. There was a tray over the bed with a plastic bowl on it, but I didn't need it yet. What I really needed was a toilet. I swung my legs over the edge of the bed and re-coiled at the feel of my bare feet on the cold tile. Once I was on my feet again, I was dizzier than I expected, and bracing myself against the wall, I made my way slowly along the corridor, looking for a bathroom.

The nurse with the dark moustache intercepted me, appearing suddenly in front of me and blocking my path.

"And just where do you think you're going?" she said. Her bedside manner left a whole lot to be desired, I thought.

"I gotta pee."

With an impatient cluck of her tongue, she grabbed my arm and pulled me a short way down the hall. "Hurry up," she said, ushering me into a small, sterile bathroom stall off the main hallway.

I stepped outside the stall when I'd finished and looked around. The nurse was nowhere to be seen, and I started to make my way back up the hallway.

Within sight of my curtained cubicle, that foul stuff I'd drunk finally hit bottom, and I doubled over, clutching my stomach. I scrambled to get to the tray with the bowl and reached it just in time.

When I'd emptied the contents of my stomach into the basin, I crawled back into the bed and fervently wished for a glass of water to wash out my mouth. I waited a long time for someone to come and check on me — or for someone to at least empty the bowl; its contents were starting to smell pretty bad. I looked around, feeling a little more alert. There was a buzzer on the wall next to my bed and I pressed it curiously, hoping it would summon a nurse. After a few minutes, the same nurse returned — the cranky one with the moustache — looking slightly aggravated.

"Did you press that button?" she asked, her tone shrill.

"Yeah."

"What for?"

"Could you get rid of that?" I pointed to the bowl on the tray. With something like an indignant sniff, she picked it up and turned to leave.

"Um, by the way ..." I croaked after her. She gave me an icy glare.

"Yes?"

"Could I get a glass of water or something?"

"This isn't a hotel, young man; I'm busy with people who are actually *sick*. I'll get to you when I have a minute."

And she pulled the curtain sharply, leaving me alone.

I drifted in and out of sleep for a little while, hearing voices around me and wondering whether or not I was dreaming. After a time – I couldn't tell how long, because they'd taken away my watch – I jerked back into consciousness. Someone was putting a blanket over me, tucking me in. I couldn't remember the last time somebody had done that. I looked up to see Vic standing over my bed.

"You look a little better," he told me. "How do you feel?"

He smiled at me, that closed-mouth grin that made his whole face kind of fold in the middle. It made me feel strange. Guilty, almost. I wondered how I could have hated him two days ago.

"I'm tired." My throat was raw, and my mouth tasted ghastly.

"Yeah? Well, heaving your guts out can be tiring." He brushed a piece of hair off my forehead. "You get some sleep."

"They don't have my health insurance number or anything," I said.

"Your name was in the computer. I just gave them your name and that was all they needed. You must have been here before."

"I had my tonsils out when I was twelve," I said. "They

must still have me on file." I stared up at him for a second, still a little woozy. "What's gonna happen to me now?"

"I'm not sure. I'm not related to you so they won't tell me anything. I guess they'll check you in overnight, at least."

He stood there silently for a moment and I looked at him, trying to figure him out. Why is he still here? I wondered. He could have just dropped me off at the emergency room and left ... that's what I would have done. I frowned inwardly then, thinking that I probably wouldn't even have done that much.

"Hey, do you think you could get me something to drink?" I asked him finally.

"Yeah, I could do that. Anything else you need?"

I thought hard, then shook my head. "You don't have to stay here, you know. You probably have something better to do with your time."

"It's not a problem." He stuffed his hands in his pockets like he felt awkward all of a sudden. "I'll go get you that drink."

A thought occurred to me then, sending a shudder through my body. "Hey, Vic? You're not gonna tell Matthew about this, are you?" I asked.

He shook his head solemnly, like he'd expected the question. "It's not for me to tell," he said, and turned to leave.

He wasn't such a bad guy, I decided, watching him walk down the hall. He'd left the curtain open behind him, and I pushed my blanket aside, reaching over to pull it shut. I was asleep as soon as I'd pulled myself all the way back into the bed.

■ ■ ■

When I woke up, there was someone else in the cubicle with me. There was a paper cup full of water sitting on the tray in front of me, and I drank most of it before looking up. I was a little surprised not to see Vic standing there. Instead, a young man in a white coat was hovering over me with a clipboard on his arm, staring at me from behind little round glasses.

"Jareth Gardner?"

I cleared my throat.

"Yeah."

"I need to ask you a few questions." Without introducing himself or waiting for a response, the man continued. "First of all, I need you to confirm that this is your correct address."

I glanced at the clipboard he had stuck under my nose.

"Yeah. That's it."

"And what is your date of birth?"

"September the fourteenth."

"What year?"

I gave him a blank look.

"Every year," I said.

The man fixed me with a dark stare.

"What year were you born?" he said carefully, like he was dealing with somebody a little slow.

"Oh yeah. Right."

I told him my height and weight, and answered a mess of other stupid questions he probably could have figured out himself. I thought he was going to tell me to open my mouth so he could check my teeth, but instead he asked me if I had a religion.

"Religion?" I echoed. "There's a stupid question if I ever heard one. No."

"Have you ever done anything like this before?"

"Like what? Answer stupid questions for a geek in a lab coat?" I shot back.

"Don't be a smart-ass. Why did you take the pills?" he said.

I shrugged.

"Because cutting my wrist hurt too much."

"And, why did you want to cut your wrist?"

"Because ..." I shifted my weight uncomfortably and looked away from him. "I guess because I wanted to be dead."

The man scribbled something else on the clipboard, all business. He was an officious-looking bastard, the kind of guy who probably got his ass kicked twice a week from kindergarten all the way up to the end of high school.

"Are you currently under psychiatric care?" he asked.

I thought of Doctor Eschen and debated lying.

"What difference does it make?" I said cautiously.

"If you already have a psychiatrist, we'll call them. If you don't, we'll assign you one."

That would be great, I thought miserably. I'll have two shrinks instead of one. I gave him Eschen's name and address. The man wrote for a minute on his clipboard before looking up at me.

"We'll get you admitted in a little while," he said, his tone softening just a little. "They're having a rough night over in psych, so it might take some time. In the meantime, someone will be here to take some blood. We just want to make sure most of the toxins are out of your system before we transfer you to the psych ward."

With that, he turned and walked away.

Psych. The Psychiatric Ward. I'd seen the sign every time I'd come through the hospital lobby to visit Brad upstairs in Pediatrics.

They're putting me in the loony bin, I thought. Suddenly I wasn't so sleepy anymore.

I lay on my back and looked at the ceiling. It looked like it must have been a hundred feet up. I wondered where Vic was. He'd probably gone home. It had to be pretty late at night. Instinctively I looked at my left wrist where my watch usually was before I remembered the nurse had taken it away.

In the cubicle beyond mine a child started to scream. I hadn't heard anyone being ushered into that cubicle; I decided it must have happened while I'd been asleep. I heard adults talking in hushed voices. Heard the word "appendix" whispered a couple of times. Finally a nurse came and took the kid upstairs to have surgery.

Up and down the hall, voices spoke in hushed tones. I listened to the clicking of hard-soled shoes on the hard tile floor, and the *pad-pad* of the nurses in their rubber sneakers. After a long time, one of them stopped outside my cubicle and pulled back the curtain. I was more than a little relieved to see it wasn't the cranky woman with the facial hair.

"I'm here to take blood from Jarrod Gardner," she said ceremonially, reading from a clipboard. Wordlessly I pushed up a sleeve and offered her my arm, not even bothering to correct her.

Usually I would have been flipping out as she fastened the rubber band around my upper arm and slapped at the inside of my elbow to find a vein. But I was more upset at the prospect of what was to come than I was at the indignity of having blood taken from me. *The Psych Ward.* Going to see Doctor Eschen was bad enough, made me feel like a bit of a freak, but at least I could stop being crazy when I left his office at the end of the hour. Now I was going to be ... what? Shoved in a room with a bunch of psychos and left to fend for myself, more than likely.

I glanced over at the nurse taking my blood, barely noticing as she jabbed away at my arm, probing with the needle.

"You've got really small veins," she said, giving me a nervous little giggle. "I'm having a hard time getting the needle in."

I shrugged and looked away. Oh well, I figured this nurse was at least nicer than the one with the moustache. I got the feeling that other woman would have sooner slit me open and let the blood pour into a waiting funnel than prod around for a vein. On the other hand, I thought, maybe moustache lady had sent the inept nurse just to torture me. Either way, what the hell. It didn't really matter; I still wasn't feeling much pain.

When she'd finally managed to dig out a vein and get a few tubes full of blood, I lay there forever until the man in the white coat and glasses came back.

"You're being admitted," he announced. "I just need you to sign a few things." He showed me a sheaf of papers and handed me a pen.

"What am I signing?" I wanted to know.

"Admission papers." He pointed at the top sheet, all business. "I'm obligated to tell you that this is a Form One."

"What's that supposed to mean?"

"It means you can't leave the hospital before you've been formally discharged. Otherwise we can call the police, and they'll bring you back."

"I can get arrested for *leaving the hospital*?"

"You're considered a danger either to yourself or to others. You need to sign there ... and there." And he gestured toward a pair of signature blanks on the sheet.

"So, what if I refuse to sign it?"

The prissy little man looked perplexed. I'd thrown him a curve he wasn't expecting.

Chalk one up for Jareth, I thought numbly ... if I'd only had the energy to argue. I didn't feel like sleeping, but I sure wasn't feeling too energetic. I held the pen loosely in my hand and scrawled in the places where I'd been told. My hand was shaking like crazy, and I barely recognized my own signature. The man looked relieved as I handed him back the papers. He pursed his lips into what I thought must be as close to a smile as he could get.

"Fine," he said. "I'll send someone to bring you over to Psych." With a small upward tilt of his nose, the man turned on his heels and stalked down the hallway again.

8

The snoring of the man in the next bed was deafening, disturbing. Terrifying. The whole room resonated with it, and I was amazed nobody else was awake. There must have been five or six other beds in the room, although it had been dark when the guy with the glasses had shown me in, so I hadn't got a good look at the place.

Every once in a while the guy in the next bed would stop breathing altogether, and then he'd cough and wheeze for a few seconds before settling back into his snoring. Out in the hall, an old man was moaning in French. Further away, a woman was singing at the top of her lungs. Across the room, someone was mumbling quietly in his sleep.

"Mr. Thibeault," one of the nurses was telling the man in the hall, "you'll have to go back to sleep now. It's late."

"My legs!" he managed in heavily accented English. "My legs are hurting!"

"Shh, Mr. Thibeault. The other patients are trying to sleep."

The man in the bed next to mine sputtered and started to choke.

"Just roll over, for crying out loud!" I shouted into the darkness. I clamped my eyes and mouth tightly shut, rolled over on my side and wrapped my arms around my knees as tightly as I could manage. A tear fought its way out of one closed eye and streamed across the bridge of my nose into my other eye.

"I don't belong here," I whimpered under my breath. "This place is for crazy people. I'm not crazy. I'm not!" I whispered the words over and over again, trying to convince myself. But the voice in my head was louder: Crazy people tried to kill themselves. Crazy people slashed their wrists and swallowed pills. Crazy people were admitted to the psych ward under a Form One.

There was a mighty crash from out in the hallway, and I hugged myself tighter, so tight my back hurt. I wanted to go home, I thought. I didn't care anymore what she'd done to Brad, to me. I just wanted somebody to hold me and tell me this was all a bad dream.

I listened to the unfamiliar, terrifying night sounds for a long while, sobbing quietly under the blanket of noise coming from the next bed, and I felt like a scared little boy.

I had to go to the bathroom, so bad it felt like my kidneys were about to explode, but I ignored the feeling, not wanting to venture out into that hallway in search of a toilet. I squeezed my fists into the tightest balls I could manage, digging my fingernails deep into my palms. For an eternity I prayed silently — most of all I prayed for sleep, and when I thought it might be on the verge of arriving, I prayed not to wet the bed.

I was still wide awake when I began to notice a big window on one wall of the room. The sun was coming up over the parking lot outside, touching the cars with a sickly pinkish light. It must be nearly six o'clock, I realized with despair.

And with that thought, I was finally seized by a brief, restless slumber.

After what seemed like only a second — but was probably closer to an hour and a half — lights in the room were flipped on and a cheery female voice woke me from my brief, troubled sleep.

"Time to rise and shine, Jareth!"

I pried my eyes open. My eyelashes separated reluctantly, still sticky with tears.

"What time is it?" I wondered aloud. I looked up to see a huge bald man sitting on the bed next to me, pulling on a pair of wool socks with the bottoms worn thin. This was the snorer, I realized. He didn't look so frightening in the daylight. He gave me a big smile, and I saw that two of his bottom front teeth were missing, making him look like a jack-o'lantern come to life, or maybe a Disney cartoon gone horribly wrong. I turned away from him, hoping he wouldn't still be there when I looked again.

"It's a quarter after seven," said the nurse who'd woken me up. She was pretty — a young black woman in a pink uniform. She gave me a welcoming smile. "If you want to take a shower, you have a few minutes now. There's a towel and soap at the foot of the bed." She handed me a plastic bag, and I hauled myself into a sitting position. "Those are your clothes from yesterday. You can put them on once you've showered."

"Where are the showers?" I asked her, my voice a dull croak.

"Right across the hall. When you're finished your shower, go on down to the kitchen and have some breakfast."

My stomach rolled. The last thing I wanted was food. My mouth still tasted lousy, but the nurse was gone before I'd thought to ask for a toothbrush. I stumbled across the hall and opened the door labelled *Shower*. I flipped over the "Occupied" sign on the doorknob — there was no lock on the door — and hung the plastic bag with my clothes on the inside doorknob while I took off the hospital gown. Before I turned on the shower, I snuck a peek under the bandage on my arm. The cut looked a lot worse this morning than it had the day before, and now that I'd cleaned all the drugs out of my system I was starting to feel it. I couldn't be sure if it was aching or itching, but whatever it was, I sure didn't like it.

I had no sooner stepped into the water than I realized I'd left the soap and towel sitting on the bed across the hall. I contemplated stepping out of the shower and running across to get them, but decided against it. I didn't feel like putting that gown back on, and I wouldn't be particularly clean anyway once I got out of the shower, wearing yesterday's clothes with no deodorant. There was a scrap of soap stuck to the rack on the edge of the shower, and I gingerly scraped it off and used it to wash myself, trying not to imagine who might have used it before me.

When I'd finished my shower, I used the hospital gown to dry myself off some, then put on the clothes in the plastic bag. I slipped my watch onto my right wrist; I probably wouldn't be able to get it on over all the bandages on my left arm. There was a knock at the door as I was getting dressed, and a voice yelling at me to hurry up. I stepped outside into the hallway. Where was the kitchen? I looked around and saw an open door at the other end of the hall where a group of people sat around a table eating. That must be it, I thought, taking a deep breath and padding on down the hall.

There were people sitting around a long, plastic-covered table, talking, laughing, eating. It seemed almost too *normal*. I decided not to sit down. Sitting down would somehow include me in this group, and the last thing I wanted now was to be included.

There was a carton of milk on the table next to a pile of plastic cups. I took a cup and started to pour myself some milk, only to discover that the carton was empty.

"There's some more in the fridge," said the man who had slept in the bed next to mine. He had a terrible lisp. I looked around and found the refrigerator behind me.

"You can have anything you want in the fridge," someone else called out to me. They were all looking at me, I thought wildly. All the crazy people were staring at *me*. I didn't want them looking at me like this. I wasn't supposed to be here.

I found a half-empty bottle of apple juice and poured some, drinking it down in one gulp. It served to kill some of the dreadful taste in my mouth. Behind the apple juice I spotted a pitcher of grapefruit juice. I decided that would do a better job of getting rid of the taste. I poured myself a glassful and all but inhaled it.

The group at the table gave me a funny look as I poured a second, then a third glass. I didn't want to look back, but could see them all staring from the corner of my eye. I just concentrated on drinking the juice, emptying most of the pitcher before setting it back in the fridge and throwing my cup in the garbage.

When I was finished, I went out into the hall and looked around. There was a little alcove halfway between the room where I'd slept and the kitchen, and in it there was a couch with a coffee table and some magazines. I went and sat down, leaning my head back drowsily and closing my eyes. I'd almost fallen asleep when I felt the couch heave with the weight of someone else sitting down. I opened my eyes to see who it was. A mousy little man with slicked-back grey hair and a pink shirt was looking at me intently.

"Where you from?" he asked me.

"Nowhere much," I told him. "Just around here." I closed my eyes again and settled back into the thin couch cushions as well as I could.

"Tired, huh?" the man asked me. He had a dreadful voice, like a squirrel scolding. "Must be the weather. It's real damp out there."

"No," I said blandly, my eyes still closed. "It's not the weather. I just didn't get any sleep."

"First night, huh? It's always hard to sleep on your first night in a new place. Oh, well. You'll get used to it. It always takes a little while."

Get used to it! My stomach did somersaults at the very idea of spending another night there, and I felt the grapefruit juice I'd just drunk rising in my throat.

"You'll like occupational therapy," the man told me. "Margaret leads that on Monday, Wednesday and Friday. It's a lot of fun."

Great. Basket weaving. I kept my eyes closed and tried not to react. This was just fantastic. I should have been in Biology with a bunch of stupid Grade Ten punks, not in a freaking psycho hospital.

"Sometimes the food isn't so good, but that's okay." The man's voice dropped to a whisper. "I've got cookies in my drawer," he said conspiratorially. "Decadent Chocolate Chip. My wife brung 'em for me. I'll let you have some if you promise not to tell anybody."

I sat back and listened to the little man chatter away at me, letting my ears become accustomed to the sound of his voice until I barely heard him. Once in a while I nodded, mumbled "oh, yeah?" or "hmm, that's good to know," just so I wouldn't seem too rude. What I really wanted to do was close my eyes and drop off to sleep, but if I was going to be stuck in this place for long, I didn't want to piss off anybody who might be a homicidal maniac. At least not on the first day.

An old man with a cane limped past us, stopping for a moment to stare. Mumbling something in French, he shuffled on. That's the old guy from last night, I realized. The moaning one from across the hall.

"I'm not really a *patient* here," I heard the man tell me. "I'm just *staying* here for a little while. Until they find a place to move me to."

"Like, what kind of a place?" I said.

"I don't know, but I hope it's out in the country."

"Like, an asylum?"

"A *treatment* centre. So I can figure things out for a little while."

"Sounds cool," I said. *Figure things out for a little while.* It did sound like a nice idea. I shut my eyes and tried to fall asleep. Then the whiny little man said something that made my heart stand still, although he wasn't speaking to me: "Doctor Eschen," he called out happily. "It's so nice to see you here."

Sure enough, there he was ... as perfectly dressed as ever, and standing out like a neon sign in this place. And he was looking at *me*. There was a file folder under his arm, and I was pretty sure I knew whose name was on it.

"Hello, Reggie," Eschen said politely to the man in the pink shirt. Then he nodded a greeting at me, a gentle, tight-lipped smile that reminded me of Vic for just a second.

"Don't you try talking to *him*, Doc," Reggie said, jerking a thumb in my direction. "He ain't too friendly."

"That may be, but I still need to talk to him." And Doctor Eschen — tightassed Doctor Eschen — actually *winked* at me. Despite everything, I smiled back at him. That wink had spoken volumes: "This guy's nuts, Jareth, but let's humour him all the same, shall we?" He knew I didn't belong in here, I thought triumphantly; he's come to let me go home.

I stood up and ran a hand through my damp, matted hair. I followed the doctor a long way down the hall, past the kitchen, to a door marked "Conference Room 2." Eschen pushed the door open and ushered me inside. There were three hard-backed wooden chairs inside. One of them was occupied by the nurse who'd woken me up that morning. I noticed now that her name tag said Desirée. She flashed me another smile. She was probably trying to make me feel more comfortable, I thought fleetingly, but she was succeeding in making me nervous as hell. Eschen sat in another of the chairs, leaving the third for me. I sat gingerly on the edge of it, feeling like it might collapse under my weight. Now that we were here, in this official-looking broom closet disguised as a meeting room, I wondered whether that wink in the hallway had meant what I thought it did. Maybe he was just patronizing me ... maybe he was here to commit me to some "nice place in the country." Me and crazy old Reggie could be roommates, share his Decadent Chocolate Chip Cookies.

Eschen set the file folder down in his lap. He opened it and took a pen from his jacket. He busied himself for a minute, flipping through the papers in the folder. Then he looked up at me with those cold, professional eyes of his and gave me a good once-over. Finally he spoke.

"Jareth, what happened?" he said quietly.

Suddenly I was that guy again. The smart-assed kid in his office. I shrugged and leaned back in the rickety straight-backed chair.

"I tried to kill myself," I said, trying to make it sound casual.

"How?" he said.

That caught me off-guard. Funny, I thought for sure he'd ask "why?"

"I took a bunch of pills."

"And what happened to your arm?"

I looked down at the white gauze bandage which covered both the cut on my arm and the burn on my palm.

"I cut myself."

"On purpose?" prompted the nurse.

"I guess."

"You wanted to bleed to death," she suggested.

I gave her a slightly superior look, like she couldn't possibly know what I'd wanted.

"I knew it wasn't gonna kill me," I said.

"How did you know that?" Eschen asked.

"Biology class," I replied. "Shroades — that's the teacher — once told us that if we ever wanted to kill ourselves we should cut *up*, not *across*. He said it jokingly, but he was telling the truth, you know? You cut your vein from side-to-side, it's easy to stitch up again, and it doesn't bleed that much anyway. But if you cut up and down, it just *gushes* blood, and there's not much anybody can do about it. I've taken that class three times and he gives the same speech every semester."

"So, if you didn't want to kill yourself, why did you cut your arm?"

I shrugged. "I really don't know. Did you know my brother died this week?"

The doctor nodded grimly. "I read about it in the paper yesterday. That must have been really rough on you."

I stared at him for a second, suddenly caught in a staring match with those weird colourless eyes of his, eyes that could tear me apart, see right into my soul.

"Look," I said finally, snapping out of the trance. "I really hate this place. I'm not suicidal. Not *really*. Maybe I was for a little while yesterday, but I'm okay now. I'm not going to do this again. Never ... I promise. Just let me go home. Get me out of this place. Tell them I can leave, please?"

Eschen leaned back in his chair, scribbling something in the folder that sat open in his lap.

"Have you got somewhere to go?" he said. "Somebody who could come and pick you up?"

I shrugged.

"Yeah, well, my mother's in jail, so I'm kind of short one official guardian at the moment," I said. "I guess my friend's stepfather could come and pick me up. He's the one that brought me here."

The doctor nodded.

"Why don't you give him a call, then?" he said. "Tell him to be here around ten-thirty. All your paperwork should be ready by then."

"Really?" I could feel a grin spreading across my face, a real one for a change, not the phony Jareth Gardner Special. "Thanks a lot," I said.

Eschen gave me a meaningful look.

"You're not off the hook, you know," he told me. "This isn't a 'get out of jail free' card; you still have to come and see me."

I nodded. "Yeah, I understand that," I said. Stone cold relief washed over me as I stood to leave. "I'll be there."

And he shook my hand.

"I'll look forward to seeing you, then." He smiled, a real honest-to-gosh friendly smile, and turned to leave me alone in the tiny interview room with the nurse.

"Where can I use the phone?" I asked, anxious to leave.

"There's a pay phone by the door. Do you have a quarter?" Her tone was less perky now than it had been when she'd woken me up an hour and a half earlier, but still a little too pert and happy for me to believe it.

"No. I don't have any pockets in these pants," I said. "I wasn't really planning to go out yesterday."

"Okay. I'll see if I can find you one." We walked together down the hall, with me just half a step behind her. At the nurses' station she reached behind the desk and found her purse. She dug around and fished out a handful of change, handing me a quarter.

"There you go, hon," she said like I was an absolute infant, and pointed to the phone.

"Thanks."

I picked up the receiver and held it to my ear. The mouthpiece smelled terrible — worse than stale smoker's breath, like nobody who'd used the phone had ever heard of a toothbrush.

I dialled Matthew's number from memory.

"Vic," I blurted out before he'd even said "hello."

I explained the situation to him, and when I'd finished, he didn't say anything for a minute.

"Okay. I'll see you at ten-thirty, then," he said, and hung up without saying goodbye.

I hung up the phone slowly on my end, wondering if I'd offended Vic. Maybe it had been a little presumptuous to assume he'd just drop whatever he was doing and come get me. Then again, what choice did I have? I couldn't stay there any longer, and I couldn't leave unless he came.

I told myself to be nice to Vic when he showed up. I was running a little low on people who were willing to put themselves out for me, and I thought it would probably be a bad idea to make any of them mad.

Vic came at ten thirty-five. When I saw him, I ran over to him and hugged him as hard as I could. He made a noise like I'd thrown him off-balance, but he hugged me back. It occurred to me that I hadn't hugged anybody in maybe three years — and that had probably been Brad hugging me — and here I was throwing my arms around this guy for the second time in as many days. I was too relieved to be embarrassed, though, and Vic didn't seem to mind much.

As we left the hospital, my night in the psych ward suddenly seemed a billion miles away. We got into the car and I revelled in the familiar sights and sounds around the hospital: the highway going past, the big park by the lake, the posh little boutiques and the downtown streets.

I didn't much want to talk on the way home, but Vic was trying to make conversation, and I sure didn't want to seem rude after everything he'd done for me.

"How's the stomach this morning?" he asked.

"It's okay. I had some breakfast. Just juice, but I'm not feeling sick or anything."

"Good for you." He was quiet for a few minutes. "Did you get everything sorted out?" he said then.

I wasn't quite sure what he meant, but I figured he was asking me if I felt better, and I told him yes. I wasn't feeling *good*, as such, but I sure didn't feel as bad as I had the day before. I didn't think it was possible to ever feel that bad again.

"I don't have my keys with me," I told Vic, just for the sake of saying something. "I locked them in the house when I left."

"How are you gonna get inside?"

I almost laughed at that. I'd gotten into much more difficult houses than my own, but I realized just in time it would be a very, very bad idea to tell Vic that.

"I'll just lift out the basement window," I said instead.

"Hmm." He half-turned in his seat to give me a good look. "What are you planning to do now, Jareth?"

I shrugged and stared out the window at the passing stores and industrial plazas.

"I don't know. Pack some stuff. Maybe go to Toronto or something."

"You're not planning to stick around?"

I laughed derisively. "What for?" I said. "All I've got here is good old insipid Matthew. No offense."

"None taken." He smiled, perhaps a little more than he should have at that. "But what do you have in Toronto?"

"Nothing," I admitted. "But there's more stuff. Opportunities. I could get a job or something."

"And live where?"

I shrugged, thinking of Lloyd's money. "I have a little bit saved up. Enough to tide me over until I find a job. I can get a room or something."

"What about school?"

I shook my head. "They won't let me go. I'm under contract; if I skip any classes I get kicked out. I haven't been at school nearly all week."

Vic gave me a funny look at that. "Jareth, I'm sure they'll make an exception. I'd venture to say you've had a pretty unique week. If you want, I can go down there with you tomorrow and help you explain it to the principal or whoever."

"No thanks. I mean, I'm grateful for the offer and everything, but I really don't think I want to be in school right now."

"So what are you gonna do instead?"

"I already told you," I said, a little curtly.

Vic was silent for a long time, and when I looked back at him I could see he was thinking hard, his long, thin eyebrows twisted into a concentrated frown.

"Can you do something for me?" he said then. "Can I ask you to just stay put for a little while? I mean, a couple of hours. Let me look into something for you. Please?"

I shrugged. "Sure. I want to shower and take a nap anyway. I didn't sleep real well last night."

When we got to my house Vic helped me lift the back window out, and I crawled in over the work table in the basement — the work table Keith, Brad's father, had set up years earlier. There were still little pink pieces of plastic all over the place from where I'd tried to break that razor. Fleetingly I wondered whether Keith knew his son was dead. Or if he even cared. Like most of the men my mother took up with, Keith had disappeared after a year or so, and we hadn't seen him since.

"I'll give you a call in a couple of hours," Vic called through the window, and I nodded.

"I'll be here."

I sat in the bathtub for a long time and let the water from the shower wash over me, just enjoying the silence and solitude of being alone in the house. Of being in control.

I didn't bother dressing when I'd finished, just wrapped myself in a towel, wandered into my room and fell sideways across the bed. I'm pretty sure I was asleep before I landed.

Part Two:

REDEMPTION

10

I lingered on the porch of the old brick
house for a few minutes, looking up at the ivy that covered the front wall and contemplating ringing the doorbell. Vic was off parking the car someplace, and I stood
waiting, juggling my knapsack back and forth from hand
to hand.

This was the "something" he'd been looking into for
me: a friend in the city with a big old house who'd be
willing to let me crash with him for a while.

After a few minutes Vic showed up with the rest of
my stuff — an old army duffel bag filled with clothes and
a couple of books. The important things, my own little
treasures, were in my knapsack. I'd grabbed the picture of
Brad, the sketchbook I'd bought from the variety store the
day he died, the big knife I'd ripped off from Lloyd's place.
Things I didn't want anyone else touching.

I almost hadn't brought the knife. I'd nearly finished
packing when I saw it sitting there on my desk. I'd picked
it up, unsheathed it slowly, looking it over inch by inch
before I grabbed it by the tip and hurled it as hard as I

could into the wall. It sank into the drywall between two posters with a satisfying *thunk*, and I walked over to pull it out, pleased with the hole it had made. It left me with a taste for destruction and for the next twenty minutes or so I'd walked around the house, using the knife to carve my name into the walls wherever it suited me. I wasn't sure what had come over me all of a sudden, but I felt like I was full of poison, and the only way I could let it out was by tearing at the walls of this house where I'd grown up. When I'd finished, though, I didn't feel any less poisonous — just tired. Somehow I justified what I'd done to the house; I figured the landlord would be so thrilled to have got rid of us that he wouldn't much care about having to fix up the walls. My mother had never been one to pay her rent on time.

Anyway, I still had the knife in my hand when Vic rang the doorbell. Without thinking, I stuffed it into my knapsack, grabbed my duffel bag and my jacket and ran down the stairs so I wouldn't have to invite Vic into the house to see what I'd done to the place.

■ ■ ■

While I'd waited for Vic to park the car I had had a good look at the front of this new place. It had probably been a real nice place about fifty years earlier — stately, even. I imagined it sitting on a sizable lot, big trees in the front yard, maybe a big stone wall around the property. It was still pretty impressive-looking, but now it was crowded on either side by houses that were considerably newer and much less attractive. The street in front of it had been widened to four lanes and a sidewalk had been added, which took up most of the front yard. And the house itself wasn't in great shape by any means. The ivy that crawled up and over the front wall looked like it was holding the entire place together, and I was more than a little concerned about the structural integrity of the porch, which creaked and groaned every time I shifted my weight. In the laneway beside the house was a rotting old Mustang with its hood up, and beyond that, an antique pickup truck that looked like someone had put a lot of work into it.

"Ah. I see Danny's home." Vic heaved my duffel bag up the three steps onto the porch and followed it up.

"Who's Danny? I thought you said this guy's name was Stewart," I said.

"Yeah. But that's Danny's car." Vic pointed at the Mustang, trying to pretend he wasn't out of breath as he rested for a second. Then he picked up my duffel bag, opened the front door and walked straight in without knocking.

He stood in the front hall for a second, turning to watch as I stepped inside. He'd been here an awful lot; his whole body seemed to relax as he stepped inside, like he'd just gotten home after a long day. Funny how he never looked that relaxed in his own house.

I cast a fleeting glance at my surroundings, trying not to make it too obvious I was gawking. The front hallway was an open white space with big globby abstract paintings on the wall. On the other side of me was a sunken living room full of musty-looking couches from the fifties, and a broad spiral staircase towered above us like a monolith. Vic called Stewart's name and a door opened somewhere at the top.

"I'll be right down," called a voice before the door slammed shut again.

I'm not sure what I expected this guy to look like, but when he finally appeared it was a complete shock to me. The guy looked like he'd just stepped out of 1967 and didn't know quite what to make of the nineties. He was a little older than Vic, maybe forty-five, with a wild mane of long yellowish-brown hair and small, sad eyes about the same colour. In fact, his whole body had this sort of yellowish aura about it, like a jaundiced glow. He made his way down the stairs like it didn't much matter to him how long it took to get to the bottom. He smiled at me with chipped and crooked teeth and extended a hand.

"Stewart Morgan," he said. "You must be Jareth."

Stewart was tall, maybe six-foot-two, and he stood too close to me as he talked. I resisted the urge to back away from him.

"Yeah," I said, shaking his hand. He had a dead-fish handshake, fingers hanging. Creepy. I dug my own hand back in my pocket as soon as I let go. "I guess you're a friend of Vic's."

Stewart tried to make small talk — asked me where I was from and how I knew Vic, although I suspected he already knew. He was the kind of guy who made too much eye contact, just stared at you unblinking to show how interested he was in what you had to say.

"Hey look, um, Stewart," I said after answering a couple of questions. "I don't want to be pushy or anything, but it's been kind of a long trip. D'you think I could maybe use the bathroom?"

I didn't really have to go to the toilet — at least not so bad it couldn't have waited — but I was already getting tired of this guy in my face. He was pretty cool about it, though, falling all over himself about how he should have thought of that earlier, and did I want anything to drink when I got out, and why didn't I come sit in the front room where it was more comfortable?

The little bathroom just off the front hallway was homey and neatly-kept, with a raspberry-scented candle burning on the vanity and a rack of magazines across from the toilet. I decided to forego the magazines as well as the too-cute guest towels hanging on the brass ring over the sink; I wiped my hands dry on my pants instead of worrying about how to refold the towels properly.

I thought the bathroom was a little strange, given that Stewart looked more like the woodsy-outdoorsy type than the floral soap and finger towels type. I was right, as it turned out. I found out much later that Stewart had inherited the house from his parents. It was in terrible condition, and he'd given some interior decorator friend free reign over the renovation of the place. I don't think he ever actually set foot inside the downstairs bathroom — or half the other rooms in the house, for that matter.

When I stepped out of the bathroom there was a stranger standing in the front hall, tall and dark and built like a brick wall. His hair, so black it looked almost blue, brushed the tops of his ears and flopped down into his eerie, almost-white blue eyes. He braced himself against the wall with his shoulder, both hands deep in the pockets of his dark blue jeans.

"Hey," I said awkwardly. This guy was making no effort to hide the fact that he was staring right at me. "Are you Danny?" I added after a second.

"Might be," the man said, the hint of a smile on his lips. "And you're my brother's new stray dog."

I started at that, too puzzled to be offended.

"You're Vic's brother?" I said.

"No, Stewart's. Might as well be Vic's, though; I've known him since I was a kid. They're in the sitting room." And he jerked his head toward the front room. Casting a suspicious glance back at him, I wandered into the living room where Vic and Stewart were laughing about some old story.

"I met your brother," I told Stewart.

"Oh, Danny?" Stewart said, like he'd forgotten about him. "Yeah, he's a little abrasive, but you get used to him after a while."

Vic nodded. "He's an interesting guy, Danny is," he said. "Abrasive, but boy, he's constant. You get Danny Morgan on your side, man, he's loyal."

"My mother always said Danny was just going through a difficult phase," Stewart added, "but he's been like this for more than thirty years now. I'm starting to doubt anything much is going to change." He scooped a big grey cat off the chair beside his and motioned for me to sit down.

"So," Stewart continued, "Vic calls me up this morning and tells me he's got this friend who's having a housing crisis. Well, I've got this great big house and nobody in it but me and Danny, so I have no problem with letting you stay here for as long as you need a place to stay."

"It won't be for very long, you know," I said guardedly. "Just until I get a job or something."

It was the first time the thought had crossed my mind. Getting a job. Growing up. It was a scary idea, but I figured it sounded good coming out of my mouth. I sat up as straight as I could and wondered how much of my act this guy was buying. I hadn't really had enough time to figure out exactly what kind of image I was trying to present to this guy, and consequently I was feeling a little frazzled. Overall it had been a strange couple of days.

I looked around the room, half-listening to what he was saying in response. Through a door at the end of the living room I saw a high-ceilinged room lined with books. A library. This place had a library.

"— room at the top of the stairs," I heard Stewart say. "It's not real big, but it's got a big window with a decent view. It's all made up for you whenever you want to move your stuff up there."

I turned to give Stewart a good look. Out of the corner of my eye I could see Vic looking on like he was watching TV — detached, like he knew it was going to come out all right in the end.

"But you don't even know me," I said. "I could be some kind of psychopath, for all you know."

Stewart shrugged.

"Maybe so. But if Vic says you're okay, I'm willing to take a chance." He winked and gave me that limp-fish handshake again. Delicate, like he was afraid of hurting me. Then he stood up, as if we'd closed some kind of deal. Like I'd just signed my life over to this guy or something. "Come on. I'll help you bring your bag upstairs."

That night I lay in the bed I would come to know as mine — a big brass thing with pristine white blankets in a little grey room at the top of the stairs — staring at the ceiling in the dark. Outside the window I could hear a tree scraping against the side of the house, and even though I knew what it was, it still made me nervous. I was exhausted, but I couldn't force myself to sleep. In the next room I could hear someone moving around, opening drawers and closing them again. I figured it must have been

Danny; I didn't see Stewart as the type who would make that much noise just going about his business. Besides, Stewart's room was up in the attic. He was some kind of artist and he did all his work up there, too. I wasn't entirely sure what Danny did for a living ... if he did anything at all. Mostly he just seemed to sit around and gripe. Stewart had made dinner, and as we sat around the table in the kitchen he tried making small talk with me. I didn't want to tell him too much, so I steered the conversation toward minor things — stuff I'd learned at school, how I knew Vic. I thought of the last thing Vic had said to me before he left.

"Stewart's a good guy," he'd told me. "But if this doesn't work out, you call me. We'll find something else for you." He'd been looking me right in the eye, made me promise not to just take off somewhere without calling him first.

I still couldn't figure out what was in this for Vic. I figured maybe he was trying to do some kind of penance for something terrible he'd done in the past. Or maybe he just had some weird Boy Scout ethic, or felt like it was his duty to help me because of Matthew. Either way, though, I was beginning to relax a little about everything he'd done for me over the past couple of days.

Which was probably a good thing, since Danny Morgan was freaking me out in a huge way. Since the second I'd arrived he hadn't said much to me, just stared right through me with those icy, washed-out eyes that seemed to see more than I wanted him to. I wondered why he was here, living with his brother. Physically, they didn't look much like they were related, but the way they acted with one another was so fraternal, almost coldly familiar, that there was no way they hadn't grown up to-gether. Still, there was a distance between them, an air of tolerance instead of love. I wondered if Brad and I would have ended up like that, or if he would have died anyway in another year or so. With this in my head I eventually drifted into a fitful, restless sleep.

■ ■ ■

I woke up around noon, blinking at the light that was shining in my window. The first thing I noticed, after the light, was the feeling of being watched. I looked around until I saw a cat sitting on the shelf of the open closet, staring at me like I didn't have a right to be there. It was a black cat, scrawny and suspicious.

"Piss off," I snarled. "I've got every right to be here."

I got out of bed and went downstairs in the shorts and tee-shirt I'd worn to bed. There didn't seem to be anyone around except the other cat, the grey one I'd seen the day before. This was biggest cat I'd ever seen, with eyes nearly the same colour as its fur, a tired bluish-grey. I tried to pick it up like I'd seen Stewart do the previous day but it hissed at me and bolted into the living room.

There was a newspaper on the kitchen table, open to a page that made me do a double-take. "No bail for sus-pected child-killer mom," said the headline. There was a picture of my brother, a really old class picture, I thought. I just stood there for probably a full minute, staring down at the paper, not reading, just staring. Wondering where they'd gotten the picture. Then I shook my head to clear it, and sat down at the table to read.

The paper told the whole story — well, most of it, at

any rate. How I'd come home from school and found Brad on the floor, how the cops had come to get the old lady, how Brad had died in the hospital. They got most of it right — although they had everyone's age wrong, and they'd misspelled the name of our street. But the meat of the story was still there.

As I sat there re-reading the article I heard the front door open and close. I glanced up for long enough to discern that Danny had just walked in, then stared back at the paper again.

"So, you're up." He brushed past me with a bag of groceries and started to put them away. "That's you in the paper, isn't it? I didn't figure there were too many sixteen-year-old kids named Jareth."

"I'm not sixteen," I said a little defensively. "And my mother's not thirty-one, she's thirty-five. I don't know where they got their numbers, but they're wrong."

"Whatever," said Danny. "I mean, I don't really care if you're sixteen or eighteen or a hundred-and-three. I just thought you might want to see the article. I figure if I was in your position I would want to know what was going on, you know?"

I stared down at the paper so I wouldn't have to look up at him. "Yeah, whatever. Thanks," I mumbled. Behind me I heard him moving around, stacking cans on top of one another and rustling through the armload of paper bags he'd brought in with him.

I read the story a second, then a third time. Seems the old lady had made a court appearance and made a complete ass of herself — screaming, crying, begging for them to let her out. The judge, understandably, hadn't paid her an awful lot of attention.

"You as much of a psycho as your Ma?" Danny said behind me. "I mean, you're not gonna freak out and bludgeon us in our sleep, are you?"

There was a hint of laughter in his voice. I bristled, but managed to control myself.

"Are you trying to pick a fight with me?" I said incredulously, turning in my chair to face him.

"Why, you want to fight?" he said, standing up straight.

"You must be out of your mind," I told him. "Look, I'm not looking to get into any trouble. I'm just crashing here until I get my shit together, you know?"

He really did laugh at that, a nasty-looking smile spreading across his broad, ugly red face.

"You're not looking for trouble, eh, Jareth? Yeah, I've heard that one before. I know your type; you got trouble written all over you. Stewart doesn't have much of a nose for it, but then again, he's a lousy judge of character."

I couldn't do anything but shrug at that. I folded up the paper, tucked it under my arm and left the kitchen.

It's ridiculous, I told myself on the way upstairs. This guy must be in his thirties and he gets his kicks cutting me down. I could hear music coming from up in the attic, something slow and familiar. "American Pie," maybe. I stopped and listened for a few seconds, but I couldn't figure out what it was.

I showered and dressed, then decided to take myself on a tour of the neighbourhood. I passed Danny on the stairs on my way out and he smiled at me and raised an eyebrow just a little, like he expected me to be happy to see him. Instead I just ignored him and kept going.

10

It was a clear, bright day as I set out on my walk, and there was a hint of spring in the air despite the cold wind that bit through my windbreaker and drove my hands deep into the pockets of my jeans. Stewart lived just a few blocks from downtown, and I hadn't walked far before I got a good whiff of exhaust fumes and pollution.

I didn't have any particular plan for my excursion; I just figured I'd get myself a good sense of the neighbourhood, get my bearings, maybe see if there was anything interesting going on.

Ever since I was a young teenager I'd always loved coming to the city and just walking around. Matthew would make fun of me: "You're spending eight bucks on a train ticket just so you can go for a walk?" he'd said every time. "What's the matter, the sidewalks here not good enough for you?"

There were some newer houses along Stewart's street, probably built in the last ten years — big brick monstrosities with steel doors and security stickers on the front windows. But there were others, too — older houses that caught my eye. There was one with rotting window frames around all the basement windows; another had a big shed with a broken lock in the side yard. As I wandered along the block I picked out three or four houses that had potential for future excursions.

Of course, after what had happened with old Lloyd I figured I'd have to be pretty careful the next time around. I wouldn't have Matthew to watch my back, for one thing, although he was always such a nervous wreck I sometimes wondered if he did me more harm than good. One thing was certain, though: I would have to be much, much more careful in the future. I didn't want to find any more old men clutching their chests on bedroom floors.

It was funny — it had been years since I'd gone for more than two days without talking to Matthew, although I had no overwhelming urge to call him. Maybe I needed a break from him, I decided. I wondered if Vic would tell Matthew where I was — give him Stewart's number, maybe. I wasn't sure why, but I half hoped he wouldn't.

I wandered to the end of Stewart's road and found myself in a place I recognized. It was only another couple of blocks until I got to a major intersection, and from there I headed toward the core of downtown: Yonge Street, the Eaton Centre. As I approached, I could hear the sounds of people going about their days ... a pair of street performers playing steel drums, a raucous bunch of young teenagers smoking and shoving each other playfully. I wound my way around the rowdy kids and through the tourists, plodding along like I actually had somewhere to go. I wondered if I'd be able to find my way back to Stewart's place when I was finished walking.

I kept on down the street, fascinated by the sheer size

of things, and by what a huge hurry everyone seemed to be in. I stopped for a second to peek through a space in a construction fence, looking at the huge hole in the ground that would soon house some bank tower or corporate headquarters or something.

There was a trio of kids wearing Doc Martens boots — the high ones with coloured laces — crouched in the doorway of a boarded-up store, wrapped in sleeping bags with a shallow cardboard box on the ground in front of them.

"Spare some change, buddy?" one of them said.

I looked down. The guy who had spoken to me had bright purple hair and a ring through his nose.

"I might have a bit." I poked around the pockets of my jacket and came up with a handful of silver, maybe a dollar fifty in all. I dropped it into the box and the guy with the purple hair thanked me.

"No problem," I said, and continued up the street. I cast a backward glance toward them as I walked, wanting to stare but not wanting to seem rude. I wondered where they slept at night ... or how long it would be until I ended up squatting in a doorway myself.

I still had most of the money from old Lloyd's house, and I hadn't eaten yet that day, so I went into a restaurant. There was a *Help Wanted* sign in the window, and for a brief second I considered asking for an application. Then I thought better of it and just asked for a menu. I didn't want to get stuck working in some greasy little café, downtown or not.

I ordered a sandwich and picked at it until it was gone, dropped a few dollars on the table and got up to continue my tour. I didn't walk very far before I started to get tired, so I turned back toward home. I was surprised how easily that word came to me … *home*. It sounded like a strange name for this place of Stewart's, which looked more like a museum than a house.

I found my way back easily enough, identifying Stewart's house from the ratty old porch and the red pickup truck in the side yard. Danny's car wasn't in the driveway when I got there, I noted with relief. I wasn't in the mood to be provoked again.

I stood for a second outside the door, wondering whether I should knock or just walk in. As I glanced through the front window I could see Stewart sitting in the living room with a book in his lap. I caught his eye and waved, and he gestured for me to come in, a big silly-looking grin on his face. Like I was the first human being he'd seen all day, and he was just thrilled to death to have me there.

"Jareth," I heard him call as I stepped inside. "Good to see you. Come on in and talk to me."

I stepped into the living room and sat cross-legged on the floor in front of a chair, which made Stewart laugh.

"You know, you're allowed to use the furniture."

"That's okay. I like the floor."

He laughed, although I wasn't sure why.

"Suit yourself," he said, and set his book aside. He fixed those funny yellow eyes of his on me, and I instantly wished I'd sat in a chair. It was a little unnerving, the way he was towering over me from his chair. I felt like a little kid getting in trouble from the teacher.

"How've you been?" he said. "Are you settling in okay?"

I shrugged. "I guess. I just went for a little walk."

"Exploring the neighbourhood, eh? That's great." He nodded, rubbed his hands together like he was trying to figure out what to say next.

"Yeah, well, I already know Toronto pretty well," I explained, for lack of anything better to say. "I used to come here all the time when I was a kid."

"That's great," he said again, like it didn't matter in the least. "Look, Jareth, you had a caller today."

I frowned at that. "Who? Vic?"

"No. He must have told them where you're staying, though."

My heart started to race. Them? "Who is 'them'?" I said, my voice squeaking just a little.

"It was, um, Detective Booker? No, Brooks. He said you'd spoken with him earlier in the week. About your brother, I guess."

"How did he find me?"

"Well, that's funny," Stewart said. "It turns out he asked your mother where you might be. I guess she suggested they check with, um ... Vic's stepson. I'm so bad with names."

"Matthew," I prompted.

"That's right. I guess Matthew wasn't home, but Vic was able to help him out."

"Great." I leaned my head way back against the seat of the chair behind me. Vic was just way too damned helpful, I thought bitterly. But I'd given the cop Vic's number, hadn't I? When he'd asked for my father's number. And as loyal as Vic might have been, I'd known him long enough to realize he certainly wasn't going to hide me from the cops, no matter what the circumstances. I couldn't help but be a little disappointed, though. I'd been enjoying the idea of the relative anonymity I thought I'd have at Stewart's. I sighed as I realized I'd left a lot of unfinished business at home.

"I guess I'm gonna have to deal with that," I said aloud.

"Well, yeah. He left his number," Stewart said, digging around in a drawer in the end table beside him. "I told him you'd get in touch."

"Swell," I muttered, taking the number from him. I dragged myself to my feet, stiffer than I expected after my long walk. "Guess I'll go give him a call."

"Okay. Why don't you do that?" Stewart looked vaguely relieved as he reached to pick up his book again.

I was poised to go upstairs when I heard Stewart calling after me. "Hey, Jareth?" His voice was soft, nervous.

"Yeah?"

"I just wanted you to know you're welcome here," he said. "Whether Danny makes you feel that way or not. I'm glad you're here."

I didn't know what to say to that, just mumbled something and headed on up the wide oak staircase to my room.

There was a phone on the table beside my bed, and I stared at it for a long time before picking it up. I held the receiver to my ear, staring at the business card in my hand, the letters blurring as I listened to my heart racing in my ears. What did this cop want with me, I wondered. I played the conversation out in my head: "Yeah, Jareth? Your mom said she wasn't the one who killed your brother. Yeah, guess what? She said it was you. We'll be over in an hour to arrest you."

I set the phone down, laughing nervously.

"Don't be ridiculous," I said aloud. "That's not the way it works. And even if it was, there's no way to prove it. Just give the guy a call. He probably just wants to double-check your address for the records or something."

And before I could chicken out, I picked up the phone and dialled.

The detective actually sounded pretty happy to hear from me. I couldn't picture him sitting behind a desk, this hulking great man with fingers so thick he'd probably have to use the end of a pencil to press the number buttons on his phone. "Hi, Jareth." His voice was less gentle than it had been when I'd last spoken to him. "How are things going?"

"Good, I guess. I mean, not good, but better than they were."

"Glad to hear it. Hey, I called you earlier. Your dad said you were out."

His words jarred me for a second before I remembered I'd told him I was going to stay with my father. With something like a thrill I realized Vic hadn't ratted me out. Man, the guy just got cooler and cooler.

"Yeah, I was out for a while," I agreed after a second.

"Well, I just wanted to let you know what's happening with your mom," he said. "I was actually a little surprised I didn't see you in court yesterday."

"I read about that in the paper this morning," I told him. "She didn't get out on bail."

"That's right. So you know she's back in court again on June 4?"

"Hmm. Yeah, I think I read that. What, do I have to go or something?" I said.

"Well, I don't think you *have* to go," he said, sounding a little surprised. "You may have to go at some point, but it won't be me letting you know about that. If you have to testify at all, it'll probably be the Crown Attorney's office giving you a call."

The Crown Attorney. Right. I remembered that from my Grade Ten Civics class. I'd grown up watching courtroom scenes on American TV shows, but everything had a different name in Canada.

"What time is it gonna be?" I said, just for the sake of asking. I had about as much interest in watching my mother cry and carry on in a courtroom as I did in driving sharp needles under my toenails.

"Ten in the morning," said Brooks. "You might want to show up a little early. You know, get a good seat."

"Yeah," I said drily. "I'll want to be right in the front row for that one."

"Look, son. Jareth. I'm actually just on my way out for the day. But are you ... I mean, are you talking to someone? Has our Victim Services office been in touch with you?"

"Victim Services? What kind of crap is that?" I said, suppressing a snort. "You gonna set me up with a grief counsellor or something?"

"Well, if you need to ..." The cop trailed off, obviously uncomfortable. He hadn't struck me as the type to get into a squishy talk about my feelings, and from the sound of things I'd been right.

"It's okay," I said. "I already have a shrink. Thanks anyway."

When I'd hung up the phone I lay back on the bed and stared up at the ceiling for a while, my hands linked behind my head. Outside the window the light was fading from the sky, dark storm clouds closing in as the sun crept lower on the horizon.

I lay for a while and watched as the rain began to fall, cold and hard against the side of the house, the wind rattling against the window and shaking the branches of the tree outside my room. This wasn't such a bad place, I thought. It sure beat having to scrape my mother off the floor three times a week, even if I did have Danny to contend with.

Impulsively I rolled off the bed and found the duffel bag I'd stowed in the closet. I started to unpack, hastily folding my jeans and tee-shirts as neatly as I could manage and stuffing them into the drawers of the dresser, hanging my one dress shirt in the closet, then folding the duffel bag and throwing it on the top shelf of the closet.

Next I set to work on my backpack, dumping the contents out on the bed to sort through them. I'd thrown in a mishmash of crap, mostly stuff I'd swept off my desk in my haste to leave the house.

I'd hidden old Lloyd's Bowie knife in a side pocket of the bag, and I looked around the room for a new hiding place for the thing before realizing I didn't really need to hide it from anybody here. If Stewart or somebody ever asked about it, I'd just say it had been a gift from my grandpa or some cheesy crap like that. I just set it on the dresser beside the bed, where I could look at it whenever I wanted.

In the main body of the knapsack there was an old pencil case from Grade Nine, a clear plastic paperweight with a bunch of pennies and paperclips embedded in the bottom, an assignment I'd been working on for English class ... and the sketchbook I'd bought that day from the convenience store downstairs from the doctor's office.

I opened the book to the first page and ran my hand over its rough yellowish parchment, remembering how much I loved the feeling of watching a few scratched lines evolve into a car, or a face or the bark of a tree. No, not *watching* them evolve — *making* them evolve. I thumbed through the pages, imagining the front of a house, maybe one of Stewart's cats, my own reflection in a doorknob. There was nothing there yet, I thought, but there *could* be. It sounds silly, but my heart started to race as I dug through my pencil case for a ball-point pen. I flipped back to the front of the book and wrote my name as neatly as I could manage inside the front cover.

Drawing was nothing new to me; I'd been at the top of my class in art since I was a little kid. It was the closest thing I had to a talent. I hadn't had many friends besides Matthew in elementary school, but they'd all wanted me to draw them pictures of their favourite superheroes and rock stars. Heck, I'd even made a buck or two off some of them: "Jareth, I'll pay you five dollars if you draw me a picture of Donny from New Kids." Or whatever.

But after Grade Nine, something had happened. One of my mother's boyfriends — Albert, I think his name was — had been looking at the course selection sheet I'd brought home from school for my mother to sign. Half the time I didn't even bother to bring stuff like that home, just signed it myself and handed it back, but for some reason I'd left this thing on the kitchen table for a day or two.

"Hey, Moira, what are you letting this kid do with his life?" the guy had said when he saw the form, all filled in and ready to go back. "Art, Typing, French ... what, are you trying to turn him into some kind of pansy?"

My mother hadn't had any kind of response to that one, although I'd tried to argue my way out of it.

"You gotta take art to graduate," I said. Albert laughed pretty hard at that one, as I recalled. He was a weedy little guy, beady-eyed and balding, but he thought he was a tough guy, and he was always right. At least, it was a good idea to let him think that. Otherwise he would get awful loud.

"Yeah, right, one credit. You go in, screw around for a semester and come out with a C. That's all the art you need. Says here you've already got your one credit."

That was how I'd wound up suffering through gym, auto mechanics and wood shop for five months. Albert was long gone by the end of the semester, but by the time the next year's option sheets came around, I just didn't care anymore. A kid in my gym class had taught me how to pick locks and jimmy windows, and by the following spring both me and Matthew had a brand-new hobby.

But here in this new place, far from the Alberts and Keiths and Moira Gardners in my life, it was as if a long-asleep piece of my soul was suddenly awake. My fingers danced over the blank pages, wondering what would fill them ... and whether I would still be able to create a picture worthy of their beauty.

11

I found my inspiration the next day in a ratty little park around the corner from Stewart's place. I set out after an uncomfortable breakfast of toast and jam, watching Danny glare at me from across the table. I hadn't even meant to stop at the park, a dingy fenced-in corner with dilapidated swings and a rusty set of monkey bars. The place was deserted: The only sign that any child had ever stopped to play there was a deflated plastic ball at the edge of an old concrete fountain. Overhead the sky was a menacing black, although the guy on the radio had said there was only a forty percent chance of rain. Ah, well, I mused, thinking of the newspaper story about my mother. The damn news media didn't seem to be very good at all about getting their numbers right.

The fountain in the park, now chipped and cracked, had probably been the centrepiece of the neighbourhood at one time — unpleasant-looking gargoyles streaming water from wide-open mouths as children in bathing suits splashed around in the basin below. Of course, little kids would be scared to death if they ever took a really good look at those gargoyles, but I figured some old rich guy had bequeathed the thing to the city and the powers that be hadn't wanted to offend him.

The wide basin beneath the spigots was boarded up now — if not permanently, then at least for the winter — but the gargoyles were still poised menacingly over the basin, their faces forever frozen in tortured, suspended animation. They were exactly what I'd been looking for, I thought with a strange feeling of exultation.

I used the sleeve of my coat to wipe most of the rainwater from one of the swings, and perched to dig the sketch book out of my knapsack. The gargoyle nearest to me sneered invitingly as I found the stub of a soft pencil in my bag. With a couple of swoops I had the shape of his head; with another, his eyes bulging out atop his bizarre grimace.

I was so enraptured by trying to recreate the shape of the creature's lips on paper that I scarcely noticed someone creeping up beside me. My mind registered a slight figure in a long dark coat, and by the time I realized I should be paying attention, the stranger was inches away.

"I don't think its ears are supposed to be quite that big," she said, nearly startling me out of my wits.

"Shit," I muttered, realizing she'd made me jump, smearing a dark pencil line halfway across the page. I scrubbed at it with the eraser at the end of the pencil, cursing under my breath.

"Sorry," the girl said. "I didn't mean to scare you."

"Who's scared?" I snapped, slamming the book shut. "I just wasn't expecting anybody to be there, that's all. I was startled."

"Scared, startled, whatever. That's a really good picture," she said, and smiled.

I took a deep breath, trying to coax my pulse to return to a normal rate, and smiled back. At first glance I thought this girl was maybe thirteen, but after a second or two I realized she was at least my age, maybe a little older. Her face was round, framed in black hair with bleached blond patches. It had an ageless look about it, smooth sepia skin with bow-shaped lips and a small flat nose. Her eyes, dark and almond-shaped, had a sad look about them, like she'd crammed too much living into not enough years.

"You just said the ears are too big," I said, and opened the book again.

"Yeah, well. It's better than I could do."

"Thanks. I haven't drawn anything since I was a kid," I told her. "This is my first drawing in a long time."

"That makes it even better, then."

She sat on the swing next to me, not bothering to wipe the water off the seat, and swayed back and forth idly for a few minutes as I worked to erase the smudge I'd made when she'd surprised me.

"It's gonna pour," she said after a minute or two.

I glanced up at the sky, heavy with dark rain clouds.

"Yeah, probably," I agreed.

"You live around here?"

"Yeah, I guess." A minute more passed before I realized I was probably being rude.

"You?" I said.

"Me what?"

"Live around here?"

She laughed at that.

"You sound like Tarzan. 'Me king of jungle. You live here?'"

Despite my irritation at being interrupted, I had to smile at that, thinking of the long-ago school photographer. "Last time somebody called me Tarzan I wound up in the principal's office," I said, and told her the story.

"That's pretty funny," she said, turning in circles on the swing until the chain was twisted as tight as it could go. "You look like Tarzan, too, with your hair all wild like that. You should cut it."

At that I slammed the sketchbook shut again and turned to face the girl. "What are you, my mother?" I growled. "You don't like my hair, you don't like my drawing, you don't like the way I talk. I'll tell you what: Why don't you either shut up or piss off?"

She didn't look particularly inclined to do either of those things, just shrugged and took her feet off the ground, spinning around until the chains of the swing started to twist the other way.

"I'm just saying, I think you'd look good if your hair was shorter. And I do like your drawing. I already said, I think it's really good."

I tucked my pencil back into a side pouch on my knapsack and shoved the sketchbook into the body of the bag.

"I don't remember asking for your opinion about anything," I said coldly, zipping up the bag and standing up. I hadn't realized how cold my hands had become while I was drawing, and I rubbed them together vigorously in an effort to return some feeling to my fingers.

"I'm sorry. I was just trying to be friendly," she told me. Her tone of voice didn't sound particularly sorry, just ... matter-of-fact.

She leaned back on the swing so far I thought for a second that she was going to fall off. I just stood there foolishly, not sure whether I should try to salvage the conversation or just leave.

"It's starting to rain," she said after a minute or two. "I felt a drop."

"You should leave, then," I said petulantly, and looped my left arm through both straps of my bag. "Unless you want to get soaked. You're the one who said it was gonna pour."

"I'm waiting for somebody," she said. "You might as well leave, though. It's not like you really want to be here ... not with somebody who keeps insulting you."

And, astoundingly, she winked at me. I just about did a double-take: girls didn't wink at Jareth Gardner. "Yeah," I echoed numbly. "Insulting me."

I didn't leave, though, just stood for a second watching her spin around on the swing, staring up at the sky like I wasn't even there.

After a minute or two the rain began to fall in earnest, icy pellets plastering my hair to my forehead and drenching my worn-out winter coat. Still the girl lay spinning in circles, her long hair streaming out beneath her head, the ends dragging in the wide mud puddle under the swings.

"Hey, Zoe!"

I looked up to see a guy leaning over the park's wrought-iron fence, gesturing frantically at the girl on the swing. She glanced in his direction, nonchalant.

"Yeah?"

"What the hell's the matter with you?" he shouted. "It's raining!"

She sat up straight, turned to look at him. He was a punk – torn jeans and high Doc Martens boots, with bright purple hair spiked with so much gunk it didn't show any sign of wilting in the driving rain. He looked familiar to me, although it took me a second to figure out why: he was one of the kids I'd seen panhandling downtown the previous day.

"Hang on a sec. I'm coming," she called back, and pulled herself off the swing with some difficulty. She grinned at me, revealing a chipped, discoloured front tooth. "What's your name?" she asked me.

"What do you want to know that for?" I said, feeling a little foolish standing there in the rain staring at her.

"You already know my name. I figure it's only fair I should know yours."

"It's Jareth," I managed.

"Good to meet you, Jareth." And she jerked her head toward the guy by the fence. "I gotta go now. My friend's waiting. See you later."

She gave me a little wave as she loped off through the downpour, then turned and half-jogged toward the fence.

Beautiful, I thought crazily, watching her run.

When I got back to Stewart's place I changed into some dry clothes, spreading my wet ones out on the floor to air. I checked my knapsack to make sure the sketchbook had stayed dry, then had another look at the picture of the gargoyle. It wasn't bad, I thought a little smugly, but it wasn't done, either. The girl in the park – Zoe – had been right. The ears were too big, and I didn't like the way the eyes looked. I'd have to go back when it stopped raining to finish the picture.

I slipped the sketchbook into the top drawer of my

dresser, then paused to look at my reflection in the mirror for a second before I closed the drawer. There was a nasty, scruffy-looking punk staring back at me, and all of a sudden I didn't much like what I saw. I ran my fingers idly over my hair; it was long and stringy, a mass of uneven tangles that reached maybe six inches past my shoulders.

I think you'd look good if your hair was shorter.

I gave the mirror a funny half-smirk, impulsively reaching behind my head with one hand to grab a handful of dripping wet hair. With the other hand I reached for Lloyd's knife, unsheathing it awkwardly. Without thinking about it, I began to hack away at the handful of hair, sliding the knife between my fist and my scalp, tearing the hair more than cutting it. Soggy, uneven clumps fell to the floor as I sawed away at it, nearly driving the knife into the base of my neck more than once.

I went about the task so vigorously I was nearly out of breath by the time I'd finished. I set the knife down on the dresser, little chunks of wet yellowish hair stuck to the blade. I shook my head as hard as I could, running my hands over the tattered remains of my hair, staring in disbelief at the image looking back at me now.

"Shit, what'd you go and do that for?" I said aloud, startled at the sound of my own voice. I couldn't answer the question, though. Why would I go and chop off all that hair? Because some weird chick in the park said it would be a good idea?

"You're an idiot," I told the mirror.

As I was wiping the hair off my knife there was a knock at the door. Danny.

"I've got dinner ready if you want some," he shouted louder than he needed to.

"Thanks," I called back, my heart suddenly racing. How was I gonna go out in public looking like this? I dug through the drawers of my dresser, hoping I'd thought to bring a bandanna along with me. I found one — black with white polka-dots — and tied it awkwardly over my head. With a final glance in the mirror, I cringed and made my way down the stairs.

The bandanna wasn't fooling Danny, who laughed when I walked into the kitchen.

"What the hell happened to your head?" he wanted to know.

I shrugged, trying to look casual.

"Haircut," I said, pulling up a chair.

Danny reached out across the table to grab the bandanna, yanking it off my head.

"With what? Hedge clippers?" he chortled.

I stared down at the table, glowering.

"Bowie knife," I muttered.

"Looks like it, too." He set a plate down in front of me, some kind of spaghetti thing.

"Yeah, well, I just got sick of it long," I said.

"Tell you what," Danny said, not unkindly. "After dinner we'll fix that up for you."

I glanced up at him in surprise. His colourless eyes danced with laughter, wide red lips pressed tightly together. I figured he was kidding, but decided not to push the issue.

"Where's Stewart?" I said instead.

Danny shook his head, hunched over his plate.

"Out. I don't know. He's not here for dinner, anyway."

"Is he at work or something?"

Danny laughed derisively at that one.

"Stewart is an artist," he said grandly. "Stewart doesn't go to work; he goes to *functions*. I don't know where he is."

"What kind of artist?" I pressed.

Danny glared.

"Why don't you ask him?" he said, signalling to me in no uncertain terms that the conversation was over.

When I was finished eating, I scraped my plate into the garbage and stuck it in the dishwasher, then tried to make a hasty exit to my room. I was hoping Danny had forgotten about my hair, but I had no such luck.

"Take your chair into the front hallway and wait," he barked. "I'll be right out."

So I dragged one of the wooden kitchen chairs out into the hallway and sat in it, feeling like a prisoner waiting to be executed. I perched on the edge of the chair as I listened to Danny rooting around in a drawer. He appeared a second later with a big pair of kitchen scissors and a dish towel.

"Sit back," he commanded, and slung the towel around my neck.

I could feel his breath on my neck as he started snipping away at my hair, circling me critically, shaking his head at the mess I'd made of myself. He didn't say a word, just hemmed and hawed as he chopped off the uneven bits of hair. I tried not to look at his face, broad and ugly, as he took those enormous scissors to my head. Instead I concentrated on his neck, marked side to side with a wide purple scar, like somebody had slit his throat and stitched it up badly. He snipped for the better part of half an hour, as the room filled with an uncomfortable, almost palpable silence. Then he took a step back and with a satisfied grunt, wiped the scissors on his shirt.

"There. Clean that up, will you?" He gestured at the clumps of hair on the floor. As I stood up to start gathering them, he grabbed the chair from behind me and disappeared back into the kitchen.

Upstairs I stared at myself in the mirror for a long time, marvelling at how short my hair was — and how dark. All those years of sun-bleached hair lay in clumps in the kitchen garbage can. I ran my hands across my skull, leaning up as close to my reflection as I could manage. Zoe had been right; I did look a lot better.

"The new me," I said with a grin — I really did look like somebody else. And I wasn't entirely sure that was such a bad thing.

12

It rained on and off for most of the next week. By the end of it I was going stir crazy, but it was far too wet to even think of venturing outside. I had nowhere to go, for one thing, and it seemed silly to wreck my only pair of shoes just wandering around.

On Monday I tried to work from memory on the picture of the gargoyle, but I got nowhere. I needed to go back to the park and see it again. Instead I plunked myself down in front of the television. Tuesday I sat in my room most of the day, trying to draw the big old tree outside. I thought maybe it was an oak, but with no leaves it was hard to tell. I worked on the thing for so long my neck was aching from staring down at the page, although I was pretty pleased with the picture by the time I'd finished.

Wednesday was when I started to go a little berserk. I'd spent the entire week avoiding Danny, leaving the room when he wandered through. I hadn't seen hide nor hair of Stewart in about three days; I could hear him banging around upstairs, doing whatever it was he did. Danny'd said Stewart was an artist, but I hadn't yet got up the nerve to ask him about it. I figured it would have been only polite to ask Stewart what he did for a living the first time I met him. Now that I'd been here a while, it seemed a little stupid to be asking.

I'd spent so much time in front of the TV during the first half of the week that by Wednesday at noon I was starting to crave a little action. I wandered upstairs and had a look through the drawer where I'd stowed the remainder of Lloyd's money. I counted it a couple of times; there was a little less than two hundred dollars in all. Not bad for a night's work so long ago.

But as I spread the bills out on the bed — tens and twenties mostly, a wide arc of green and purple — I started to feel strange. I felt an emotion I couldn't put a name to, but whatever it was just ripped through my stomach like some kind of wild animal, vicious sharp teeth tearing me. In my mind I caught a picture of Lloyd stumbling across the bedroom toward me, trying to speak, clutching at his chest, his face a grotesque mask of fear and rage. He'd died for this money, defending the house where he and his lovely wife Constance had lived since 1934.

I piled up the money, rolled it and stuffed it in the back pocket of my jeans. Suddenly I had to get out of the house; I had to get rid of this money. Just having it near me was freaking me out, making me feel dirty.

I'd killed Lloyd as surely as my mother had killed Brad, I told myself. And here I was with my pocket full of money while the old lady was sitting in jail, and my brother was — where? Rotting in the ground someplace, I supposed. They must have buried him by now. I knew where he'd be, too; when my grandmother had died a few years earlier, my mother had bought into some two-for-one deal at the cemetery and picked up a plot for Brad. You were supposed to use it to buy a spot for your husband or wife or whatever, but Mom had bought a place for Brad. At the time I'd thought it was macabre; like she was looking forward to having him drop dead on her. Now it seemed eerily prophetic. Had she been planning to kill him, or was it all a big accident, like she'd told me?

I shook my head, decided it didn't matter. I certainly hadn't set out to kill old Lloyd, but he was just as dead as if I had. The same went for Brad.

I decided maybe that was my punishment for killing Lloyd: Brad dying, I mean. Nobody but me and Matthew knew he'd died of anything but a plain and simple heart attack while he was at home alone; me and Matthew and God ... or whoever was up there keeping score.

With Lloyd's money in my pocket, I decided that rain or no rain, it was time for me to get out of the house. I went downstairs and pulled on the leather high-cuts I'd left by the door. I figured they'd get wrecked in the rain, but that wasn't my biggest priority at the moment. What mattered was getting rid of the wad of bills in my back pocket.

"Hey, Jareth."

I jumped, startled, and looked up to see Stewart coming down the stairs behind me.

"Hey."

"Where you headed?" he asked casually.

I shrugged. "I don't know. I just thought I'd go for a walk or something."

He laughed. "It's a little wet out for walking. I'm just headed out to get something to eat. How about we go for lunch? It's on me."

I shrugged, taken aback. That sounded like such a grown-up thing to do. Doing lunch, I mean, and not with Matthew or my little brother. But it meant I wouldn't have to spend another meal with Danny. Stewart almost never ate with us — sometimes he came down and got food from the kitchen, but he usually brought it back upstairs to eat.

"Sure, I'll go," I said easily. I flashed him the grin. "I mean, if it's on you. How can I turn that down?"

"No worries. Come on, let's go."

Which is how I wound up in some trendy little uptown café, watching the rain come down outside while I tried to make stilted conversation with Stewart. His pickup was parked outside, this brick-red relic from the 1940s. On the way over he told me he'd spent more than a year restoring the thing. There wasn't much more I could say to that than "Oh, yeah?" and the conversation had fallen pretty flat.

So I sat across from him, looking out at the rain and the truck, glancing over at Stewart cutting his food into absurdly small pieces. He'd ordered some bizarre thing — bean sprouts and bits of zucchini stuffed into a pita. I'd played it safer — a turkey sandwich and a bowl of soup. We sat there for a long time in silence, just looking up at each other once in a while, both of us trying to think of something — anything — to say.

"So Danny says you're an artist," I eventually said awkwardly between bites.

"Yeah. I'm a sculptor. Sometimes I teach, but I'm taking a sabbatical at the moment." He leaned forward across the table, staring right at me, intimidating. "Jareth, tell me something, will you?"

I wasn't sure why, but my pulse suddenly speeded up.

"What's that?" I said, my voice squeaking a little.

"What's your dream? What do you want to do more than anything else?"

I frowned. I couldn't think of anybody who had ever asked me that before ... not since I was a little kid, younger than Brad.

"I don't know," I said awkwardly. "I like to draw. But I don't know about a dream, you know? I always figured I'd just get out of high school, get a job, whatever."

"Sounds pretty vague."

"I guess."

I took a bite of my sandwich and looked down at the table, its blue-and-green marble veneer with little yellow place mats. I was hoping he'd change the subject or stop talking altogether, but he kept on asking questions: whether I was looking for a job, if I planned on going back to school, whether I'd made any friends in the neighbourhood. His tone wasn't threatening, not like he was going to kick me out if I didn't make something of my life, but more like he was just interested. Making casual conversation.

Finally, though, I got tired of being interrogated and started to get a little snippy. "Look, Stewart, I'm not trying to be rude, but what exactly are you after?" I said, feeling an edge creep into my voice.

"After?" The man sounded genuinely bewildered.

"I mean, are you trying to hint that I should be out trying to get a job or something? Because I've heard enough of that from my mother, you know?"

Stewart laughed again, which threw me for a loop.

"You've been here what, a week?" he said. "Jareth,

from what Vic says you've had a hell of a time lately."

"You don't know the half of it," I muttered, thinking of Lloyd.

"Well, I don't want to put any pressure on you ... I'm sure you've got enough on your plate right now without me trying to act like your mother." He leaned back in his chair a little, his eyes taking on a faraway look. "When my wife died, I don't think I even left the house for about three months after the funeral," he said.

"Wow," I said, feeling stupid. What else could I say to that? I tried to picture what kind of woman Stewart would marry; I couldn't.

"Now, my mother — mine and Danny's — she was quite a woman," Stewart continued, like he was oblivious to the fact that I was even there. "When Vic was a kid, she had him staying at our place probably three weeks out of four. Whenever things got to be too much for him at his own place."

"Vic?" I echoed. It was incomprehensible to me that Vic had ever been a kid, let alone one who had troubles at home.

"Yeah. His dad was kind of a skunk. Kicked him out pretty regularly. Anyway, when my mother left me the house, she was pretty adamant that I not keep it all to myself. She always said 'God didn't give us this big house so we could live like kings while there's people who don't have any place to go.' "

"Hmm. You know, I've never had any particular use for God," I said, not coldly, just matter-of-fact.

"That's okay," Stewart said with a funny smirk. "One of these days you might just find out He's got some kind of use for you."

We ate the rest of the meal in relative silence, and by

the time we'd finished, the weather had cleared some. The sky was still ominously overcast, but it had stopped raining for the moment.

As I saw Stewart pulling out his wallet to pay the bill, I was reminded of the wad of cash I had in my own back pocket. Money I had to get rid of.

"Hey, Stewart. Tell you what," I said, standing up. "I'm just gonna visit the washroom, but maybe I'll walk home, you know? It's clearing up a bit, and I just feel like walking around a while."

Stewart frowned, puzzled. "That's a pretty long walk, Jareth."

"Yeah, it's okay. I want to walk."

He looked like he wanted to say something else, maybe ask if he'd offended me, something like that. But instead he just nodded, a friendly "see you later."

Once I was out of sight of Stewart's funky red pickup, I ducked into an alley between a Greek restaurant and a boarded-up dollar store. I hid behind an overflowing dumpster, eyes watering from the stench, and pulled the money out of my pocket. It wasn't a fortune by any means, but it was truly all the money I had in the world. But as I snuck a look at it, that strange feeling I'd had back in my bedroom washed over me again. This time I picked a name to go with it: guilt. This money wasn't mine; I didn't want it anywhere near me.

Impulsively I wadded up the pile of bills and dropped them over the side of the open trash bin, where they wedged between several bags of garbage from the restaurant. I didn't even look back at it as I walked away.

Stewart was right; it was an awfully long walk back. I lost my bearings a few times, and it drizzled on and off as

I walked. By the time I approached Stewart's place, I was soaking wet and feeling pretty miserable.

"What did you go and throw all the money away for?" I muttered aloud. "If you'd saved a couple of bucks, you could have at least taken a cab or something."

I dug my icy hands deep into the pockets of my drenched jeans, which didn't help a bit, and slunk along home, feeling worse and worse. The cold seeped through my skin into my bones, making me ache all over, my lips quivering as I concentrated on just putting one foot in front of the other. "Just a few more blocks," I told myself. "Nearly there now."

At the time it didn't seem strange to me that as soon as I started to feel a little sorry for myself about how wet I was, I started to feel a lot sorry about getting rid of that money ... especially since I didn't see where or when I was going to get my hands on any more. "Even if you get a job tomorrow, it'll be weeks before you see your first pay cheque," I grumbled.

Suddenly the problem seemed insurmountable, and the remorse I'd been feeling over what had happened with Lloyd took a distant back seat to the fact that I had no source of income, no mother to con, no Matthew to manipulate.

That's when it happened — an opportunity for the perfect crime. At least, that's what I thought at the time.

After an eternity of walking, putting one wet, frozen foot in front of the other, my shins on fire, knees ready to give out, I rounded the corner onto Stewart's street. I counted down the houses as I plodded along, exhausted — six doors away, five, four, three — and then I heard something that made me all but screech to a halt.

"Come on, Dad, do I *have* to go see Grandma? I'm old enough to stay home by myself."

I paused, two houses away from Stewart's, and bent down to make a big production of tying my shoelaces.

The scene unfolding beside me was like Norman Rockwell for the nineties, a family of four packing up the minivan for a few days away. Nobody looked terribly happy about going, least of all a kid of about fourteen. He was a real cool-looking cat with a skater haircut, long on top and shaved on the bottom, and a pair of those drop-ass jeans that start about mid-thigh, with the crotch hanging down around his knees.

"Now, come on, Tiger." This was his dad, a real smarmy type with a button-down Polo shirt under his Mountain Equipment Co-op rain jacket. Very trendy. "If I have to put up with your grandmother for four days, so do you. Besides, you get to take the rest of the week off school. You can't beat that, can you?"

"Yeah, well. What if I sneak back in the middle of the night or something? I know where you hide the key."

"Don't be ridiculous," the kid's mother said, piling a stack of artfully-wrapped gifts into the back seat. "It's your grandmother's birthday. Would it kill you to be a little bit nice to her?"

The kid dug his hands in his pockets, grumbled something under his breath. He wandered around to the back of the van, uncomfortably close to where I was standing, and hawked up an enormous gob of spit. He let it fly a little too close to my head, and I glanced up to give him a nasty look. The kid smirked and gave me the finger, and I resisted the urge to take a piece out of him.

"Come on, Princess," Dad called toward the house.

The girl — a prissy-looking kid about two years younger than her brother — had gone back inside for a second to get out of the rain, which had begun to fall steadily once again.

"I'm *coming*," she shrilled, louder than I thought was necessary. Then again, if my parents were anything like these Leave-It-To-Beaver wannabe yuppies, I'd probably want to scream, too.

By the time the girl came back out of the house I'd finished retying both shoelaces a couple of times, and I stood up slowly to resume walking. Strangely enough, my feet didn't hurt quite so much as I turned to watch the happy foursome climb into the van and back out of the driveway for their trip to Grandma's house. I cast a glimpse at the house itself, took note of the cutesy folk-art sign on the front door: *The Petersen Home*.

As I walked away I was smirking some, and there was a bit of a spring in my step. And by the time I'd gotten to Stewart's front door, I'd suddenly stopped feeling quite so sorry for myself.

13

It was sometime long after midnight when I woke up, like a kid on Christmas morning, and stepped out into the hallway. I'd come in after my walk and had a long, hot bath, then gone to bed right after dinner.

Now I tiptoed down the stairs, a black hooded sweatshirt over black sweatpants and socks. I'd left my grey cotton gloves at home, so tonight I would have to make do with a pair of yellow rubber ones I'd found in the kitchen. My heart was racing as I pulled on my sneakers – which were still damp, despite having spent half an hour in the dryer while I took a bath – and headed out the door. I'd left my Adidas bag at home, but I brought along my knapsack instead, figuring it would serve the purpose just as well as anything. In the pocket of my sweatshirt, along with the gloves, I had a little flashlight I'd ripped off from somewhere. It only took two AA batteries, but it was pretty powerful for its size. I didn't dare turn it on outside, so I was slightly relieved to discover it wasn't too dark out.

The sky had cleared up, for the most part, as small

dark clouds raced back and forth over a sliver of moon. I checked my watch by the glow of the street lamp: it was a quarter to three.

I pulled the front door closed behind me, then looked up and down the street to make sure there was no one around. It was beautiful; there wasn't so much as a porch light on, as far as the eye could see. As casually as I could manage, I wandered down the driveway toward the Petersen house.

Young Tiger's words were still with me as I ducked behind the high hedge that surrounded the Petersens' front yard: *What if I sneak back in the middle of the night or something? I know where you hide the key.*

I doubted he would have made it back from wherever the family was; it looked like they'd been packing for a fairly long car trip. But wherever they were, good old Tiger had inadvertently given away a little secret: there was a hidden key somewhere for the taking. I slunk around to the back of the house, although there was really no need to be quite so careful. There was a high privacy fence behind the Petersen house, and the only thing behind that was some kind of old warehouse. Still, after old Lloyd, I didn't want to take any chances at all.

The back door of the house was up a flight of stairs, off a wooden deck that occupied most of the yard. I crept up the stairs, hoping they wouldn't creak, and crouched under the partial cover of the stair rail. There was a black rubber mat by the sliding glass doors, and I flipped it over to check for a key. There wasn't one there. I stood to run my hand across the top of the door frame. Still no key. I made a cursory check of the rest of the deck before creeping back down the stairs and around to the front of the house.

My heart was racing as I made a similar search of the front doorstep, checking the mat, the mailbox, the top of the door.

Nothing.

I was beginning to think better of the whole idea when I noticed the little garden beside the front step. It was obviously well cared for, with evenly spaced cedar trees and rosebushes wrapped in burlap bags for the winter, and a little circle of fist-sized rocks all the way around it.

If it weren't for the moon casting strange shadows over the yard, I would never have noticed the one rock that didn't seem to fit — the only rock not glistening with moisture from four days of heavy rain. I ran a hand over it curiously. Plastic. I picked it up, turned it over, and slid the Hide-A-Key out of the slot on the bottom. Just who did these people think they were fooling?

Now, I was better-than-average at picking a lock, but I was certainly no professional. And without Matthew watching my back I didn't want to take the time to do any real breaking-and-entering ... especially not on a street where the houses were so close together. No, with the Petersens' Hide-A-Key I would simply be entering — no breaking involved — although I'm sure neither the Petersens nor the police would have seen it that way.

With a self-satisfied grunt I pulled open the screen door and inserted the key into the lock before I remembered I wasn't wearing any gloves. I paused to put on the dishwashing gloves, then used them to wipe the screen door handle and the key as well as I could. The key turned easily in the lock, and with a last quick look around I stepped into the front hallway.

I shut the door carefully behind me, tucking the key

into the pocket of my sweatshirt and letting my eyes adjust to the dim light in the foyer.

The layout of the Petersen house was fairly unoriginal — the living room off to one side, the kitchen beyond it, the bedrooms upstairs. In daylight, I figured the place probably looked like a photo spread from some women's magazine. It was one of those houses that looks like they hired an interior decorator to decide what colour toilet paper went best with their towels. They probably had a maid in twice a week. Yes, sir, these people had money, and they didn't care who knew it. I just hoped they'd have some sitting out in the open to share with yours truly.

With a deep breath, I wiped each shoe on the leg of my pants, then made my way up the stairs.

I could hear Matthew's voice in my head: "Stay out of the bedrooms! You want to get caught? What if somebody's in there?" But I ignored it. I wasn't after stereos or televisions or silly trinkets people kept in the living room. I was looking for cash: jars of loonies, a couple of fives sitting around, anything.

The first room at the top of the stairs belonged to the little girl, all pink and frilly with a canopy bed and pictures of kittens and teddy bears all over the walls. I didn't find much worth taking — a couple of CDs, mostly teenybopper crap, and a roll of quarters on the dresser.

As I tiptoed past the bathroom, the flashlight caught my own reflection in the full-length mirror on the wall opposite the door, and I nearly jumped out of my skin. A split second after I'd done it I realized I'd let out a pretty decent squeal, and I froze where I was for a full minute, waiting to see if somebody was going to react. When I didn't hear anything, I continued on my way down the hall, shining the light on what could only be my buddy Tiger's room.

The door was shut, for starters, and plastered generously with the yellow-and-black "Crime Scene" tape you see on TV. Gingerly I reached out to turn the knob, standing to the side of the door so I wouldn't be in the line of fire if the kid was crouching in there with a gun or something.

The kid's room was a little disturbing, all army posters and bloody-looking pictures from the kind of comic books that have women in metal bikinis on the cover. Quite a contrast to his little sister's room — or, in fact, to the rest of the house.

I had a quick look at the dresser — not much there, a jar full of pennies, a tube of hair gel, a loose key, a couple of grimy-looking baseball caps. I decided not to bother with any of it for the time being.

The floor was a study in dirty dishes and laundry, the kind of mess my mother would never have tolerated for more than a day or two. The open closet door revealed a similar pile. I kicked my way through the mess to the bed, mischief on my mind. Obviously young Tiger's mom didn't make her way in here very often, judging from the mess. The whole place smelled like an unwashed kid, and I resisted the urge to plug my nose and flee.

I thought of the encounter I'd had with the little punk at the end of his driveway, how he'd nearly spit on me, then flipped me off when I got annoyed. I chuckled a little as I formulated a plan of revenge, only a little disappointed that my poor friend would never know why he was being punished.

Gingerly I reached between the mattress and box spring

of Tiger's bed. If he was anything like Matthew, whose mother had refused to make his bed from the time he was about four years old, there was treasure to be had in there. When Matthew was a kid, he'd hide candy and stolen comics under his mattress. When the Puberty Fairy had arrived, he'd upgraded his collection to include a variety of questionable magazines from the top shelf of the rack at the corner variety store. I was hoping young Master Petersen would have a similar reading library. I figured scattering a couple of copies of *Hot Babes Monthly* throughout the living room would make for some interesting family conversation when they got back from Grandma's house.

What I found, though, was much, much more interesting.

As I felt around carefully under the mattress, my hand hit something harder than I'd expected. Puzzled, I stood and lifted the mattress a little way off the bed.

"Well, well," I heard myself mutter. "What have you been up to, Tiger?"

I had to give the kid credit; this was one of the more ingenious hiding spots I'd ever seen. Young Tiger, it seems, had hollowed out a section of his box spring, actually removing some of the springs — sawing them off somehow, from the looks of it — and replaced them with a small metal tackle box. It must have been pretty uncomfortable to sleep on, but I'll bet nobody had ever checked there. He'd even left a flap of fabric over the hole, so if you just happened to be changing the sheets or something you might not notice. Unless you actually went through the effort of running your hand over the spot, you'd think it was just a little tear in the cover.

My hand quivered a little as I pried the box from its

cocoon; it was wedged in there pretty tight. It took a minute or two to wrench it free, and when I had finished, I sat on the edge of the bed for a second examining it.

The box was locked, of course, but a quick trip back to the dresser revealed that the key sitting there matched the lock on the tackle box.

"Pretty stupid, junior," I said with a grin. I sat the tackle box on the bed and opened the lid, half-expecting a mutated frog or something to leap out at me.

The first thing that hit me when I opened the box was the smell: strong and sweet, and strangely familiar, like the back stairwell at school where no one ever went except the stoners and jocks. It was the corner of the school where the vast majority of shady dealings were done, the most isolated place you could hope to find in a building with twelve hundred bodies floating around all day.

My guess was that Tiger's elementary school had a similar corner somewhere, and that in that corner, he was most likely the king of the hill. The top half of the tackle box was full of clear plastic baggies, each carefully sealed, each holding a carefully measured portion of something leafy and green — and while I didn't have any real intimate experience with the substance in question, I knew immediately what it was.

"Gee whiz, Mom and Dad," I laughed, not worrying too much about the volume of my voice. "Looks like ol' Tiger's got quite a little dealership on the go."

I took a couple of the baggies out of the box, finding an assortment of junk in the bottom of the box ... and a white, legal-sized envelope stuffed thick with cash. I flipped through it greedily, figuring there must be at least a thousand dollars in the envelope, most of it in twenty- and fifty-dollar bills. I laughed out loud as I stuffed the entire envelope into the pocket of my sweatshirt.

"All these years I've been in the wrong racket," I muttered, reassembling the contents of the box in roughly the same order as I'd found them.

My thoughts of leaving Tiger's dirty little secrets for his family to find were long gone; the money in my pocket would more than cover any kind of damage he'd done me. I just wished I would be around to see the look on his face when he came home and discovered it gone.

I retraced my steps up the hall, replacing the quarters and the CDs I'd taken from the other bedroom. I didn't need that kind of small change ... and besides, she'd never done me any harm. What did I want to go stealing from some little girl for, anyway? That was almost as bad as robbing a helpless old man ... maybe even worse, since she had so much less that was worth stealing.

I'd spent longer than I'd intended to in the Petersen house, and by the time I got outside it was approaching four in the morning. I wasn't as tired as I'd expected, having slept for several hours after dinner, but all the same I was anxious to get home and find a place to stash my new-found cash.

I stowed the Petersens' key back under the fake rock in the front yard, then took a quick look around to make sure I hadn't been seen before wandering as casually as I could back over to Stewart's.

Which was where my little plan hit a bit of a snag.

The first day I was at Stewart's, he'd said something about giving me a key to the house. But I'd never yet come home when nobody was there, so it had completely slipped my mind that he hadn't given me a key.

"Damn it!"

It didn't occur to me how loud I'd yelled that, although after a second or two I figured nobody had noticed.

With a heartfelt sigh, I sat down on the damp, rickety porch to think for a minute. I wasn't going to go ringing the doorbell at four in the morning, that was certain. I didn't even want to think about trying to come up with an excuse about why I was out at that hour. Of course, I didn't relish the idea of sitting around in the yard for three hours until the sun came up. On the other hand, I didn't exactly want to be out on the streets with that kind of money on me. In all my years of wandering the streets alone I'd never been mugged, but I sure didn't want to try it out tonight.

Finally I came up with a solution, childish and risky, but the best I could think of on short notice. I lay flat on my stomach on the porch, leaning way over the edge, and cleared aside a pile of dead leaves and branches that had been pushed up against the front of the house. Then I raised up enough to ease the envelope out of my pocket and bury it under the pile. I slung my backpack over one shoulder and headed off for an early morning walk.

I was halfway down the street when it occurred to me that I should have grabbed a twenty from the envelope and gone to sit in an all-night coffee shop or something. It was a little chilly to be wandering around in just a sweatshirt.

14

My feet were still sore and blistered from my walk home that afternoon, and I hadn't gone far before I wanted to sit down awhile. I found myself close to the park where I'd been drawing the previous week, and I sat down on a swing to rest. I looped my backpack over both shoulders and slung my arms around the chains of the swing, burying my hands in my pocket as I swayed gently back and forth. The park was well-lit, presumably to discourage troublemakers from hanging out there at night. I glanced around at the collection of broken beer bottles scattered across the playground and decided the lighting hadn't been particularly effective. Nor was the sturdy iron fence around the perimeter of the park, which had taken me about three seconds to scale.

As I sat looking out over the small park, I considered my evening's activities. The Petersen house was a one-in-a-million chance, I thought sleepily. There was no way something like that was ever going to fall into my lap again. And suddenly, without ceremony, I knew — that was the end of it. My last late-night house visit, the last time I was going to take a stupid chance like that.

I wasn't thinking about Lloyd now, I was thinking about the Petersen kid. How invincible he must have felt, his little stash hidden away under his mattress, unknown to the world, just raking in the profits from his business while he sold pot to his schoolmates.

But I'd found him out, hadn't I? He was going to come home from Grandma's house and discover he wasn't so untouchable after all. And while I didn't have any great feeling of sympathy for the kid, I didn't feel particularly good about having ripped him off, either. I just felt ... empty. Empty and tired.

I wedged my head firmly between my shoulder and the chain on the swing and closed my eyes. I was just drifting off to sleep when a voice jarred me awake.

"Well, well. If it isn't Zoe's little friend."

I looked up, startled, and saw a pair of menacing-looking figures approaching me. One of them I recognized — the tall, skinny punk with purple hair. I scrambled to my feet as they drew closer, instinctively gripping the straps of my knapsack tightly.

"Hey, look, Martin. Buddy thinks we're gonna jump him. What'd Zoe say his name was ... Jareth? What's the matter, Jareth, you think we're gonna jump you?"

This was the other guy, a little shorter and stockier than his friend, with a shaved head and a ratty-looking green parka with a furry hood. He grinned as he crossed the park, and even from a distance I could see one of his teeth was missing.

"Yeah, well, what's to say we aren't?" said the punk with a nasty smirk. "Didn't your momma tell you not to hang out alone in the park at night, Jareth?"

"Didn't your momma tell you if you kept making that face it'd stick?" I retorted, regretting the words before they were all the way out of my mouth. But instead of pounding on me, the pair of them laughed. It wasn't a particularly reassuring laugh, more like they were willing to put off torturing me until they'd finished intimidating me a little more first.

The punk — Martin — sat on the swing to my right, the other guy on the swing to my left, and they started to rock side to side casually, like they came here all the time.

"So, you live around here, Jareth?" Martin said. "Or you just got a thing for playing on the swings?"

"Maybe both, maybe neither," I said, sitting back on the swing. "So you're friends of Zoe's?"

"You know it," Martin said.

The other guy, the one whose name I didn't know, stunk something awful — a combination of cigarettes and a first-class case of B.O. "So Zoe says you're quite an artist," he said. "Are you, like, professional or something?"

"Not really," I said, trying to sound grown-up. "I mean, not yet. I'm sort of between professions at the moment."

"Oh, yeah?" said Martin, laughing softly. "Hear that, Pete? He's between professions. So tell me, Picasso, what did you do at your last job? I mean, before you retired or whatever."

"I used to be a cat burglar," I told him. "But there wasn't much room for advancement."

"You're funny," Martin said. I couldn't tell whether or not he was kidding. "You should be on TV or something, you're so funny."

"Well, maybe if the artist thing doesn't work out I could get on *Saturday Night Live* or something." I stood up and took a few steps away. "Look, this is all very stimulating, but I've gotta go."

"Yeah?" The bald guy, Pete, stood up and took a step or two after me. I stifled the urge to take off running, and dug my hands deep into the pocket of my sweatshirt as he stepped uncomfortably close to me. "Where you think you're going?" he said.

"Home," I told him. "I kind of got locked out, and I'm just waiting for everybody else to get up so I can get back inside."

"Yeah? Mommy and Daddy didn't give you a key?" said Pete, an edge to his voice.

"I don't live with my parents," I said a little defensively. "And I do have a key. I just left it inside." A bold-faced lie, I thought, but what does it matter? It just sounded a little odd not to have a key to your own house.

"Oh, gee. What luck. And on a school night, too." Pete laughed, though I was beginning to see less and less humour in the situation. "What are you, fifteen?"

"Eighteen," I said automatically. "Well, almost. Why, how old are you?"

"He's twenty," said another voice — Zoe's — from behind me. "But he acts a lot younger."

I turned around to find she'd taken my place on the swings, relaxed as could be, like there was nothing unusual at all about this whole situation.

"Hey," I said awkwardly.

"Hey yourself," she said. "I like the haircut. It makes your head look a lot smaller."

"Great. I hadn't realized my head looked big."

"Well, you know. It wasn't that bad. And it looks fine now."

"Well, that's a relief," I said, not feeling at all relieved. "Hey, Zoe, unless I'm mistaken, your friends are just about to beat the crap out of me. And you know, I wouldn't mind half so much if I had the slightest idea what for."

Zoe giggled wildly at that.

"These guys? No, they're, like, totally harmless," she said, very Valley Girl. She was pretty, I thought, and a little flaky. Her straight black hair was cut strangely, all different lengths flying around her face with a chunk caught up in a ponytail on top of her head. Sections of her bangs were bleached white, and her eyes were lined with a thick layer of black makeup. She was wearing the same voluminous trench coat I'd seen her wear the first time I met her.

As Zoe kicked her legs to start the swing moving, her friend Pete backed off some, wandering over to a set of monkey bars in the shape of a rocket. He perched up at the top and pulled out a cigarette, lighting it and puffing away as he looked out over the park.

"Did I hear you say you were locked out of your house?" Zoe asked. She was swinging pretty high, her coat flying out around her like a cape as she kicked.

"Yeah, you heard right," I said, wondering how long she'd been listening in on the conversation before she'd made her presence known.

"You could come stay over at our place for the night, you know."

"Our place?" I echoed, looking back and forth between Pete and Martin.

"Yeah, the three of us," she said. "Why don't you come stay over with us?"

"Actually, I can think of a few reasons why not," I said with a nervous laugh.

Zoe grinned at that one, and hopped down off the swing.

"Come on. We're not gonna jump you in your sleep or anything."

Obediently Martin got off his swing and Pete climbed down off the monkey bars. It was pretty clear to me that Zoe was the one in charge of this little crowd. I figured if she told them not to kill me, I'd probably be okay.

"All right," I said after a moment's consideration. "Where do you live?"

It wasn't a long walk, as it turned out. I'd been picturing them living in some run-down rooming house, but instead they took me to a boarded-up building about two blocks from Stewart's place. It was an old factory of some kind, surrounded by plywood construction boards that were covered in rotting posters for concerts and night-clubs and X-rated cartoon festivals.

"This is it," said Pete, grabbing the top of the wall with one hand and scaling it easily.

"You *live* here?" I said incredulously.

"Yeah." Zoe grabbed my arm and pulled me toward the end of the building. "There's an easier way to get in, though. He's just showing off."

She pulled up a loose board at the end of the wall and crawled through it, then pushed it open from the inside for me to do the same. I took off my backpack and shoved it through the hole first, then followed it into the yard surrounding the dilapidated building.

"Just how long have you lived here?" I said, looking over the property. Even in the dim light I could see that the walls of the building weren't sitting straight: one of them jutted out at a funny angle, like the whole place was ready to cave in at any second.

"A while," said Pete, who was leaning against the wall, lighting another cigarette. "Me and Martin, maybe a year. Zoe about half that. On and off. Is that right, Zoe?"

"Yeah. Something like that," she said, and disappeared into the shadows around the building.

I tossed a glance back at Pete before I wandered off after Zoe. I figured I'd rather be killed by a collapsing building with Zoe than be outside with her friend, who was still giving me a look I didn't like.

"Hey, Jareth. In here," I heard her say. I ducked through an empty doorframe and found myself in a dark, mouldy-smelling room. Zoe lit a candle, illuminating a small corner with a sickly yellowish glow.

"You know how unsafe this place is?" I said. "I mean, of course you know. Just take a look around. How can you live here?"

"It beats the alternative," Zoe said. She took off her coat, hung it tidily from a nail on the wall. It was such a strange, homey gesture in a place like this that it took me a few seconds to notice what that enormous coat had concealed: Zoe was pregnant. She was pretty far along from the looks of things, her belly protruding conspicuously from her slight frame.

I didn't say anything, just sat down on a musty old mattress in the corner and plunked my knapsack down in my lap. But she must have noticed me looking at her funny, because she cupped her hands self-consciously around her stomach as she slid down the wall to sit beside me. She gathered a grimy-looking blanket around her shoulders.

"It's due in July," she said, very matter-of-fact.

"Is that why you ran away from home?" I asked. "Because you were pregnant?"

Zoe gave me a funny look. "What are you, twelve?" she said derisively. "I didn't run away. I just left. I go back sometimes. Just not when my dad's around, that's all. He's an asshole."

"So whose baby is it?" I managed, hoping it wasn't a stupid question. The expression on her face told me it had been.

"What difference does it make?" she snapped. "It's not like he's gonna be around anyway. I don't even care if I ever see him again."

And she clammed up, like the subject was closed for further discussion. I stared down at the faded daisies on the mattress and thought that it might make an awful lot of difference to the baby someday.

It was a few minutes before Pete came inside, and Martin followed a few minutes later. I sat on the mattress feeling uncomfortable and out of place as the two of them went about their business. Zoe sat silently beside me, watching as Martin dug a little camp stove out of an old filing cabinet and set it up in the middle of the floor. Pete produced a can of ravioli from someplace and opened it with an attachment on his Swiss Army knife. They were settling down beside me on the mattress to share the can and a single, rusty-looking spoon between them, before anybody spoke again.

"So, Jareth," Martin said, "how come you got locked out of your house?"

"It was an accident," I told him. "I went out to do some stuff, and by the time I got back everybody was in bed."

"A likely story," said Pete with a nasty-looking grin. "What kind of stuff?"

"I told you. I'm a retired cat burglar. Tonight was my last job."

"You're so full of shit," Zoe said, laughing. "Come on, tell him the truth."

"I'm not lying," I said earnestly. "Truth is, I'm just not very good at the whole career criminal thing. So after tonight, I've decided to look elsewhere for income."

"You're really a burglar," Martin said around a mouthful of ravioli, sounding sceptical. "You're talking house break-ins?"

"That's right."

"You ever get caught?"

I thought that one over for a second and decided against telling them about Lloyd.

"Almost, once," I told them instead. "But then I didn't. So everybody lived happily ever after."

"You ever do time, Jareth?" said Pete, leaning uncomfortably close to me. "Ever been in jail?"

"Nah. Like I told you, I've never been caught."

"Pete has," Martin said quietly. "He just got out."

I looked over the pair of them, gorging themselves on canned pasta, looking less scary than sad as they crouched in this disintegrating old building.

"Is that supposed to threaten me in some way?" I said.

"No ... it's just a fact. Like you saying you're a cat burglar. Of course, now that you're giving it up, I guess that makes you an ex-cat burglar." Martin's voice was calm, rational, not sarcastic.

"I guess it does," I admitted.

We sat and made uncomfortable small talk for a long time, probably a couple of hours, although I didn't check my watch at all. I wanted to; I was dying to know whether it was nearly dawn yet, but I didn't want to be rude.

Pete dominated the conversation for the most part, alternately bragging about his own criminal exploits and interrogating me about mine. He was a real tough guy, or he liked to think he was, anyway. I was much more interested in hearing about Zoe's life — or about Martin, who sat quietly off to the side throughout most of the conversation. He was a long, scrawny guy with a thoughtful look about him. There seemed to be an awful lot going on behind those pale green eyes of his, eyes that seemed to see right through Pete's act — and mine too, for that matter.

So I sat, my shoulders against cold concrete, my hands buried deep in the pocket of my sweatshirt, listening as Pete told us about this store he'd robbed, this building he'd broken into, this guy he'd beat up. Zoe and Martin looked bored; they'd heard these stories before. But I felt obligated to listen, to nod politely, to look impressed as he went on and on.

Out in the park, Martin had scared me perhaps more than Pete. The way he'd just sat and quietly mocked me as Pete pranced around ... somehow Martin's self-control had been much more worrying to me than Pete's bluster. I'd always been pretty good at pushing people's buttons: If I'd wanted to infuriate Pete, or even make him lose interest in me altogether, it wouldn't have been difficult. But with Martin, I couldn't tell if he even had buttons to push. He was unflappable. Unreadable. And there was something very appealing to me about that.

As the night ticked on, I could tell Pete and Martin were both starting to fade. After a while Martin just leaned his head back against the wall and closed his eyes. Half an hour later, Pete, who wasn't one to do anything at all without a good amount of fanfare, stood up, yawned loudly and stretched.

"I'm going to bed," he announced.

"Okay, so go," I said indifferently.

He answered that with a relatively soft kick to my left thigh.

"So get your ass off my mattress," he said.

I scrambled to my feet.

"Fine." I tilted my watch so it caught enough candle-light for me to read the time. It was nearly seven in the morning. "It's time I was leaving anyway."

Zoe stood slowly.

"I'll walk you home, then," she said. "You said it was close by, right?"

Pete gave her a suspicious look.

"You going someplace with him?"

"That's what I said. What's your problem?" Zoe retorted. "You said you were going to sleep, now shut up and sleep."

She put on that enormous trench coat and grabbed me by the hand before she ducked back through the doorway, out of the musty, dimly-lit room into the cold light of early morning.

"You don't like Pete, do you?" she said once we'd gone a block away.

"Not especially."

"He's not really that big a jerk, you know. Not once you get to know him. He just feels like he has to show off whenever he meets somebody new. He's actually really sweet."

"Sweet. That's terrific."

"What, you don't believe me? He's a really nice guy."

"No, I believe you. I'm sure he's great."

And with that, Zoe let the subject drop. She grabbed my arm as we walked, stepping closely beside me to keep warm. I tried to keep in step with her, but we both tripped over each others' feet a couple of times.

It wasn't completely light out, but all around us things were coming to life. Lights were coming on in houses, cars were starting, joggers and people with dogs were passing us on the sidewalk.

"So, Jareth," she said when we were about half a block away from Stewart's place. "What about you, now?"

"What d'you mean?"

"Well, you listened to Pete all night ... you didn't get a word in edgewise. Tell me about you."

I shrugged.

"I talked some," I said.

Zoe snorted.

"Yeah, that cat burglar stuff? That's such a load of crap."

"It's not, though. I've been doing it since I was thirteen. Me and my friend Matthew."

She pulled away from me.

"Yeah, but who cares?" she said. "You broke into a couple houses, you never got caught. So what? Is that all you've done in your life? I know you're an artist. What else is there?"

I looked at her, five-foot-nothing, her round, earnest face looking up into mine, and something unfamiliar washed over me. A feeling of — what? Love? No, that was stupid; I'd only just met this girl. Hormones was more like it. But there was something else — pity, maybe. Empathy. I'd had a rough couple of months, but I was willing to bet it was nothing next to Zoe's life. She had the look of somebody who'd lived through a whole lot.

"I don't know what you want me to say," I told her. "It's not like I know anything about you, either."

She gave me this mysterious little smile and stood on her tiptoes to give me a kiss on the cheek.

"Well, I suppose you could always find out," she said, grabbing my arm and walking on. "That's much more interesting than breaking into houses."

15

I woke up around two in the afternoon, curled up on top of the covers, my hand buried deep under the pillow, still clutching the envelope of money I'd stolen from the Petersens.

That was to be my first task for the day — getting rid of the money. I don't mean throwing it in a dumpster like Lloyd's cash; I had something much more productive in mind for this windfall.

I'd left Zoe a few doors down from Stewart's place — I didn't want anyone to see me fishing the money out of its hiding spot beside the porch — and had passed Stewart on my way up the stairs.

"You're up early," he had said, not looking quite awake himself.

"Yeah. I went for a jog," I told him, my head suddenly aching from exhaustion.

"Really? I'd no idea you were a runner. I've been meaning to take it up myself," he said.

"Mmm. Good for you," I said, trying to sound sincere. "I'm not feeling great, though. Think I'll lie down for a while."

Suddenly he'd looked awfully concerned. "Yeah? You want some Tylenol or something?"

"Nah. I just need to rest a bit."

Now, as I made my way out of the house, the bulging envelope padding the inside pocket of my jean jacket, I felt a little bad about lying to Stewart earlier in the day. Not that I could have told him the truth about why I was coming in at that hour, but still. The guy had been pretty cool to me — I had no call to be lying to him.

■ ■ ■

The woman at the bank gave me a strange look when I plunked the envelope of money down in front of her.

"You want to open an account with this?" she said suspiciously, flipping through the pile.

"Yeah. I just moved to town." I gave her the grin, wide and innocent, although it didn't look like she was buying it. "I figured it was time to clean out my piggy bank, you know?"

She looked at the pile of bills again, trying to figure out where I might have ripped off such a lot of money, but she didn't say anything else about it. She just took my name and address, gave me a bank card and a passbook. The whole time she was entering my name into the computer the woman didn't look like she was buying my story, but I didn't much care. The money I had was safe; I was reasonably sure it would never be reported stolen. It was all mine.

My next stop was a shoe store. The leather high-tops I'd ripped off a couple months earlier were looking a little ragged, so I picked up a couple pairs of shoes — legally this time.

That is to say, I paid for them: a pair of black-and-white canvas runners and a pair of brown leather dress shoes.

It was a nice day as I wandered up Yonge Street — warm and clear, the promise of spring in the air. The sad little trees that grow in cages along the main street were beginning to show the first signs of buds on their aenemic branches.

I caught my own reflection in a store window, and thought for probably the hundredth time that week that my hair really did look a lot better. Hell, I looked like a completely different person — I was downright respect-able-looking.

I stopped at a little alcove south of College Street that had a couple of park benches and changed my shoes. If I was gonna look like somebody else, I figured I may as well go whole hog, so to speak. I took off my old shoes and put them on the bench beside me, then took the dress shoes out of their bag.

"Hey. Those sure are nice shoes."

I looked up to see an old guy sitting beside me, tooth-less, grimy, reeking of alcohol.

"Yeah. Thanks." I slid the left shoe on and laced it up awkwardly, holding the box with the right shoe carefully in my lap. I wasn't sure what the old guy was after, but I certainly didn't want him making off with my new shoe.

"Listen, son. I don't suppose you could spare a dollar or so for an old soldier to go get himself something to eat," he said.

I shrugged, dug one hand in the pocket of my jean jacket and came up with a couple of quarters. I held onto them, though, giving the guy a suspicious look. His eyes were yellowish and bloodshot, his breath bad enough to knock out a buzzard.

"I don't suppose you're gonna buy food with that," I said drily. The old guy laughed wildly, little drops of spittle flying everywhere. I inched away from him on the bench, although there wasn't really anywhere for me to go.

"I'm starvin', sonny. Cross my heart and hope to die," he said, slapping me on the back with one hand while he held out his hand with the other.

"Great." I put on the right shoe and laced it up, then put my old sneakers into the box. "Hey, look, you want an old pair of running shoes?" I said.

The guy's face lit up.

"You don't want 'em?"

"Nah." I glanced down at the old guy's feet, which were probably two sizes smaller than my own. There wasn't much left of his shoes. My ratty old sneakers looked like Guccis in comparison. "I mean, I don't know if they'll fit ..."

"Oh, hey. I'm sure they'll fit fine," the guy said. He grabbed my hand and shook it hard, and when I finally managed to extract my fingers from his I saw that he'd given me the quarters back. "Thanks a lot, son. God bless you." And he leaned down to pry his nasty old shoes off his feet.

I gave him a little wave as I wandered on down the street, wiping my hand on my pants as I walked, the bag with my new running shoes in the other hand.

It was too nice a day to go straight home, and I wandered in and out of a couple of stores as I walked. I bought a couple of tee-shirts at one place, a pair of jeans at another.

By the time I was a few blocks from home, the new shoes were rubbing at my heels and I was ready to sit down. But as I rounded the corner to head home, something in the corner of a video store window caught my eye. It was a "help wanted" sign, one of those yellow-and-black ones you can buy at the variety store. I looked the window over, all blinking lights and posters for some Bruce Willis movie that was due out on video the following week. "Tinsel Town Video," said the black-and-silver sign over the door. It was more than a little cheesy, but what the heck.

"Yeah, I could work here," I said to myself, and went inside.

The girl behind the counter was a little older than me, maybe nineteen, with flaming red hair and an eyebrow ring. She was discussing some movie with a customer, every sentence a question.

"So, it has, like, *way* too much violence for little kids, right? But it was okay for like, probably *older* kids?"

I poked around in the comedy section for a few minutes as I waited for the customer to leave. It was a cool store, not too brightly lit, with a decent selection of obscure movies. The clerk was playing some cheesy romance on the little TV behind the counter, which made me think it wouldn't be a bad place to work at all — I mean, if you could watch movies while you worked.

I walked up to the counter and flashed the girl a ten-dollar grin.

"Hi. Could I get an application for the job?" I said, all salesman.

"Okay, we're, like, hiring for daytime hours?" she told me, lifting an eyebrow.

"Yeah, that's fine."

"You're not in school?"

"Not right now." I chewed on my lip a second, trying

to come up with a reasonable excuse for being out of school. "I'm taking a semester off," I said after a second.

The girl fished around behind the counter a second and came up with a pile of blank job applications. I took one, folded it, and shoved it into one of my bags.

"You'll probably want to bring it back really soon?" the girl said. "I think they're looking at hiring somebody, like, this week?"

"Sure. I'll bring it back this afternoon," I told her, flashing the grin again as I turned to walk out of the store.

■ ■ ■

When I walked in the front door I heard a familiar voice coming from the living room. I closed the door hard and squatted down to untie my shoes.

"Speak of the devil," said Vic, and stepped out into the hall. He gave a throaty chuckle. "Well, look at this. New haircut, new shoes. Where's Jareth and what have you done with him?"

I pulled off the shoes and stood up straight.

"Ha ha, you're funny. How you doing?" I said, re-arranging my armload of packages.

Vic shrugged, leaning back against the wall. "You know me, terrific as always," he said, giving me a forced smile. "Been out shopping?"

"Yeah. I'm applying for jobs and stuff, so I figured I should have some decent clothes." The words came out easily, and for a second I wondered why, before I realized it was the truth.

Vic's smile widened and spread to his eyes as he looked me over. "Stewart says you're holding up okay," he said, expecting a response.

"Yeah, I guess."

"Why don't you go put that stuff away and come on back downstairs? We should have a conversation."

I wasn't sure why, but those words sent a shiver down my spine. I jogged up the stairs to dispose of my purchases and came back down to the living room, where Vic was sitting with Stewart. A knowing look passed between the two of them as Stewart excused himself, walked past me and up the stairs.

I sat in a chair opposite Vic, my rear end on the edge of the seat, fingers clutching the padded wood of the armrests in a nervous death grip. Vic had the same look on his face as the guidance counsellor at my school when I'd been summoned down to the office to talk about the switchblade incident — eyes locked onto mine, lips pressed tightly shut, rubbing his hands together slowly in front of him. Like we were going to have some big conference about my attitude or something, which was usually just a fancy way of saying I was going to get a strip torn off me. The only thing was, this time I didn't have the faintest idea why I was getting in trouble. He couldn't know about the incident at the Petersens; and if Stewart had figured out I'd been out all night, I couldn't see why he would call Vic instead of just talking to me about it.

All of a sudden Vic burst out laughing, a loud, nervous chuckle, and sat back in his seat. "It's funny, Jareth, I've had about a hundred different conversations with you in my head on the way here, and now here I am and I haven't got the foggiest idea where to start," he said.

"Did I do something wrong?" I asked, my voice coming out surprisingly small.

"I don't know: Did you?" And he laughed again, pulling himself together. "Seriously, Jareth, here's what's happening. I went to see your mother today."

I sat back hard in my chair, like Vic had just slapped me hard across the face. I felt angry tears spring into my eyes; my mouth opened but no sound came out. He'd gone where?

"W-what for?" I managed.

"I'm sorry, Jareth. I should have told you first. But I thought she should know you're okay."

"Why should she know anything about me?" I said, louder than I needed to. "And how is it any of your business?"

Vic shook his head, looked away from me, trying to change the subject. "It's funny. We've known each other a long time, haven't we?" he said.

I wasn't about to let myself be swayed that easily.

"What difference does it make? You think that means we're friends? You think that means I like you? Well, you're wrong." I stood, wishing I had something in my hands so I could throw it at him for emphasis.

"Maybe so," Vic said, calm as could be. "Maybe you hate my guts, and maybe you've got a good reason to." He leaned back in his chair, his eyes steady, looking up into mine. "But listen to me for a minute, will you? You're a good kid. And your mother's —"

"She's what?" I cut him off, eyes blazing into his so hard I could feel my eyeballs drying out. "You're gonna tell me she's not so bad? You went to see her and she said she was really sorry, didn't she? I bet she even cried. Told you how much she missed her little boys. I've got news for you, Vic: It's all an act. I've seen it before, about a hundred thousand times. So don't tell me she's actually a real nice lady when you get to know her, because it's all bullshit."

And I stood for a second, out of breath, not sure whether to storm out of the room or sit back down.

"I was gonna say," Vic continued, like I hadn't said anything at all, "that your mother has made an awful lot of bad choices in her life." And he looked away, surrendering our little staring contest.

I sat back on the chair behind me and stared down at the carpet, an intricate pattern of golds and greens.

"This isn't over, is it?" I said, blinking back tears. "I mean, with my mother and Brad and everything. It's not over by a long shot."

"Well, no. There'll be a trial. You'll probably have to testify about what happened with your brother. People might say some pretty awful things."

I frowned. Then I looked up at Vic, who was giving me a strange look of concern.

"What do you mean by that?" I asked cautiously. "Awful things about what? About me?" And by the look on his face, I knew. "She said it was me, didn't she? She said I hurt Brad. She turned it all around and told you I'm the one that killed him."

"I know that's not what happened," Vic told me. "And so does everyone else. But I thought you should know that somebody might ask you about that. Whether you had anything to do with ..."

"Yeah." I wiped my eyes with the back of my hand. "You know, I shouldn't be surprised." There was a long pause, and I could feel Vic staring at the top of my head as I stared down at the carpet. "So, what do you think I should do? I mean, obviously you have some opinion as to how I should handle this situation, right? Otherwise you wouldn't be here."

Vic settled back in his chair. "I was thinking maybe you could go and see her," he said.

I shook my head. "Not a chance. Where is she, anyway? Not that I care, but I don't even know. Where do they put baby killers?"

"Well, they put *convicted* baby killers in prison," he told me. "Your mother hasn't been convicted yet. She's in jail."

"How is that different?"

"Well, jail's a lot nastier, or so I'm told. You've got people who've been thrown in there overnight, people who are there for a week, people who are there for two years waiting for their trials. It's a rough, brutal place. She's not having a lot of fun, I assure you. Prison's a walk in the park by comparison. In prison, people generally have a pretty good idea of how long they're gonna be there. They settle in. None of this open-ended stuff. And if you behave yourself, you could end up in some real nice treatment facility, get your own little cottage with a couple other people ..." He gave me a cynical smile. "It's sort of like a vacation, only without the beach."

"And so you want me to go to this horrible place so I can see my mother in all her suffering. Is that right?"

"Well, I just thought if you talked to her ..."

I laughed at that, harder than I'd laughed in a long time, so hard my throat hurt. It wasn't funny, though, not at all.

"You obviously didn't get a real good read on my old lady, did you?" I said. "You don't talk to my mother. Not unless you like the sound of your own voice a whole lot."

I stood up, wiped my sweaty hands on my pants.

Nope, I thought, walking stiffly past Vic and up the stairs to my room. You couldn't talk to my mother — all you could do was watch her little act: "Oh, poor me. The world is conspiring against me." Personally I had no interest in going through that: I'd seen that show too many times already to give it another chance.

16

I stewed over Vic's visit for the next couple of days, although as time went on I was a little less angry at him for having gone to see my mother. He was a good guy, I reasoned. Helpful. He was just looking to help the wrong person, that was all.

Outside, the cold, grey weather was slowly but surely turning bright and green, and every day I spent longer and longer outside – walking around, drawing pictures, whatever. I was bored sitting around the house all day, and it was intimidating having Danny around all the time. By the first week of April, I was nearly a quarter of the way through my sketchbook, filling it with everything from mindless squiggles and silly cartoons to a half-decent picture of an old church downtown and an elaborate two-page sketch I'd done of a homeless guy sleeping on a bench.

I passed my days drawing, wandering around, using the Petersen kid's money to buy lunch from grimy-looking hot dog vendors and fast-food places. Every once in a while I'd pack my own lunch, but more often than not I would wind up throwing it in the trash in favour of some greasy-spoon hamburger or something.

Every once in a while I would stop at a store or a restaurant with a "help wanted" sign in the window and fill out an application. Some of them I took seriously; others I filled in with fake names and addresses, and listed stuff like "crocodile wrestler" and "deodorant tester" in the spaces where it asked for job experience. I didn't do that very often, though. Without somebody like Matthew following me around all the time, that kind of stuff just wasn't fun at all.

I'm not sure what brought me to that old factory on one particular Tuesday afternoon. Maybe I was bored, maybe I just needed somebody to talk to ... either way, I found myself searching the place out, wondering if I'd be able to find it in the daylight. As it turned out, the place was right where I remembered it, and it certainly didn't look any better for seeing the light of day. I hopped over the flimsy plywood wall, my knapsack securely over both shoulders, and made my way to the side door to see if anyone was home.

Now, I'd never had any particular qualms about showing up at peoples' houses unannounced — that was, after all, how I'd managed to score dinner off Matthew's mother three or four nights a week for much of my life — but my heart was beating a little faster as I approached this door. I wasn't the type to worry whether I might get a frosty reaction, but I was a little concerned that Pete might answer the door with a .45 or something.

I tapped gingerly on the door with the tips of my fingers, about the wimpiest knock in recorded history.

"Hello? Anybody there?" I called softly, then again, a

little louder. The door fell open a few inches, and I peered into the dusty room, tiny rays of sun sneaking through cracks in the painted-over windows, casting a strange yellow light over everything in the place.

"Who wants to know?"

Martin's voice. I held in a sigh of relief, and pushed the door open a little further. It groaned loudly on its hinges, and I could feel a coating of grime rubbing off on my fingers.

"It's Jareth. Can I come in?"

"Nobody's stopping you."

Martin was crouched in the middle of the floor, staring under a rusted metal desk with the intent look of a cat watching a piece of string. He didn't look up when I came in, just motioned wildly with one hand for me to come in and be quiet.

"What are you doing?" I said, my voice a near-whisper.

"Look at this."

I squatted beside him, my knees cracking loudly as I imitated his position. I followed his gaze to see a quartet of yellow eyes staring out at us — a pair of baby raccoons looking mesmerised, terrified at being discovered.

"You think they've got rabies or something?" he whispered. That was a thought that hadn't occurred to me.

"I don't know; maybe." And I stood up nervously, taking a step back toward the door.

Martin laughed at that.

"What are you, chicken?" he said, his voice a little louder. "A little rabies never hurt anybody. All they do is give you a needle and it goes away."

"Yeah, a little needle. In the stomach." My pulse raced

at the thought of it, and I backed up against the wall, trying to put as much distance between me and those raccoons as I could.

"I wish I had some cookies or something," Martin was saying. "Maybe I could get them to be friendly. I hear raccoons are really smart. You can train 'em to do shit."

"Yeah, like spread disease and break into your garbage." I slid my knapsack off my shoulders and set it on the floor. "But I've got a sandwich if you want to try."

I handed him my lunch, untouched from the day before. He broke off a piece and put it on the floor a little way from the desk, then another, placing it a little farther away, and another, until he had a trail of sandwich pieces leading over to the mattress.

"You think they like peanut butter?" I said, mostly to hear the sound of my own voice, and leaned back against the wall to watch. We didn't have long to wait, as it turned out. The bolder of the raccoon cubs poked its head out from under the desk after a minute or two and made straight for the first chunk of sandwich. He sniffed it carefully, eyeing Martin suspiciously even as he seemed to decide it probably wasn't poison and swallowed the piece without chewing.

The first raccoon had polished off nearly half of the sandwich pieces before the second one decided to be brave. The second one, a little smaller than its sibling, headed straight for Martin, who was holding the biggest chunk of sandwich in the palm of his hand. The creature seized the food with its paw and shoved a corner into its mouth, dragging the entire piece with it as it scurried back under the desk.

After it had consumed the trail of sandwich chunks, the first raccoon made its way back to its hiding spot to wash itself. I watched it for a second before I turned to look at Martin, who was leaning back with a big grin on his face. "That was great. I bet I'll have them eating right out of my hand in a week."

"Yeah. They'll probably tell all their aunts and uncles and cousins about this place, too. Before you know it, you'll have *Wild Kingdom* right here in your living room."

Martin chuckled.

"You're just a ray of sunshine, aren't you, Jareth?" He motioned for me to come and sit down. "What else do you have in that magical bag of yours?"

"Nothing much," I said, sitting beside him and looking inside. "I've got a can of ginger ale."

"Give it here." He opened the can and drained it in three gulps. "Anything else?"

"Nothing to eat. I had an apple, but I ate it."

"Mmm. What else is there?" He motioned for me to give him the bag, and I slid it toward him reluctantly. He pulled out a pile of junk I'd been carrying around: a bandanna, my Swiss Army knife, an extra pair of socks, a pamphlet from some religious guy on Queen Street, my little flashlight.

Finally he came to my sketchbook. It was the biggest, most obvious thing in the bag, but it seemed like he'd been saving it for last. He pulled it out and opened it, angling himself so a beam of sunlight fell right across his lap. He leafed through the book silently, stopping here and there to stare at a page for a minute or more. I sat uncomfortably, watching him look at my scrawlings, things I'd never shown anyone, and scarcely breathed as he contemplated each page.

Finally he reached the first blank page, and gave a

cursory flip through the rest of the book to make sure there was nothing he'd missed. Then he handed the book back to me, his face unreadable.

"Those are pretty good," he said simply.

I busied myself putting my belongings back into the bag, relieved he hadn't hated my work, crushed he hadn't said more. "Thanks," was all I could manage.

I was zipping up my knapsack, thinking I should just leave, when Martin spoke again.

"If you're looking for Zoe," he said, "she's gone home for a few days."

"Home? You mean, her parents' place?"

"Yeah. She'll be back pretty soon, though. I thought I might go see her tomorrow if she's not."

"Oh yeah?"

"Yeah. You can come, if you want. I mean, if you don't have anything else to do. I think she'd like to see you. She's been talking about you all the time since you left here that time."

I raised my eyebrows, flattered — although I'd told Zoe things I didn't necessarily want her repeating. Not to Martin, and especially not to Pete. I got the impression Pete would see everything that had happened to me in the past couple of months as an indication of how tough I was — or more importantly, of how tough I wasn't. I was fairly sure he would have a story that made him sound just a little tougher, just a little meaner than I was: "Your old lady killed your brother? Well mine killed my brother, two sisters and a dog. Then she came after me, but I managed to fight her off with a broken bottle." Something stupid like that.

"She's been talking about me?" I echoed, forgetting about Pete for the time being.

"Yeah, like nonstop."

"Cool." I could feel a goofy-looking grin creeping across my face at the idea. "Where do her parents live?"

"Out in Scarborough. It's easy to get to on the subway."

"Great. What time are you going?"

"I don't know. Afternoon, sometime."

"Okay. Well, why don't I show up around then?" I suggested.

"Yeah, okay. If I'm still here, we can go," he said.

I checked my watch. Outside the shadows were starting to get longer, and I figured I should be heading home for dinner pretty soon. Danny had given me nasty looks for about two days after I'd skipped dinner without telling him one time. He wasn't much of a cook, but it seemed to be a matter of personal pride with him that there was *somebody* there to eat what he made. Stewart was usually home, but like I said before, he almost never came downstairs to eat.

"Look, I should be going," I said, and stood. A cloud of dust escaped from the mattress as I shifted my weight, flying up into my nostrils and making my eyes water.

"Already?" Martin sounded vaguely disappointed. "Well, okay. But you're coming back tomorrow, right?"

"Yeah, sure." I slipped my arms into my backpack and headed for the door. By the time I pulled it shut behind me, Martin had already gone back to crawling around after the raccoons.

■ ■ ■

It's funny how everything seems to happen at once some days. Day after day is completely boring and routine, and then you'll suddenly have a day where everything that happens seems to have lasting significance. Or maybe every day's like that — we're just not paying enough attention most of the time.

At any rate, I was nearly home when I saw him: the Petersen kid, resplendent in those drop-ass jeans of his and a dark blue tee-shirt with a horizontal yellow stripe across the chest, hands buried deep in his pockets. He was walking down the driveway of his house on the way somewhere or another, and he turned toward me onto the sidewalk.

I estimated it had been a week and a half since he'd come back from Grandma's house, and in the meantime someone had given him a lovely shiner. It was a few days old, but his eye was still puffy, surrounded by a brown-and-yellow bruise that must have been every colour of the rainbow a day or two earlier. I couldn't help but give him a good stare as I approached him on the sidewalk, and he looked up at me, struggling to remember where he might have seen me before.

I was about two feet away from the kid when he suddenly realized when we'd met, and he did a double-take that just about knocked both of us over. He turned to stare at me as I passed, and as I glanced back over my shoulder, I could see him still watching me as I walked up Stewart's driveway and into the house.

■ ■ ■

As I kicked off my new running shoes in the front hall, I wondered how smart it had been to walk into the house in front of the kid. Now he knew where I lived — and I could tell from the look in his eye that he suspected something was up.

Oh, well, I reasoned, heading up the stairs to my room. That's all he could do: suspect. There was no way he could know anything.

There was a note taped to my bedroom door — a name and phone number I didn't recognize. "Call Miriam."

I pulled it off, puzzled, dialled the number.

"Good afternoon, Tinsel Town Video," said the voice on the other end.

I had to think about that for a second — about why I knew that name. Then I remembered the application I'd dropped off, what? A week ago? More? The night Vic had come to visit.

I told the woman who I was, and she sounded so thrilled to hear from me I wondered if anyone else had filled out a job application.

"I'm really hoping you can come in for a job interview tomorrow afternoon," she said. "I'm looking for somebody to start by the end of the week."

I thought that over carefully. I'd told Martin I'd go with him to see Zoe, and I really didn't want to stand him up. It wasn't like I could call him to cancel, and I really did want to see Zoe again.

"Could we make it the morning?" I said carefully. "I actually have another commitment in the afternoon."

"Hmm. I hadn't planned on coming in tomorrow until about noon. How about this evening? We're open until nine tonight. Why don't you come in around seven?"

I checked my watch; it was five-thirty.

"Seven sounds great," I told her, my hand shaking a little as I hung up the phone.

A job interview. I looked down at my clothes, still dusty and smelling of mould from the old factory. I figured I should clean up before I went anywhere. I ate supper in silence with Danny, had a shower and changed into a new pair of jeans and my one and only dress shirt. It was a little wrinkled, and since I hadn't worn it in probably two years, it was a little tight. But I figured with my jacket on, nobody would notice.

I checked my reflection in the bathroom mirror, ran a comb through my hair. I looked strange, respectable. Grown up.

"Wow," I said under my breath. "Looking sharp, buddy."

And with that, I headed for the door.

17

"Why do you want to work in a video store?"

The store owner, Miriam, seemed like a nice enough lady. Her daughter, the redhead with the eyebrow ring, worked in the store as well, although she was going up north someplace to plant trees for the summer. Which was why they needed to hire somebody.

"Well, who wouldn't?" I said, laying on the charm a little thick. "It looks like a nice little store, I'd get to meet lots of people ..." I started reciting all the crap we'd learned to say in my Business class unit on job interviews, although it didn't look like this woman was buying any of it. She was a real friendly soul, a little touchy-feelie for my tastes, but she seemed pretty cool. If she didn't mind her daughter's slacker clothes and body piercings, I figured she'd be easy enough to get along with.

"Plus you'd get to watch movies all day," Miriam interrupted, and winked. "That's why everybody wants to work in a video store. Of course, you'll have to do some real work, too, you know."

"That's fine. I mean, otherwise what's the point in hiring me? Assuming, of course, that you're going to hire me." I laughed. We'd been talking for a while, just shooting the breeze, before she actually got around to asking me any questions, and I could tell she liked me. We stood, the pair of us, leaning over opposite sides of the store counter, just like I was a customer stopping by for a chat.

"Well, Jareth Gardner," she said after a few more lame questions. "Here's what we're looking at. I hate doing these interviews, and you seem like a nice enough boy. My daughter's leaving for up north in a couple of weeks, so I thought you could maybe start right away. She can show you around, teach you how to do everything, and then you could take over for her for the summer. She usually works from ten to five, and then we have another young man who comes in evenings and weekends. I'm in for part of most days, and then I fill in for the other fellow when he can't come in. He's got night school tonight, which is why I'm here today."

"That sounds fine," I said. "Actually, it sounds great."

"Great. Why don't you come in tomorrow morning and we'll show you around?"

I hesitated for a second, thinking about Zoe. Wondered how mad Martin would be if I started a job instead of going with him to see her.

"Um, tomorrow's the only day I can't make it," I reminded her. "But I can get out of it if —"

"Oh, right, right. Of course." She reached out, grabbed my arm with both hands, gave it a friendly squeeze. "I'm getting forgetful in my old age. Make it the day after, then. I'll let my daughter know. Her name's Rebecca."

"Great. Terrific." I shook her hand, a natural grin on my face this time. "I'll see you later, then."

■ ■ ■

I walked home quickly, a bit of a spring in my step as I leapt up every couple of houses to give a tree branch an exuberant slap. I had a job. My own source of income — a legal one, no risk of getting arrested, no risk of somebody dropping dead on me. I couldn't help but skip a little as I went.

I was a few doors away from home when I suddenly skidded to a stop.

There, leaning against the post of the street lamp in front of Stewart's house, was the Petersen kid. He'd been standing there for some time, by the look of things. And by the way he stiffened up when he saw me, there could be little doubt that he'd been waiting for me.

"Hey," I said, trying to look indifferent as I approached the kid. "How you doing?"

"I need to talk to you," the kid said, his voice tight, anxious. "Can we go someplace?"

I thought about that for a second, trying to figure out what would be the least incriminating way of answering that question.

"What do you need to talk to me for?" I said, forcing myself to hold eye contact with the kid. His lip was swollen and cracked — either a new wound or one I hadn't noticed earlier in the day.

"I think you know why," he said. There was no spite in his voice, though; just fear. I took a deep breath, trying to keep my composure while I thought about the situation.

"Why don't we go inside?" I said amicably. "We can talk there."

If it sounds crazy to have invited this kid into my house, there was method to my madness. As I led him up the walkway to the front door, there was only one thought in my mind: Danny. Tall and scary and built like a brick shithouse, as my grandmother used to say. I'd never met a more frightening-looking human being, which made him good to have around in a pinch of this type. His car was in the driveway, and although I figured he didn't have any particular loyalty toward me, he would more than likely intervene if this kid tried something stupid.

It was Stewart, not Danny, who was in the kitchen when we got in, emptying out the dishwasher as I showed the kid inside. He came out with a surprised look at the sound of a strange voice in his house.

"Hi, Stewart," I said as casually as I could. "This is ... a friend." I trailed off awkwardly as I realized I still didn't know the kid's name.

"I'm Richard Petersen," he said, and extended a hand to Stewart. Even with the black eye and thick lip I could tell the kid knew how to turn on the charm when he needed to, grinning as he shook hands.

"Your face looks like it's seen better days, Richard Petersen," Stewart said, a polite smile on his own face.

"Yeah, well. I got in a fight at school."

"That's too bad." Stewart wiped his hands on his pants. "Look, I was just cleaning up in here, and I'll get right out of your way."

"That's fine. Take your time. We'll go in the living room."

"Is that your dad?" the kid — Richard — said as he sat on the couch.

"No. He's just this guy. It's his house; I just moved to Toronto maybe a month ago."

"I didn't think I'd seen you before." The kid frowned at me, adjusted his baseball cap nervously. "How do you know Curtis?" he asked.

That threw me off slightly.

"Curtis? Who the hell is Curtis?" I said. I sat in Stewart's big chair, leaned back like I owned the place. "The only Curtis I know was in the Special Ed class at my old school. Somehow I don't think we're talking about the same guy."

Richard leaned forward intently, like he was trying to convince me of something.

"No way, man. You gotta know him. Nobody knew I was going away until you saw me leaving. Nobody except my home room teacher, and I'm pretty sure she didn't tell Curtis about it."

Suddenly I realized what he was talking about. Richard thought this Curtis guy was the one who stole his money while he'd been away, and he thought I was the one who'd told Curtis when he was leaving.

"I'll have to give you part marks for effort, Richard, but I've never met this Curtis guy in my life."

Richard's frown intensified, his thick brown eyebrows nearly meeting over his nose. A couple more months of puberty, I thought, and he would just have one big eyebrow going from one side of his face to the other. After a few seconds of thinking a look of understanding crossed his face.

"You're the one who stole the money?" he said, a little louder than I would have liked.

"Shh." I winked at him humourlessly. "You don't want to ruin my good name, do you?"

"But how — how'd you know it was there? I never showed anybody but Curtis where I hid the stuff."

In a low voice, glancing up at the doorway to make sure no one was there, I gave Richard an abbreviated version of how I'd found his hiding spot.

"You were mad 'cause I gave you the finger, so you decided to rob my house?"

"No, no, no," I said, even quieter. "That's not it at all. I just figured you'd be a safe target. A little drug money ... who would ever report it missing? What are you gonna do, go tell your Mommy and Daddy about it?" I laughed. "Come on, Richard. We both know that's not smart."

I sounded like a complete bastard, but I actually did feel a little sorry for the kid, who looked like he was about to burst into tears.

"Here's the thing," he said. "The money's not even mine. Not all of it, anyway. Just a little bit was mine. The rest belongs to this other guy."

"Curtis?"

The kid looked at me like I was an idiot.

"No, stupid. You think Curtis is gonna steal his own money? No, Curtis is this other guy, he works for me sometimes. The money belonged to this other guy, Boswell."

"Who's he, your dealer?" I grinned wryly, feeling like I was on an episode of *Law and Order* or something.

"Yeah, kind of," said Richard. "Bos gets me the stuff at cost — pot, hash, sometimes acid or whatever — and I sell it around school. I get to keep twenty per cent and as much weed as I can smoke. The money you took — maybe three hundred bucks was mine. The rest was Boswell's. And now he's gonna kill me if I don't give it to him."

The kid's voice broke, and I could see his good eye brimming with tears.

Suddenly the whole thing didn't seem so funny anymore. From the look of the kid's face, this Boswell guy was for real, and here I was with his money sitting in my brand-new bank account. My mouth was awfully dry as I spoke next, although the words came out sounding like I knew what I was talking about.

"Tell you what, Rich. Can I call you Rich? I appreciate your situation, here. You're in a bind; I can see that." I sounded like some sleazy business tycoon in a bad TV movie, but I didn't care. I was in control of this situation, and nothing this kid did or said was going to change that. "And I feel bad for you. I really do."

"Bullshit," the kid muttered. He stood up to leave, wiping his hands on his baggy pants. I figured they were probably real sweaty by now.

"No, wait. Don't go," I said, meaning it. "Sit down. I'm not finished talking yet."

The kid eyed me dubiously, but he sat.

"Look, guy, I don't want you jerkin' me around," he told me. "You want to keep the money, that's fine. But I should tell you I think Bos is really gonna kill me. I'm not talking about a black eye and a fat lip, I'm saying he's really gonna kill me. And when I tell him you stole his money, he'll probably kill you, too."

I had already considered this possibility, and I didn't much like the idea. But I didn't let Richard know that.

"Oh, come on. You probably already told him this Curtis guy took his money. What's he gonna believe? Curtis took it, some other guy took it ... old Bos is just gonna think you're jerkin' *him* around. But I can help you out, here. Exactly how much money do you owe Boswell?"

Richard thought about that for a second.

"A thousand fifty," he said. "And he wants it now. I was supposed to give it to him last week."

I did some math in my head. I still had about nine hundred dollars in the bank, but I wasn't crazy about handing it all back to this kid. Especially when it would probably be a few weeks before I got a cheque from Tinsel Town Video.

"You have some pot, too, though. I saw it in the box with the money."

"I have a little bit. Maybe six hundred dollars' worth."

"That's if you sell it, right?"

Richard looked at me like I was a couple logs short of a good bonfire. "Yeah. If I sell it, I'll maybe get six hundred for it. What else am I gonna do, eat it?"

I made a face. "Yeah, well. I don't want you to sell it. How much did you pay Boswell for it?"

"About two hundred. What do you mean, you don't want me to sell it?"

I thought for a second.

"About two hundred," I repeated. "Okay. Here's what's gonna happen. I want you to give the stuff back to Boswell."

"What?" The kid's voice squeaked a little. "You want me to give it *back* to him?"

"That's right. Tell him ... I don't know, tell him your parents are on to you. Something. Tell him you can't sell for him anymore."

"Oh, yeah, that's great. Here you go, Boswell. I lost your money, and now, by the way, I'm not gonna earn you any *more* money. Yeah, that's terrific, buddy." He stood up again. "I'll see you later."

I stood up, grabbed the kid by the arm.

"Listen," I hissed between clenched teeth. "I'm trying to help you, here. But this drug shit's gotta stop. What are you, thirteen years old?"

"Fourteen next week," he said defensively, pulling away.

"Terrific. Fourteen next week. It's a perfect time for you to smarten up, then." I sat down in my own chair, pointing Richard back toward the couch. I didn't feel like a stupid TV villain now — more like the sitcom dad who sits his teenage kid down for a Serious Talk. "I'll tell you what we're gonna do. I'm gonna give Boswell eight hundred dollars. This is a gift, from me to you, and Boswell never finds out I took his money. You're gonna give the two hundred dollars worth of pot back to Boswell, and he can sell it or smoke it or feed it to the pigeons. The other fifty bucks? Well, that's up to you. Rake some leaves, or wash some windows or something, but come up with the money. Simple as that. That's the plan. Take it or leave it."

Young Richard Petersen thought this over carefully, his nostrils flaring as he tried to decide whether to thank me or punch me.

"I guess I'll take it," he said finally.

"Good boy," I told him. "I knew you'd make the right decision." It was my turn to stand up, and I showed him toward the front door.

The kid eyeballed me strangely as he put his shoes back on.

"What's with you, anyway?" he wanted to know. "You're okay with stealing my shit, but you don't want me selling pot."

"I don't like drugs," I said with a shrug. "I'm not really

a big advocate of stealing, either, but sometimes in this life we just have to choose our battles."

He gave me an even stranger look after that, but finished lacing up his shoes without further comment. When he was finished he stepped outside, motioned for me to follow. I leaned my head out the front door, not really wanting to go anywhere with him in his current state of mind.

"So when are we gonna do it?" he asked. "Just so I can tell Bos, you know?"

"Saturday," I said, just picking a day out of the air. "I'll let you know when and where. Your number's in the phone book, right?"

"Yeah."

"See you later, Rich."

And I locked the door behind me on the way inside.

I had no sooner turned the latch, though, when I found myself blindsided, up against the wall with one arm twisted behind my back, a huge hand planted firmly in the middle of my back, pinning me firmly in place.

"You want to tell me what the hell that was all about?" Danny said, soft and dangerous in my ear.

I let out a gasp, the wind all but knocked out of me, as a jolt of pain tore through my arm.

"What — was what — about?" I managed, the heel of his hand digging into my spine.

"Don't give me that shit, Jareth Gardner. I knew you were a little delinquent the second you walked in here. And don't think a new haircut and a new pair of shoes are gonna change anything, either."

I could hear the seam along the arm of my shirt tearing as he twisted my wrist.

"What is it you think I did, exactly?" I said raggedly. "I mean, if you let me know what I did, I could maybe apologize or something."

Danny's hand came off my back, and I was relieved for about half a second, until he used it to bounce my face off the wall. I could hear my nose crack, and a second later I felt a blinding pain, like a spike straight into my brain.

"Don't even try that shit," he said. "I thought you were a hood, maybe into shoplifting or something, all these new clothes you're bringing home. But I'm sitting upstairs and I'm hearing you talk about drugs and house break-ins. So what's it all about, Jareth? What are you up to?"

I could barely see, and my mouth was full of the taste of blood as I struggled to understand what he'd just said to me.

"How did you — ?"

"How did I hear you from upstairs?" he finished. "This is an old house, Jareth. Big old vents. They carry sound pretty well. Now, I wasn't trying to eavesdrop, but when you hear things like that being said in your own house ... well. Let's just say I pricked up my ears a little bit."

"It's not what you think," I told him. "I mean, it's not great, but it's not what you're thinking. Just — let me go and I'll tell you about it."

That earned my face another good bounce off the wall, and the world went blank for a second.

When the wall started to come back into focus again, the first voice I heard was not Danny's, but Stewart's.

"What do you think you're doing?" he said, the anger in his voice sounding strange, foreign. He didn't seem like a guy who boiled over very often, but now that he was, I wanted nothing more than to disappear under the floor-boards.

"Get out," I heard him bark, and I automatically stumbled toward the doorway, dazed, seeing spots. Then there was a hand on the back of my neck, steadying me, and Stewart's voice, a little more gentle: "Not you."

I heard the door slam as Danny stormed out, and a second later the sound of his car starting, tires squealing as he pulled away.

Stewart sat me down at the kitchen table, got me a bag of ice for my nose.

"You know, I think he might have broken it," he said, looking me over carefully.

"S'okay," I muttered, my head aching. "I broke it before. At camp when I was a kid. A kid bashed me in the face with a tree branch. My grandma said, 'Well, a target that big, it'd be hard to miss.' "

"She sounds like a charming woman," Stewart said, a pained smile on his lips.

"Yeah, well. She's dead, no great loss to the world," I said, pulling the bag of ice away from my face when it got too cold.

Stewart sighed, looking me over sadly. I had this sick feeling in the pit of my stomach as he stared at me, knowing what was coming next.

"Jareth, what's going on with you?" he said after a minute or two.

I put the bag back on my face just so I wouldn't have to look at him.

"I can't tell you," I said. "If I do, you'll throw me out."

He reached over and moved the ice pack out of the way.

"Try me," he said. "Or should I start guessing?"

I thought it over a second, feeling those muddy eyes of his boring into me.

"That kid who was over tonight?" I said. "I ... um, did something to him. I shouldn't have done it, and now I'm trying to make it up to him."

"And what does that have to do with Danny smashing your face into the wall?"

I shrugged. It hurt my head to even move it.

"He said he heard us talking through the air vents. I guess he thought that would be a good way to confront me."

Stewart let forth a pained sigh.

"I'll be honest, Jareth. I've wondered about you. I mean, I don't know where you go all day, who you talk to, what you do. And the way you're always about five seconds away from boiling over ..." and he trailed off, frowning. "But Vic says you're a good kid, and for the moment I'm prepared to let it go at that. You say you're fixing things with this kid, so go ahead. I'm not gonna kick you out because my brother thought he heard something through the air vent. But you have to understand, I can't kick him out, either. You're both staying, and you're both going to have to coexist. Is that clear?"

I nodded, my head throbbing. I felt like a little kid in the principal's office.

"Yes, sir. It's clear."

"Good." Stewart looked me over again, checking my pupils, shaking his head grimly. "I think you'll be okay," he said. "Just ... take it easy, will you? Keep the ice on, let me know if you think you've got to go to the hospital or something."

"Yeah, sure."

Stewart gave me an awkward pat on the shoulder.

"I've got some paperwork to do. I'll be upstairs if you need anything."

■ ■ ■

Stewart had a little apartment of sorts on the top floor of the house. I'd never been up there, but I figured that must be where he did all his work, since that where he always seemed to be. I let an hour go by, holding the bag of ice on my face until I thought my nose was going to drop off. I turned on the TV in the living room but it made my headache worse.

I kept thinking about what Stewart had said. It must have looked strange, the way I lurked around the house all night, disappearing all day. I hadn't even told him I'd been looking for a job. I'd just figured he thought I was busy mourning or something, after what he'd said to me that day in the café.

I could hear music playing upstairs, another old rock and roll song — the Beatles, maybe. Impulsively I plodded up the stairs to my room to grab my knapsack, then continued on up the next flight of stairs to the third floor. I tapped on the door at the top of the stairs, not much harder than I'd knocked on the door of the old factory earlier that day.

"Stewart? Can I come in?"

He was at the door in a second and a half, opening it halfway, his face a mixture of concern and suspicion. This was his space; not even Danny ever came up here, and I wondered suddenly if I'd made a mistake going there.

"What's up, Jareth?"

I pulled my sketchbook out of my bag and offered it to him, my hand shaking .

"I, um, just thought I'd show you what I've been doing all day," I said.

His face softened a little as he took the book from me and started to look through it, even slower than Martin had, pausing to examine even the pages where I'd only made a scribble or two. He didn't speak for a long time, just peered at each page intently. For the second time that day, I watched someone looking through my drawings.

"Jareth Gardner," he said slowly, the ghost of a smile appearing on his thin, greyish lips. "I knew you had a soul in there somewhere."

And he closed the book, handing it back to me with a look of — what? Triumph?

"Thanks, Jareth," he said. He turned and disappeared behind the door again, closing it behind him.

18

I woke up with a splitting headache and stumbled to the bathroom to find some Tylenol or something. I'd been a little surprised to wake up at all. I'd had visions of Stewart finding me dead of a concussion or something. That would have been ironic, I thought dryly. A little more than a month earlier I'd been sorely disappointed at having woken up alive — now that I actually had something to look forward to, dropping dead would have just been bad timing.

A sorry sight looked back at me from the mirror: swollen, discoloured nose between two puffy red eyes. I was going to have quite a pair of shiners — enough to rival little Richard Petersen's and then some.

I went to meet Martin a little before noon. I tried to hop gently over the fence, jarring my nose as little as possible, although I still let out an involuntary groan as I landed on the other side.

I knocked a little more assertively this time than I had the previous day, and was a little disappointed to hear Pete's voice telling me to come in.

He let out a chortle when he saw me, and came over to get a better look.

"Aw, gee. Somebody messed up your pretty face. What's Zoe gonna say?"

I gave him a pained smile at that one, flinching as he poked at my face with his grubby fingers.

"Yeah. I had a bit of a run-in with a wall," I told him.

"Oh, come on. You expect me to believe that?"

"It's true. I had a little help running into the wall, though," I said. He found that hilarious, and let out a long, horsy chortle.

"You want me to thump the guy for you?" he offered, still laughing.

"No, thanks." I couldn't help but think of my meeting with Boswell, though, and I wondered if I was going to be in for another thumping. "I might need to take you up on that another time, though," I said.

"Sure, buddy. No problems." He cracked his knuckles and wandered outside to light a cigarette.

"Hey, listen. Is Martin around?"

"Yeah, he's around someplace. He said if you came I should tell you to wait. He'll be back in a few minutes."

I wandered around the outside of the building while Pete was smoking, looking at the buckled cinder blocks that were due to cave in any second now. I wondered if anybody would be inside when the thing finally did go over.

When I got back to the other side of the building, Martin was back, the front of his bomber jacket bulging.

"Hey, Jareth. Have a look." He unzipped the jacket halfway and one of the raccoons poked its head out. "I got it to come right over to me yesterday after you left.

Now he thinks I'm his Daddy." He pulled a peanut out of his pocket and handed it to the creature, which inhaled it greedily.

"That's great," I said uncertainly, still thinking about rabies.

Martin glanced up from his new pet for just a second before digging in his pocket to find it another peanut.

"So what the hell happened to you?" he said.

I shrugged.

"Ran into a wall," I said vaguely, and that was the end of it. Martin was far better than Pete at picking up the message that I didn't want to talk about what happened to my face.

■ ■ ■

I was a little relieved when Pete told us he didn't want to come and see Zoe. He couldn't stand her father, he told me, and sent Martin and me off with a wave.

"I'd love to ice that bastard, but I wouldn't want to do any time on account of him," was how Pete phrased his feelings for the man.

We sat in the corner of the subway car, Martin with the raccoon still wriggling around in his jacket, which earned him some strange looks from fellow passengers. We made quite a pair, him with his spiked purple hair, me with my rainbow-coloured nose.

The trip from downtown to Zoe's place took about three quarters of an hour, and by the time we got there my head was aching so bad I wanted to pass out. I wondered if Zoe's folks would be able to spare some Aspirin or something.

Once we got off the subway it was another ten-minute bus ride to Zoe's parents' house. Either Martin wasn't in the mood to chat or he sensed that I didn't want to. Either way, we didn't have much of a conversation until we'd arrived on her street.

Their house wasn't much to look at, but I'd expected much worse. It was a smallish bungalow, probably fifty years old, with a well-kept hedge and a carport on the right-hand side of the house. Martin had obviously been here enough times to know they used the side door more than the front, and he wandered through the carport to the side yard with the ease of someone who was familiar with his surroundings.

He hadn't even rung the doorbell yet when the door came flying open and a tall, heavy-set guy with an enormous beer gut stepped out onto the porch.

"I thought I told you punks not to come around here anymore," he barked, giving Martin a shove. Martin coiled back, trying to shield the raccoon with his arms.

The man looked at me, his eyes narrow slits in his yellowish, unshaven face.

"And who the hell are you?" he said.

"I'm a friend of Zoe's," I said, standing my ground. He was drunk; that was no problem. I'd handled my mother in worse condition dozens of times. And after tangling with Danny the night before, I felt a little invincible. "Who the hell are you?" I shot back.

"I'm her father, punk." And he reached out, grabbed me by the collar. "Don't you talk back at me, I'll slap you silly." He laughed and let go of me, shoving me backwards into the tool shed. "Except it looks like somebody already beat me to it."

I recovered my footing and stood staring at the guy, my heart pounding in my ears as my head throbbed with pain.

"Where's Zoe?" I said. I was too freaked out to make eye contact; instead I concentrated on his hair, a bad comb-over that was doing a lousy job of covering his sizable bald spot.

Zoe's father looked at Martin with the look of someone who was sharing a joke with an old buddy.

"What's with this guy?" he said. "He too stupid to keep his mouth shut?"

Martin shrugged, running his hands slowly over the front of his jacket to ensure that his raccoon was okay.

"I guess maybe he is," Martin said with a wry smile. "Yesterday he ran into a wall."

"Ran into a wall, eh?" The guy turned around, headed back up the three concrete steps into the house. "That's awful funny, 'cause so did Zoe. She's not here; she's in the hospital."

He slammed the door behind him, and I heard the sound of a deadbolt sliding shut.

I looked over at Martin, who was unzipping his jacket to check on the raccoon.

"What hospital do you suppose she's in?" I said.

He looked up, a little surprised.

"What do you mean?"

"Well, her dad just said she was in the hospital. Where do you suppose that would be?"

"Oh, that. He says stuff like that all the time. She's probably just downstairs or something."

I frowned, not sure what to make of the whole situation. My head was pounding so hard I could barely see straight, let alone figure out why Zoe's old man would say something like that. Or why Martin would hardly even react to it.

"Well, shouldn't we find out?" I probed. "I mean, what if he's telling the truth?"

Martin shrugged. He seemed more interested in that damned raccoon than he did in Zoe all of a sudden.

"I don't know," he said mildly. "You wanna try knocking?"

I paced up and down the driveway a couple of times, debating whether I should try the door again. I'd already taken enough of a beating in the last twenty-four hours that I didn't want to do anything else that was going to cause me any amount of physical damage.

"No, I don't really want to try knocking," I said after a minute's contemplation. "But we can't just leave, can we? Is there a hospital close by? Maybe we could check there."

The answer to my question came, not from Martin but from a small woman who suddenly tapped on the side window of the house — the kitchen window, from the looks of it — and gestured for me to come around to the front.

She met us on the porch, still wearing a bathrobe at two in the afternoon, looking like she hadn't slept in a good long while.

"Are you looking for Zoe?" she said, her voice a near whisper. "My husband's asleep inside."

"Hey, Mrs. G." Martin loped over, casual. "Is Zoe here?"

"No. No, she's not here. She ... fell down the stairs," her mother said. "The baby came early; they're still in the hospital."

Suddenly she had Martin's rapt attention.

"She had the baby? It's not supposed to be born until July," he said, his face finally cracking a little.

"It's real sick," her mother said. Somehow I got the idea this woman was a little slow ... something about the way she held her mouth when she talked, or maybe the way she chose her words so carefully, tilting her head to one side as she talked. All the same, it was obvious she was pretty worried about Zoe.

"What hospital is she in?" I pressed. She gave me a funny look.

"It's okay," Martin said. "He's a friend of ours."

That sounded funny, "a friend of ours." Like I was part of their little gang or something. After a little more coaxing, she let us know where Zoe was: "a big yellow hospital near the mall," was how she put it, and we said our thanks and goodbye.

"You don't tell Patrick about this, okay?" she called softly after us. "You don't tell him I talked to you."

"Sure thing, Mrs. G."

And we walked quickly on down to the corner.

"How 'bout that guy?" I said when I thought we were a safe distance from the house. "I mean, treating people like that."

"Mmm."

Martin opened his jacket far enough to let the raccoon poke its head out. It actually seemed to be pretty happy in there – it had been sleeping most of the afternoon, and when Martin unzipped his jacket, it showed no sign of wanting to bolt. I wondered silently what had happened to its sibling.

"Her father said she ran into a wall," I continued,

mostly to hear the sound of my own voice. "Her mother said she fell down the stairs. Which do you suppose it was?"

"Don't be an idiot," Martin said. "The old man beat her up."

I fell into silence, suddenly feeling very stupid. On some level I'd known that's what had happened, but I hadn't wanted to admit it to myself. Like my mother with Brad, I just hadn't wanted to believe it.

We walked in silence to the bus stop, where Martin tucked the raccoon back into his coat and tried to look casual as the bus approached. The driver, a pretty young woman with a blond ponytail, gave his bulging jacket a worried glance as Martin climbed aboard, but she didn't say anything.

"I hope you know this is my last bus token," he said, dropping it in the fare box. "So you're paying for the trip home."

"That's fine," I said, and deposited a two-dollar coin. We sat near the back, Martin next to the window and me with my legs out in the aisle.

"That's my old school," Martin said at one point, and at another he pointed out the apartment building where he'd once lived with his mother.

"You grew up around here, eh?" I said idly.

"That's what I said." His voice was tight, irritated. He didn't say anything else for a long time, not until the bus stopped a block or so away from the hospital.

"We can walk from here," he said, stepping over me to get off the bus, just about knocking me over in the process.

I chased after him, my head feeling like it was going

to explode with every step. He wasn't running, but he was a good six inches taller than I was, and I had to jog to keep up with his long, determined strides. He just walked right up to the front door of the hospital, through a flock of patients and nurses milling around smoking, and stopped just inside the front door to let me catch up.

I gave him a careful look as I approached, certain I'd offended him in some way but not able to put my finger on exactly what I'd said or done to make him mad. He held the door open for me, then followed me inside.

"'Scuse me," I said to the woman behind the front desk, a middle-aged lady in a blue uniform with a patch that said "Hospital Auxiliary." "I'm looking for Zoe ..." I turned to look for Martin, realizing suddenly that I didn't know her last name.

"Gibbons," he said from behind me. "Zoe Gibbons."

"Hmm." The woman entered the name into the computer on her desk, finger-pecking uncertainly. "I'm not usually here," she said with an apologetic smile. "I'm usually in the gift shop, but we're short-staffed today."

After a second or two the woman's expression turned to mild triumph.

"She's in 304," she said pleasantly. "But I'm afraid you can't go upstairs with ... whatever that is."

She was looking at Martin, and as I turned to look I realized the raccoon had chosen this moment to come to life, and was crawling around his shirt front.

He gave the woman a nasty look.

"You wanna watch him while I go upstairs?" he said coldly.

"Actually, son, you're not even supposed to be in the building with ... er, him," the woman said gently. "There's actually a sign on the door that says 'no pets.' "

I took a deep breath and looked at the wriggling mass inside Martin's jacket.

"Tell you what," I said diplomatically. "Why don't I go up and see Zoe for a few minutes, and you can stay down here with the raccoon. Then I'll come down and we can switch."

Martin gave me a suspicious glare.

"You don't even wanna touch him," he said darkly. "I'm not leaving him with you."

I stood stupidly for a second, the throbbing in my head so intense I could scarcely think. A man came up to the desk as I stood baffled, and I moved out of his way. When he left I could hear the woman behind the desk saying something to Martin, but it didn't register until he started to lose control.

"I told you I'm not leaving," he said, agitated, his voice getting louder.

"I'm sorry, but if you don't step outside I'll have to call security."

"Hey, Martin." I put a hand on his arm, trying to calm him down. "Look, I'll take good care of him. I'll even let you go upstairs first if you want."

"Forget it." He slapped my hand away, spinning on his heel to storm outside. "We shouldn't have even come. This is such bullshit."

I watched after him for a second, debating whether I should run after him or just turn and go upstairs. My question was answered for me, though, when I felt someone behind me, lifting me nearly off the ground by the arm and escorting me to a chair along the wall.

"You okay, son?"

It was a security guard in a dark uniform, his face inches from mine. He wasn't that much older than I was — certainly not old enough to be calling me "son."

"What?" I said numbly.

"You looked like you were gonna pass right out there, buddy. You were just swaying back and forth. I figured if I didn't grab hold of you, you were going right over."

I blinked, trying to focus.

"No, I ... just need some Aspirin or something. Tylenol, whatever. I've got a mother of a headache."

"You've got a mother of a nosebleed is what you've got."

Instinctively I lifted a hand to my upper lip, and pulled it away bloody.

"Come on, then," the guard said, hauling me to my feet. "Let's get you over to Emergency."

■ ■ ■

An hour later I was sitting on the edge of a stretcher, letting myself be poked and prodded by some less-than-gentle old doctor who looked like he'd rather be getting root canal surgery than dealing with the likes of me.

"So how exactly did this happen?" he was saying for about the hundredth time.

"I told you, I bashed my face off the wall."

"You were just sauntering along and you managed to walk into a wall hard enough to break your nose?"

"That's what I said."

He gave a strangled sigh.

"You kids these days. If you got beat up, you could at least have the courtesy to say you got beat up. Tell me the other guy was seven feet tall and weighed four hundred pounds, but don't insult my intelligence."

I flinched as he probed away at my face.

"Ow!"

"Does that hurt?" he asked mildly.

After a while he stopped and stepped back.

"Well, you've broken your nose," he told me, "but you don't seem to have a concussion. There's not much I can do for you except maybe prescribe some painkillers."

"That'd be nice," I told him, a hint of sarcasm creeping into my voice. It seemed I couldn't go into a hospital anymore without being treated like some kind of criminal.

The doctor gave me a stern look as he scribbled something on a pad of paper.

"I'm only going to prescribe ten. That should be enough to get you through the next day or two, at least until you can get in to see your family doctor. I should warn you that if you try to sell them —"

"Oh, give me a break." I took the paper from him and stood up, getting a terrific head rush. "I'm not gonna sell them. I need them so I can get stoned tonight."

And with that, I stomped on out of there.

■ ■ ■

I stopped at the hospital pharmacy to fill the prescription, using a chunk of Richard's money to pay for it. When I finally got on the elevator to go and see Zoe, I popped open the bottle and dry-swallowed one of the pills. I didn't want to take more than one; after my last experience with pills, I was kind of turned off by the idea of them.

I was a little surprised to see that the third floor of

the hospital was the children's ward. I figured I must have got the room number wrong, but when I got to 304, the little card outside the door said "Sharma, C., Gibbons, Z."

"Excuse me, son."

I turned slowly. All of a sudden I was everybody's son, I thought crankily.

"Yeah?"

"You can't be up here. Visiting hours are for family only right now. Other visitors can stop by between two and four, and between seven and nine."

I checked my watch. It was four-thirty. I gave the nurse a foul look.

"Pretend it's three-thirty," I said, turned back and walked into Zoe's room.

She was sitting in the bed by the window, propped up and watching TV, although from the look of her eyes — vacant, bloodshot — she'd been doing some pretty serious bawling. Her hair was looking limp and hung around her blotchy face. She turned her eyes, but not the rest of her head, as I came in.

"Hey, Jareth. I thought that was your voice."

She didn't sound real surprised to see me. There was a dead sound to her voice, like she didn't much care to be surprised by anything at all.

"Me and Martin stopped by your parents' place. Your dad told us you were here," I said. I figured I owed her some kind of explanation about how I'd come here.

"What happened to your face?" was all she said. I shrugged, sat down on the bed beside hers. There was no one in it, although the blankets were messed up, so I figured whoever belonged to the bed was probably down the hall, or gone for tests or something.

"Well, you know. Stuff. I broke my nose."

"Yeah? I couldn't tell."

It took me a second to realize she was kidding, and when I did I forced a laugh.

"Your mom said you had the baby," I said, not sure whether I should be bringing it up. But she perked up a little when I did, gave me a wan little smile.

"Yeah. He's real tiny. You should see him, he's so cute. But he's not finished yet. He was like two and a half months early. The doctor said he might die, or at least be real sick. Maybe even retarded."

"That's what they said about my brother," I said.

"Yeah? And did he turn out okay?"

I thought about that for a second, whether I should tell her what happened to Brad.

"Yeah," I said finally, my voice weak. "He turned out just fine. A real neat kid." I stood, shifting my weight from one foot to the other, the painkiller I'd taken on the way up finally starting to kick in.

"So your dad wasn't too happy to see us," I said then, just to break the silence. "Your mom seems ... um, nice, though."

Zoe prickled at that one.

"She's retarded. That's what you're thinking, isn't it? My mom's a retard and my dad's a drunk, so that's why I don't like to go home. You're thinking no wonder I'm so screwed up."

"I'm thinking ..." I trailed off, wondering what Vic would say in a situation like this. He always knew the right thing to say. Of course, I figured Vic probably wouldn't have stuck his foot in his mouth like that in the first place. "I'm thinking I wish you had an easier life," I said.

"Yeah, well. You're not the only one."

I stood there for a minute or two more before I decided it was time to leave.

"Hey, look, Zoe. I should probably head out. I have to start a job tomorrow, and —"

"Yeah, yeah. That's fine." She waved her hand without looking at me. "Have fun. Say hi to Martin for me, okay?"

"Sure."

And I wandered out, feeling like a complete heel.

■ ■ ■

To my surprise, Martin was standing on the lawn outside the hospital, smoking a cigarette, the raccoon still in his jacket.

"Hey," I said, checking my watch. "You been waiting out here for two hours?"

"Yeah. I saw the security guy haul you off. Thought I'd stick around and see how it turned out. Plus I ain't got any money for the bus."

I nodded.

"I should have figured," I muttered under my breath. When I'd first met Martin I'd found him interesting, complicated. Now I just found him moody and it was starting to grate on me.

On the bus home he was all sweetness and light, chatting with me, opening his jacket and trying to get me to pet the raccoon.

"I'm all out of peanuts or I'd show you how to feed him," he said.

"That's fine. Thanks anyway," I told him. The raccoon didn't look too healthy after spending the entire day inside his jacket, although I knew better than to tell him that. It curled up listlessly in his lap as he stroked it intently.

The ride home seemed to last about three hours, although it was probably less than one. I said goodbye to him at the subway station and walked home alone. It was a nice evening, warm enough to take my jacket off and throw it over my shoulder as I walked.

I thought of Zoe, alone in the hospital, and wondered if her parents would be going to see her. I wondered where she'd go when they let her out of the hospital — or more to the point, where the baby would go.

I would go back to see her, I decided, when my nose hurt less and when Zoe might be in a better mood. When I wouldn't be as likely to say something stupid.

19

I was up at five-thirty the next morning, dressed and pacing around the house, ready to go to work. By the time ten o'clock rolled around I was already a little tired.

Miriam's daughter — Rebecca, the girl with the eyebrow ring — was ten minutes late in showing up to open the store, and she laughed when she saw me standing outside waiting for her.

"You're the new guy, right?" she said. "What is it, Gareth?"

"Jareth," I told her. "But you're closer than most people."

"Jareth, whatever. Okay, like, lesson number one? I'm always late. Like, one hundred percent of the time. So nobody's gonna shoot you if you're not here at exactly ten o'clock every day. Wow, you look like you just got run over by a truck."

I fingered my nose self-consciously.

"Yeah, well. The doctor said I should be the right colour again in a week or two," I said as she unlocked the door. "I mean, purple and green are lovely colours, but ..."

There was no point in trying to be witty, though, because she was already inside.

"Okay, this is the night return slot, right?" she was saying, emptying out a padded milk crate under the door. "That's the first thing you gotta do in the morning, is mark all the movies back in. We close at ten o'clock at night, right? Most of the big stores are open all night, or at least until midnight? But we've got the, like, *ambiance*. Plus we've got pornos in the back." She laughed. "Just kidding. We had them when my Mom bought the store, right? But they're sexist and demeaning to women, so we got rid of them." And she fixed me with a glare, daring me to disagree with her. When I didn't, she looked a little smug.

"Anyway," she said. "That's where we keep the kids' movies now."

And so the day went. Rebecca flitted around the store, showing me this and that, giving me capsule reviews of every movie in the store, quizzing me on her favourites later.

"I can't believe you've never seen *City of Angels*. You *have* to watch it. Okay, I'm putting it aside for you. You can take it home tonight and watch it."

An hour later it was a different movie.

"Okay, forget *City of Angels*. You're watching *Benny and Joon* tonight."

By the end of the day I had enough movies stacked up that the shelves were starting to look a little bare.

"Why don't you make me a list?" I suggested as gently as I could. "That way I can work through them a little slowly."

By the end of the day, though, I was really starting to enjoy myself. The occasional customer wandered in — most of them making some kind of comment about my nose — but for the most part it was just me and Rebecca.

"Evening's the really busy time," she said. "That and weekends."

A little after five o'clock, an older guy, a real seasoned ex-hippie type, rolled into the store. I was about to ask him if I could help him with anything when he dropped his knapsack behind the counter and started to straighten things on the shelves.

"Oh, hey," the guy said, noticing me. "You must be the new kid. Jerry, was it?"

I decided that was close enough and let it slide.

"I'm Lance," he said, offering me a blunt, grimy hand.

"Hey, Lance."

Rebecca seemed less than ecstatic to see the guy.

"Hi, Lance. You're late. See you tomorrow."

She grabbed my jacket from the hook behind the counter and ushered me unceremoniously out of the store, following close behind.

"What was that about?" I said, slipping my jacket on.

"That guy is *such* a pain in the ass, you know? Just pray you never have to work with him on a Saturday; he is *so* useless. If he wasn't a friend of my mother's, I swear she would have *so* fired him by now. And he is *so* late, like every single night?"

I grinned, sending a stabbing pain up the middle of my face. "Well, hey. I guess everybody's entitled to be late once in a while, eh?"

She saw the humour in that and grinned back. "Okay, well. But I only like to be late when I *get* to work, not when I *leave*."

■ ■ ■

Rebecca offered me a ride home, but I turned her down. It had been a long day in close quarters, and I wanted to walk. Besides, I wasn't planning on going straight home.

On the subway I stood crammed in among smelly guys in overalls and stressed-out yuppies in business suits, gripping the overhead steel bar and wondering how many sweaty, germy hands had touched the bar before me. By the time I got off the train it was dark, and I wasn't overly familiar with the territory, but I still felt like walking.

Things in this end of town were a lot more spread out than they were downtown, and the hospital was further from the subway station than I'd remembered. By the time I got there my feet were sore, the runners I'd worn to work that day rubbing at my heels.

It was a little after six o'clock when I got to Zoe's floor, and there was a huge crowd of people in her room, spilling out into the hallway, milling around, chatting. The girl in the bed closer to the door — a little kid of maybe eleven or twelve — had a whole host of visitors. I fought my way through the swarm to the far side of the room, most of the people at the kid's bedside scarcely taking any notice of me at all. The kid looked none too sick, sitting up in bed and opening presents. I guessed it must have been her birthday, since not all the cards hanging over her bed were of the "Get Well" variety.

Zoe had a visitor, too, sitting quietly in a chair on the far side of her bed, looking out the window as Zoe slept. For a second I thought it was her mother — small and slight, with the same wide, worried eyes. But there was something different, something in the way she held her eyes a little steadier, looked a little more at ease with herself, that told me it wasn't her.

"Hi, excuse me," I said, hoping my voice carried over the noise of the party on the other side of the room. The woman looked up, startled. Most of the people in the room weren't speaking English ... and if they had been, I doubt she would have noticed one more speaker. As it was, my throaty, stuffed-up voice caught the attention of more than one of the other kid's visitors.

The woman by Zoe's bed stood, suspicious.

"Hi. Are you here to see Zoe?" she asked.

"Yeah. I'm a friend of hers. Jareth," I told her, offering a hand. She ignored it for a second, and eventually I just shoved it deep in my pocket.

"I'm her aunt," the woman said. "She's not supposed to have visitors."

The frosty reception was throwing me off a little, but I decided flashing her the grin wouldn't be particularly appropriate. Besides, it hurt my nose to smile.

"I just wanted to make sure she's okay," I stammered. "I was here yesterday, and I think she was a little upset when I left."

The woman looked me over carefully.

"Why don't we go out in the hall and talk?" she said. "Zoe will be asleep for a while."

The woman was incredibly small, even shorter than Zoe, maybe four-ten and eighty-five pounds. Still, the no-nonsense look she had about her made me feel about an inch tall.

"I, um ... I'm sorry, I didn't know she wasn't allowed visitors," I said. "I was just worried about her."

"I'm sure you are," the woman said. "But Zoe's been through enough. I don't think she needs to see you right now."

I frowned, baffled.

"What do you mean, she's been through enough?"

The woman sighed.

"Her father showed up today, drunk as a skunk, tried to drag her out of here. The police came, Zoe had to be sedated. He's in jail now, and I hope he rots there, but somehow I doubt that'll happen. He was already charged after he beat Zoe up the other day, and he was out in a matter of hours."

I chewed on my lower lip thoughtfully.

"Sounds like Zoe's father and my mother would make a great couple," I muttered. "Look, when can I come back and see her?"

"You can't. I mean, there's not much point. She's leaving tomorrow for Montreal," her aunt said. "We thought it would be best if Zoe stayed with someone who can look after her, so we're bringing her to live with us for a while. But I'll be sure to tell her you stopped by."

"But ... what about the baby?" I managed. "Is he —"

"Zoe's mother will stop by and take care of him for a few weeks, until he's well enough to be moved."

The tone of her voice suggested the conversation was over, but I wasn't prepared to leave it at that.

"Look, can I just leave her my phone number or something? Even if she can't call me tomorrow before she leaves ... I'll leave my address and she can write me. How's that?"

The woman blinked slowly, deliberately, like her patience was wearing awfully thin.

"That's fine," she told me, and I bolted down the hall to the nurse's station to borrow a pen.

I handed Zoe's aunt a used envelope with my address and number on the back. "You'll make sure she gets it, right? I mean, she can call me collect when she gets to Montreal. Anything."

She nodded indifferently and took the paper from me like it was contaminated. "I'll see that she gets it."

I kept my hands deep in my pockets as I wandered back down the hall, my head down, feeling Zoe's aunt's eyes burning into the back of my neck as I walked. It felt like the longest hallway in the world.

I took a bus back to the subway, and as I sat in the nearly-empty car I leaned my aching face against the window, watching the blackness zoom by outside.

"Who are you kidding?" I muttered to myself. "That note's gone. It was down the toilet before you were out of the building."

I was wrong, as it turned out — but I wouldn't know that for several months.

■ ■ ■

On the way home from the subway station I stopped at the Petersen house. It felt strange, walking so boldly up the walkway to the front door. The last time I'd been so close to the house I'd been creeping around in the bushes. And now here I was, making amends. Well, more or less.

Richard's younger sister answered the door, gave me a funny look.

"Are you a friend of my brother?" she said, knitting her eyebrows — not quite as large as her brother's but still pretty impressive.

"Yeah, I guess you could call me that." I grimaced awkwardly at that. It was the second time I'd called this kid my friend, after what I'd done to him. I had to admit, it made me feel a little bad.

"What are you, like, the Black Eye Club?" the girl said, and invited me in. "Richard!"

A sullen "Yeah, what?" came down the stairs, followed by Richard. His eyes widened when he saw me.

"Hey, Rich," I said, casual as all get-out.

He looked around, paranoid. "What the hell are you doing here?" he whispered. "I thought I was gonna come to your place."

"Yeah, well. I just happened to be in the neighbourhood, you know? So I thought I'd come by and let you know what's up with Boswell for Saturday."

The kid gave me the evil eye. His shiner had faded but was still dark enough to make his face look a little lopsided. "Okay, you don't tell me what's up wit' Boswell, man. I tell you what's up. You got that?"

I had to laugh at the sudden, silly posturing.

"Sure thing, rapper boy," I said with a painful grin. His dark look intensified, but he didn't say anything else. "Tell you what," I continued. "You tell Boswell we'll meet him at the little park around the corner at noon on Saturday. You know, the one with the fountain."

"What if he don't come?"

"If he doesn't come, he doesn't get his money. I'm sure he'll react to that kind of logic," I said.

"Look, you wanna keep your voice down?" he said frantically. "My parents are in the family room."

"Well, why don't you go join them?" I said. "Go do family stuff. Bake a pie or play *Monopoly* or something. I'll see you on Saturday."

I closed the door hard behind me on the way out.

20

I'd expected Boswell to be some big, middle-aged guy with a bunch of tattoos and a big cigar hanging out of his mouth.

I got to the park early; it was a sunny day, and I was relieved to see a bunch of kids playing on the slide while their parents watched from a nearby bench. If Boswell was going to do anything stupid like pull a gun, he might think twice before he tried it in a park full of kids. Then again, it was hard to say. I sat and waited on the edge of the fountain, looking around the park, my pulse a loud, steady pounding in my ears. I fingered the envelope in my wallet.

Richard showed up next, and followed me over to sit on the edge of the fountain. The boards around the bowl of the fountain had been removed, and I figured it wouldn't be long until the water was turned back on.

"Hey, Rich. Sleep okay?" I said with a smirk that belied my nervousness.

"Yeah, screw you. Did you bring the money?" He had a red-and-white Adidas bag, not unlike the one I'd had at Lloyd's place such a long time ago.

"Of course. Did you bring the shit?"

A pained look crossed his face as he nodded toward the zipped-up bag.

"I got the other fifty, too," he said. "I told my Mom I was going to the Science Centre with my class."

"Oh, hey, the Science Centre. I went there with my class in Grade Five." I smiled, probably a little patronizingly.

"I'm in Grade Eight," he told me, defensive.

"Sure, whatever." I kept my perch on the edge of the fountain and waited until Richard gave me a good solid nudge. More of a punch in the ribs, really, but I decided to let it slide. Instead I hopped down and followed him over to the fence where Boswell was standing.

I looked at the greasy, stringy mess that was Boswell — the Chicago Bulls jacket he'd probably ripped off from somewhere, the nasty, stringy little moustache that wouldn't grow in the middle of his upper lip, the stoned, sleepy look in his eye — and I nearly laughed. *This* was what I'd been afraid of?

"Boswell. What's up?" I said casually.

"Who the hell is this?" Boswell asked Richard. "You told me to come alone, I figured you were gonna do the same thing."

"I'm his financial advisor," I said, standing too close to him. I was feeling cocky now, like I could take this guy on if I needed to.

"Yeah?" Bos snickered. "What happened to your face, you give him some bad advice?"

"Yeah, I told him to grow a moustache like yours." I pulled out the envelope full of cash and slid it through the bars of the chest-high fence that surrounded the park. "Now here's some advice for you: take this, and the shit Richard's got in his gym bag, and get your ass out of here."

Boswell took the money and shoved it inside his jacket.

"Let's go for a walk," he said, his eyes flitting nervously around the park. "I wanna count it, make sure you ain't trying to shortchange me."

I glanced over at Richard, then decided there would be no harm in it. It would be better to finish the exchange where there were fewer people around — although I didn't want to get off the beaten path entirely. Better to have a few witnesses in case this guy went nuts.

"Yeah, all right," I said cautiously.

I kept my arms crossed over my chest, trying to hide the lump in the front of my jacket. I'd taken the liberty of bringing Lloyd's knife along with me on this little excursion, although to be honest I had no idea what I would do with it in a fight. It was two cumbersome to pull on somebody with any speed, and as much as I was fascinated by knives, I'd never been keen on the idea of actually putting one in somebody.

"So, Boswell. How old are you, buddy?" I asked. The three of us walked in a triangle, me and Bos out in front and Richard trailing along behind. I was steering us a little, trying not to make it obvious that I was going anywhere in particular. When we got to the old factory I looked the place over, making a big show of examining the plywood boards around the decaying building as if I'd never been here before.

"Let's go in here," I suggested, fighting the smirk that was playing with my lips.

Boswell shrugged like it didn't matter, hopped up on a concrete block along the fence and climbed over.

I couldn't have thought this out better if I'd tried, I told myself. Of course, I had to hope the rest of the scene played out the way I wanted it. But we'd passed the first hurdle, no pun intended. Richard gave me a suspicious look as he waited for me to hop over, then followed along behind.

"So, Bos. How old are you, anyway?" I asked.

"What difference does it make?" he shot back. "Old enough to mess you up if I feel like it."

"Yeah, well. I've been messed up before. If you ask me, it's overrated." I wandered along the building, stopping close to the door, but not close enough to make it look obvious.

"So, Boswell. Did Richard tell you what the deal is here?" I was talking a little louder than normal, but — I hoped — not so loud Boswell would think anything was unusual.

"Deal is, you give me my money and I don't kill you," he said. "That's the deal."

I turned to look at Richard, who was standing there looking like he was about to wet his pants. "I'm sorry, man," he told me. "I couldn't tell him on the phone."

I gritted my teeth, not sure whether to smack the kid or take off running. But somehow I managed to keep it together, and I turned back to face Boswell.

"Tell me *what* on the phone?" he was saying. He was my height, more or less, and his watery blue eyes locked onto mine as we faced each other on the sidewalk.

"Okay, here's the scoop," I told him, my voice low and even. "I just gave you eight hundred bucks, and little Richie here's gonna give you another fifty."

"Little Richie owes me more than that," said Boswell.

I kept my eyes right on his, giving him my best poker face. It's not as good as the grin, but it's pretty impressive.

"Why don't you consider the rest a severance package?" I said. "Because after this, Richie's not gonna be working for you anymore. We're gonna give you the rest of the crap back — Rich says it's worth about two hundred. That covers the money he owes you, and after that you never talk to him again."

Boswell was giving me his best poker face right back, but when I said that, I saw a flicker of rage in his eyes.

"That's a fact, is it?" Bos said. "And you want to remind me exactly who you are again?"

My heart was in my mouth; *keep it together, keep it together, keep it together* was a steady mantra in my head. "I'm not somebody you want to be messing with, and that's a fact." I suppressed a giggle, thinking how much I sounded like a bad gangsta movie.

It was exactly then that the door at the side of the building opened and Pete poked his head out.

"Hey, Jareth." He looked uneasy as he saw the three of us standing here. "Something up?" He stepped outside, wearing a tight black tee-shirt with suspenders and a ragged pair of army pants.

"Oh, hey, Pete," I said, trying as hard as I could not to crack a smile. I gestured toward Boswell with my eyes. "I was just talking to my buddy, here. We were discussing the fact that he's gonna be leaving my young friend there alone. Wasn't that right, Boswell?"

It took Pete a second or two to catch on, but as soon as he did, he was magnificent.

"This asshole's bothering your friend?" Pete took a step or two toward Boswell, who took a step or two backward.

"Hey, look. I didn't know you were gonna ambush me, man."

Pete loomed over the guy, a day or two's stubble dulling the gleam of the sunlight on his head, a dark look in his eye. "You don't go messin' with my friends, man," Pete said.

I really did crack a grin then, a sharp pain in my nose reminding me that it might not be such a great idea.

"So, what do you think, Bos? You gonna take the deal?" I said. "We got another couple big guys in there in case you need a little more convincing."

Now it was Boswell who looked like he was about to pee himself. "You ambushed me, you son of a bitch!"

"Hey." I gave him an angelic face. "It was your idea to leave the park, man."

Richard opened up the Adidas bag and handed Bos a green plastic shopping bag from some upscale boutique. He was still too scared to say anything, but watched nervously as Bos checked its contents and disappeared back over the fence.

When he was gone, Pete gave me a good glare.

"You wanna tell me what the hell that was all about?" he demanded.

I gave him an abridged version of my deal with Boswell.

"So that's it?" Richard cut in. "You think he's gonna leave me alone?"

Pete gave him a patronizing wink.

"Well if he doesn't, you come see me. I'll give him a good thump for ya."

Richard looked like he'd just met Santa Claus, but I figured it would be a good time to make our exit.

"Hey, Pete. I've gotta get Junior home. It's way past his bedtime."

"Ha, ha." Richard looked like he wasn't sure whether he should be insulted or shell-shocked.

"Yeah, sure thing, buddy." Pete grinned that big nasty grin of his, and pulled a rumpled pack of cigarettes from his back pocket. "You want one?" he offered. I shook my head.

"Terrible habit," I said. "Come on, Rich. Let's go."

■ ■ ■

Richard chattered away like a little monkey all the way home: "That was so cool, when that big skinhead guy came out, man? Did you plan that? That was *so* boss."

I was feeling pretty cocky, like that big dog in the Saturday morning cartoons. The one who always has the little dog hopping around him yipping: "Hey, Spike, we's pals, ain't we?"

We were a few doors away from his house when he stopped dead, looking thoughtful.

"Hey, Jareth?"

"Yeah?"

"Um, I'm having a birthday party tomorrow. Just a stupid little kid party my Mom's throwing me, but if you want, you can come. I mean, if you're not doing anything. Around three o'clock."

I thought that over for a second.

"Yeah, sure," I said. "That sounds cool."

21

April had soon transformed into May, the budding trees and blooming gardens bringing a strange sense of normalcy to everything. I had always lived in Toronto; I had always worked at Tinsel Town Video; I had always wanted to be an artist.

Once in a while I would think of my previous life, the life where I'd had a mother and a brother and a friend named Matthew — but I usually shrugged thoughts like that out of my mind. I had enough on my plate; I didn't want to trouble myself with leftovers from that other place.

As strange as it sounds, I'd found a friend in Richard Petersen. It was as if seeing me deal with Boswell had been enough to make him forget I'd robbed him in the first place. In some bizarre way, I'd made amends to the kid.

And in his own bizarre way, it seemed Danny was trying to patch things up with me. He'd given me a stiff, rehearsed-sounding apology the day after he'd broken my nose, and since then he'd made a point to avoid being in the room with me. But I'd find little things done for me —

laundry folded and stacked outside my bedroom door when I'd left it in the dryer, sandwiches made and left in the fridge — that made me think he really was sorry.

■ ■ ■

It was the Friday evening after the May long weekend when I got a call that brought the old world I'd left behind crashing right into the new one. I was sitting in the living room watching some movie Rebecca had told me about — some stupid romance, I don't remember which one — when Danny appeared in the doorway. Wordlessly he held his hand up to his ear, thumb and baby finger extended. Phone.

I went into the kitchen to pick it up, a little puzzled. Nobody ever phoned me, except maybe Richard, and I'd been pretty sure he'd gone up north with his parents for a weekend at the cottage.

"Jareth, honey, is that you?"

I was silent for a full thirty seconds while I processed that voice. I felt my stomach contract, and took a couple of deep breaths before I could answer.

"Why are you calling me?" I said, my voice hard.

"Is that any way to talk to your mother, young man?" she snapped. "I'll have you know I went through hell to figure out where you're staying. Just who do you think you are, that you can desert your only family at a time like this?"

I let out a short, barking sound, somewhere between a laugh and a cough. "You've got to be kidding. You're not much on the small talk, are you? Just call me up and launch right into the stupid guilt trip."

"Jareth, honey, you haven't been to see me at all! Not

once," she said, like that was some kind of shock to her.

"Yeah, Mom, I noticed that. What's your point?"

I could hear her voice change, a forced, phony weepiness creeping into her tone. "Jareth, you don't understand how hard this is for me, being all alone in here."

"Yeah? Well, I'm pretty much all alone out here, too, thanks."

"Now, who are these people you're staying with? Matthew's father said —"

"Matthew's *step*father! For crying out loud, how long have I known Matthew, twelve years? You remember in Grade Eight, when his mother got married? Or maybe you don't ... you were pretty drunk that year."

"Fine, then, Matthew's *step*father. You always have to correct me, don't you?"

I could feel my entire body tense up, ready to lay into her. But I kept it under wraps for the moment, sitting on the kitchen counter, gripping the edge, trying to dig my fingernails into the yellow-and-white Formica top.

"See? That's what you always do. You turn it around so it's *my* problem," I said. "Of course it could *never* be your problem. You're so damned self-absorbed you never hear what anybody says to you. You're not even listening to me now, are you? You're just using the time I'm talking to figure out what you're gonna say when I'm finished."

"Darling, you know that's not true," she sniffled, phony as all get-out. "I've heard every word you said. Now, as I was saying, this man, Matthew's *step*father, if you must, he said he was going to bring you to visit me. When he didn't, I called him to find out why he never did, and he said it was because you didn't *want* to come. Personally I think —"

"Know what?" I was nearly shouting now, not caring if anyone upstairs heard me. "Vic's right. I don't want to see you. I don't want to talk to you; I don't even want to be *related* to you. Understand?"

There was a long silence. I wondered how she'd spin that around, but as it turns out she just changed the subject.

"Jareth, honey, I need your help," my mother said. "I can't stay here anymore. This place is terrible ... you couldn't understand what it's like in here."

"So what? You made your bed, as you've always been so fond of saying. Why would I want to help you get out of it — even if I could, which I can't."

Her voice brightened a little.

"But you can, honey. You just have to tell them I didn't do it."

I could just about see the little timer ticking away in my head, counting down the seconds until I went off.

"I should have figured this was coming," I snapped. "What am I gonna say: 'Oops, I'm sorry, I should have mentioned it earlier, but, you remember when I found my brother dying on the floor? Yeah, well, it was actually me who killed him. Hey, we can still be friends, though, right?' "

She actually had to think that over for a second, either missing the sarcasm completely or choosing to ignore it. "You don't have to say that, exactly, honey. I'd hate for you to get charged —" and here her voice dropped to a confidential near-whisper, "but you're seventeen, darling. You're still a Young Offender: don't you read the papers? You won't be tried as an adult ... Just say it was an accident. You were just wrestling with him and he fell."

I nearly choked at that.

"Oh, yeah, *that*'ll stand up in court," I said.

"Well, you just make something up then."

"I'm not making anything up!" I thundered, jumping off the counter and giving the nearest chair a good kick. "Shit, why are you calling me?" I said, my voice breaking.

"I told you, Jareth, I need your help."

"Yeah? Well, you should have thought of that before you killed my brother."

And I slammed down the receiver so hard it hurt my hand.

■ ■ ■

I gave myself half an hour to calm down, heading back to the living room and beating up on a throw pillow for a while. Then I wandered back into the kitchen, picked up the phone and dialled Vic's number from memory.

I shouldn't have been surprised when Matthew picked up the phone, but for whatever reason I was.

"Jareth?" He sounded cold, distant. "That's you, right?"

"Yeah." I tried to keep my tone aloof, like I'd just talked to him yesterday. "I guess you think I'm a major asshole, huh?"

"You know, I'd like to think that," he told me, "but Vic told me you were dealing with some pretty serious shit, so I should just let you have your space and let you call me when you were ready. Funny thing is, in the *five months* since I last talked to you, I've sort of stopped caring quite so much whether you called or not."

"Look, I'm sorry," I said. "I really am. But I needed to get away from everything for a while. Start over, you know?"

"Sure, whatever."

"But you know, I've wondered about you. How you're doing, all that. What's new, anyway?"

"What, you wanna know if I've got a new best friend? Or if maybe you can still come back and push me around on the weekends. Yeah, why don't you come and visit? Maybe you could still use me every once in a while."

"I —"

I couldn't say anything to that. It hit far too close to the truth. As a friend to Matthew, I'd pretty much sucked. I'd used him, sure enough — for company, for dinner, for somebody to vent on ... and not because I liked him, just because there was nobody else who would have put up with me treating them that badly.

"Look, Jareth, I'm sure you're real sorry and all, but I'd bet ten bucks you're not even calling to talk to me, are you?"

I just sat there, stupid, on the other end of the phone line until he spoke again.

"No, of course you're not," he said. "Hang on, will you? I'll go get Vic." And I heard a *click* as he hit the "mute" button on the phone. A moment later, I heard another *click*.

"Jareth," Vic said amicably. "I understand you're probably pretty upset with me."

"So why'd you do it, then?" There was an edge in my voice. "You knew exactly how I felt about talking to her, and yet you go and give her my number? I thought you were an okay guy, Vic, but it's a good thing you're not here right now. I don't know what I'd do to you if you were."

"That's probably valid. Listen, Jareth, she's been calling here every day for a month, sometimes once or twice a day."

"So what? Change your number. Call the phone company or the jail or something and tell them she's harassing you. But don't sic her on me, man. That's just not fair."

"Out of curiosity, Jareth, what did she have to say for herself?"

"What you said," I told him. "That I should just turn myself in ... lie and say I did it. She said I'm still seventeen so I probably wouldn't get charged as an adult."

"She's full of crap," Vic said. "You're seventeen and you kill somebody, you're pretty much guaranteed an adult court trial."

I thought of Lloyd and shuddered.

"So why'd you do it?" I repeated. "Why'd you give her my number?"

"I thought maybe you should hear what it is I've been up against," he said, the hint of a smile in his voice. "And I thought it might put you in the mood for a trip to court with me next week."

I thought that over for a second. Damn it, that cop had told me she had another court date the fourth of June. I hadn't planned to go, but I was a little annoyed at myself for forgetting about it completely.

"Why would I want to go to court?" I said. "I'd just have to watch my mother do her weeping and wailing and screaming about how this is all some big mistake."

"I don't know," Vic said thoughtfully. "I think it would be good for you. And it would show everybody you're really concerned about what happens in this case. That you want to see your little brother's death avenged."

"Hell, if he was really gonna get avenged — I mean, an eye for an eye kind of avenged — I might show up for that. But that's not gonna happen, is it?"

"No, this is Canada. We don't stone people here. We bury them in bureaucracy, and eventually they die from an infected paper cut or something. But I still think it would be good for you to make an appearance."

"Why? What am I gonna miss if I don't go?"

"Oh, they'll probably bring her in, let her lawyer put on a little show, then set a date for her next court appearance. But you never know. Something interesting might happen."

I let out a deep sigh and thought about my conversation with my mother. If she was gonna stand up in court and tell the world I killed my brother, I figured it might be a good idea if I was in the room to refute her.

"I tell you what," I told Vic. "I guess I owe you one. I'll see if I can get the day off work."

"That's great. I'll pick you up at seven-thirty, then."

■ ■ ■

I felt a little overdressed in the courtroom, in my new jeans and a dress shirt I'd bought specifically for the occasion. I was surrounded by motley-looking guys in Metallica tee-shirts and greasy jeans, a couple with very pregnant wives or girlfriends by their sides, some with their mothers or male friends. I sat with Vic in the third row, next to a drunk guy with long oily hair and a lightning bolt tattooed on the side of his neck.

"Hey, buddy." I could smell the alcohol on his breath as he leaned over to whisper to me. "Got a smoke I can borrow?"

I shook my head: "No, sorry."

"No worries. Hey, this your first time in court?"

I nodded yes.

"S'okay. They'll just read the charges and ask if you got a lawyer. If you don't they'll let you talk to duty counsel, and he'll tell you to ask the judge to put it over until another date. What are you up for, anyway?"

"I'm not up for anything."

"Your Dad, then." He nodded in Vic's direction. "What's he charged with?"

"Nothing," I said a little louder than I'd meant to, and Vic looked up from the newspaper he was reading and gave the guy a patronizing little smile.

I sat through six other cases before my mother's came up: a drunk driver who pleaded guilty and had his license suspended for a year; two guys who pleaded not guilty to beating their wives and had their cases put over until another date; an old woman charged with shoplifting who was ordered to have a psychiatric evaluation; a freaky-looking guy who pleaded guilty to forging a cheque and had to pay a fine; and a girl who celebrated her nineteenth birthday by getting really drunk and wrapping her car around a tree. Her case was put off until another date after her lawyer didn't show up.

When the girl — who was limping around on crutches — made her way out of the courtroom, I checked my watch and was surprised to see that the whole process had taken little more than an hour.

"That was six cases in sixty-five minutes," I whispered to Vic. "Talk about McJustice."

"Yeah. They should put in a drive-thru window," he muttered back.

The judge was a crusty-looking old guy with a shock of white hair that made him look like Einstein. He kept leaning his chin heavily on his hand and pushing up the little half-glasses he wore on the end of his nose.

"Do we have anything else we can get to before we take our morning break?" he muttered into his palm. He looked more exhausted by the whole process than anything else, and had made no effort to conceal his disgust at the stupidity of some of the morning's defendants.

I was getting a little tired of the whole process myself, and my rear end was numb from the hard wooden bench where it had been planted for quite some time.

"We have Moira Gardner, in custody, Your Honour." This was the Crown Attorney, Vic had told me, a tall, heavy-set woman with a no-nonsense tone about her. She flipped through her notes. "I believe she's here to set a date."

The judge sighed like he was doing the world a big favour just by being there.

"Bring her in," he mumbled, scarcely taking any notice as my mother was led through a side door into the courtroom. She sat down in a little box facing the judge.

I barely noticed as the charges were read. Instead, I stared at the back of this woman who'd given birth to me. She looked horrible, slumped and pale, and she'd lost probably twenty pounds since I'd last seen her. Her face hadn't even flickered when she'd been led into the courtroom and I wondered if she even recognized me.

When the Crown Attorney had finished reading the description of what she'd done to Brad, I had a good look around the courtroom. The only two people who looked unfazed by the brutality of the crime were my mother herself and the judge. I figured there was nothing he hadn't heard before, and of course my mother didn't seem to see anything wrong with what she'd done.

"And what would you like to do with your matter, Ms. Gardner?" the judge said in a monotone.

"I'm going to plead guilty," she said calmly.

That made everyone, especially the judge, sit up and take notice.

"I beg your pardon?" he said, his voice going up about half an octave.

"Um, I'm going to plead guilty, Your Honour?" she tried. A couple of people in the courtroom tittered nervously at that, but everybody was still too surprised to give it a real reaction. Myself, I thought my heart was going to bust out of my chest, it was pounding so hard. I looked up at Vic, but I couldn't read his face. He glanced over at me impassively, raised his eyebrows to say he was surprised, too.

"Ma'am, have you retained the services of a lawyer?" the judge was saying.

"No. I don't need a lawyer. I did it."

"These are very serious charges, ma'am. You could spend a very long time in prison for this. I would advise you to speak to a lawyer before making any kind of plea," the judge said.

"Yes, sir," my mother said. "But I understand the charges. I just want to get this over with as quick as possible so I don't cause my family any more pain and cost the taxpayer a lot of money with a trial."

I cocked my head to one side, double-checking to make sure it was really my mother up there.

"Ms. Gardner, I'm going to put this matter over until after our morning break. I'd like you to talk to duty counsel, and we'll take this up again in twenty minutes."

"Yes, but —" My mother trailed off as the judge shot her a withering look.

The guard who'd brought my mother in led her back out the same door, and everybody stood as the judge left the courtroom.

I was sitting back down again and turning to say something to Vic when I felt an enormous hand fall on my shoulder.

"Jareth? I thought that was you."

I turned around to see Detective Brooks towering over me in his dark suit. His shaved head seemed to glow in the fluorescent light of the sparse courtroom.

"Hey, Detective." I gestured vaguely at the spot where my mother had been sitting. "How about that, eh?"

"Yeah, how about that?" he said. "Listen, have you talked to the Crown?"

"What? Oh, the Crown Attorney. No. I haven't talked to her."

"You probably should." And he caught the woman's eye as she shuffled frantically through her papers, gestured for her to come over.

"Well, if she wants to plead guilty —"

"Genevieve, this is Ms. Gardner's older son Jareth," the cop said as the woman approached.

"Jareth." She had this deer-in-the-headlights look, like this whole situation had caught her off-guard. "Do you think we could talk in my office for a few minutes?"

I looked over at Vic, who nodded like that was a good idea, and followed the woman upstairs to a little closet of an office filled floor to ceiling with bulging binders and stacks of paper.

"Look, Miss, I know this is a real big surprise and everything, but I don't see what the big deal is. I mean, she's admitting she killed my brother. Why don't you just let her?"

"Well ... this is so unusual," she stammered. She was considerably less together when she didn't have her notes in front of her, I mused. "Do you think she knows what she's doing? I mean, is she ..."

"What, is she stable?" I shrugged, leaned against the wall while the woman sat in the single chair behind the small desk. "Heck, if she was stable she wouldn't have killed my brother, would she? But I don't think she's nuts. I think she knows what the consequences are here, you know?"

I was genuinely baffled. My mother's motivation for doing anything was usually attention, and I couldn't see why she would bypass all the hoopla of a trial in exchange for a quick trip to a long stint in prison.

When we got back to the courtroom my mother stuck to her guns, though.

"I'm still going to plead guilty," she said. "I don't understand why you won't just let me say I did it."

The judge sighed again, scribbling something in the file on his desk.

"I tried to convince her otherwise, Your Honour," said a weedy little man in a checked suit who I took to be the lawyer who'd spoken to my mother during the break. "I explained it would be in Ms. Gardner's best interests to retain the services of a lawyer and put the matter over to another date, but she insists she wants to plead guilty today."

"Very well, then." And the judge had my mother stand as the charges were read aloud again.

The whole thing took less than five minutes, and at the end of it the judge flipped through his notes a couple more times. "I'm not going to pass sentence today," he said thoughtfully. "I'd like a little more information first."

"Well, what do you need to know?" my mother interrupted. "I'll tell you whatever you need."

"You will refrain from interrupting, Ms. Gardner. I'm going to ask for a pre-sentence report to be filed, and we'll meet back here in a month to decide what kind of sentence you'll receive."

"A month!" she wailed. The judge shot her a look that would have melted concrete, and checked his calendar.

"I have July 28," he told the Crown Attorney. "Is that agreeable with you?"

It was, and the judge ignored my mother's protestations as the guard led her back out of the courtroom.

"What do you think, Jareth?" Vic said, putting a hand on my shoulder as we left the courthouse. "You think she's had a sudden onset of remorse?"

"I don't know what to think," I said numbly.

"Here's my theory," Vic said. "I think maybe somebody had a good talk with your mother. Told her if she hated jail so much, the surest way to spend a lot more time there would be to plead not guilty. They'd take her back to jail, the lawyers would do their little dance for about a year, putting the evidence together, shuffling papers, trying to set up trial dates, interviewing witnesses. Then there'd be a long trial, her name and picture would get smeared all over the papers ..."

"Actually, I think she'd like that part," I interrupted, catching on. Vic flashed a mischievous grin and continued.

"And through it all, through the whole trial, there she'd be in that nasty provincial jail, surrounded by all those terrible hardened criminals who are waiting for *their* trials. She'd be found guilty, of course: she knows she did it, and so does everyone who matters. And then she'd still have her whole sentence to deal with. Of course, if she did the *right* thing and pleaded guilty right off the bat, the judge might see fit to send her off to some minimum-security place in the boonies. She'd have her own little room in a nice cottage, lots of friendly armed robbers and child-beaters to play with. Heck, it'd be just like a really long vacation."

"Only without the beach," I chimed in with a grin.

■ ■ ■

I told Vic I'd take the train home. I was grateful for his help, but I needed to be alone for a while. I figured the forty-minute train ride would do me some good.

So this is how the story ends: a double-decker, green-and-white commuter train with blue vinyl seats, and yours truly sitting on the top level, staring out at the scenery rolling past — an industrial park, a deserted warehouse, a soccer field under a stretch of hydro wires. The conductor's voice at every stop: "Stand clear of the doors, please. Clear the doors."

This is how the story ends: with justice acknowledged, if not necessarily served; with new friendships built and old friendships fallen away. It ends as happily as anything ever really does — with some things left undone but with plenty of time to worry about them later.

And, best of all, it ends with a new start.

Epilogue:

HOPE

It seems like a long time ago that I jumped out of Lloyd Clemence's bedroom window. It's been five years since I found my brother on the bedroom floor, and it seems like forever since my mother was sent off to some federal resort. I doubt it was everything she'd dreamed it would be. Maybe someday I'll go and see the place for myself, but I'm still not ready. She'll be there for a while yet, so I guess I've still got some time to think about it.

Halfway through that first summer, I decided to stop by the old factory and see if Pete and Martin were around, but I didn't find them. I didn't find the factory, either: it had been torn down and replaced with a sign that said a big new condominium complex was going to be built there in time for spring of the next year. I haven't seen either of them since.

I got a letter from Zoe that fall, though, so I guess her aunt gave her my address after all. She said the baby was doing okay, said she was planning to stay in Montreal but I was welcome to come and visit her some day. I think about that kid a lot — another little kid with no father and a mother who's not really finished with her own messed-up childhood yet. Nothing unusual, I suppose. I just hope he turns out okay.

I haven't talked to Matthew since that last awkward phone conversation, but I've thought about him an awful lot lately — about how I treated him, the way I shoved him around. Sometimes I imagine I'm going to run into him on the street one day, just bump into him in a store or something. I wonder what I'd say, whether he'd feel as uncomfortable as I would. Maybe we'd talk about old Lloyd, maybe we wouldn't. Or maybe we'd just have a good laugh about some dumb thing that happened back in elementary school. Maybe I'd even manage an apology. I wonder if he thinks about me, about what happened with Lloyd — if he feels bad about it, or if maybe he's decided the whole thing was my fault.

But I figure if I ever do see him again, we probably won't have much to say. He'll tell me what he's doing: maybe working, maybe fresh out of school ... or maybe out of jail, if he's hooked up with some other punk who likes to follow trouble around. Or maybe he's got an ordinary life, married with kids ... or maybe he's living in a gutter someplace. Either way, I guess I'd like to know.

And what about me? Well, I guess you could say I landed on my feet after Vic brought me to Stewart's place. I stayed there for a couple of years; I went back to school that September, and I finally managed to pass the Biology course I'd been working on for a couple of years. I even came out with a halfway decent mark. I guess showing up for class once in a while helps.

I'm out on my own now, taking part-time art classes in college while I work shelving groceries at a supermarket. It's not a great job, but it pays the rent. My real passion, I've discovered, is art. Someday I'd like to make a living at it, but for now I'm content to scribble away madly in my spare time.

I still meet Stewart for lunch once in a while. He asks me how the drawing is going and tells me about Danny, who hasn't changed much. Sometimes he even mentions Vic — some old story from when they were kids.

The last time I talked to Vic was maybe three years ago. I got to thinking about him one day a little before Christmas and decided to give him a call. One of his daughters picked up the phone on the first ring, and it was clear from the way she called her father to the phone that she had no idea who I was. When Vic said hello he sounded an awful lot older than I remembered.

"Jareth. Glad to hear from you," he said, although he didn't sound convinced. We talked for a few minutes, stiff, like strangers making small talk.

"So you're doing well," he said, after I'd filled him in on what was up.

"Yeah, I guess I am." And there was a long, awkward silence.

"Say, Vic," I said after some thought. "I don't suppose Matthew's around, is he? I wouldn't mind talking to him for a sec if it's okay."

The silence that followed was even longer and more awkward. "Jareth, Matthew and his mother don't live here anymore. They moved out a few months ago," he told me.

I didn't know what to say to that, and after a short, clumsy goodbye I put down the phone and walked away.

I guess that's the way it works. People drift in and out of your life with varying degrees of consequence — one person changes your life for a week, another forever. But everyone's got their own lives going on, and unless we're awfully lucky, all we really see of one another's lives is a quick snapshot in time. It's funny — as if we each have cameo roles in the lives of everybody we meet. I guess it's up to us whether we want to be heroes or villains.

KEVIN HAWLEY

Elizabeth Wennick began writing *Changing Jareth*
after graduating in 1991 from high school, where
she found herself frustrated with the characters
portrayed in conventional teen fiction. Elizabeth
worked at a camp for inner-city kids in Toronto
before returning to her first love — writing. In 1995
she graduated from the journalism program at
Sheridan College in Oakville, Ontario and her work
has subsequently appeared in numerous southern
Ontario newspapers, including *eye Weekly*, the *St.
Catharines Weekly News* and the *Niagara Falls
Chronicle*. She currently lives in Burlington,
Ontario and is working on a variety of freelance
writing projects.